RAY TAYLOR
AND THE TORN AND TATTERED TREASURE MAP

By N. Degen

The fantastic World of Ray Taylor
Ray Taylor And The Torn And Tattered Treasure Map
by N.Degen
Translated by A.Cigale

Table of Contents

Chapter One
Never Skip Ahead While Reading a Book 6

Chapter Two
Never Take Anything that Doesn't
Belong to You 21

Chapter Three
The Dead Never Forgive 38

Chapter Four
The Lost City of Sacro-Luxe,
or The Hidden World 50

Chapter Five
The Devil's Smirk, or Death's
Empty Eye Sockets 89

Chapter Six
The Gentle Tread of Evil Intent,
or the Meowling Wind of San Felis 97

Chapter Seven
The Turquoise Lagoon 135

Chapter Eight
San Stella Diurna,
or the City Where Lives Not a Soul 144

Chapter Nine
He Saves Himself
Who Destroys Himself 185

CHAPTER TEN
San Liberi,
or the Upside-Down World 196

CHAPTER ELEVEN
The Black Wings of the Heavenly Host 234

CHAPTER TWELVE
The Winged City of Sant Avis....................................243

CHAPTER THIRTEEN
The Ship Graveyard 285

CHAPTER FOURTEEN
San Dulcedo,
Or
The Bittersweet Life of a Sweet Town 293

CHAPTER FIFTEEN
A Hair's Breadth from Certain Death........................342

CHAPTER SIXTEEN
Sanct Tempus,
the City of the Most Precise Clocks...........................350

CHAPTER SEVENTEEN
Escape From Safe Haven 387

CHAPTER EIGHTEEN
The Paradise Isle
Of Tuki -Tuki 395

Forewarning

Dear Reader: You are holding in your hands the story of Ray Taylor. It is not a tale for weaklings and wusses.

This is a story for brave boys and courageous girls.

And everything that happened to Ray is the whole, unvarnished truth.

And just one more thing: if you ever happen upon an ancient tome bound in dark leather with the inscription:

"Bloodthirsty Cook's Secret Book," never, remember this well, never open it! Wrap it in a rag and weigh it down with a heavy stone,

a stone so heavy only you will be able to lift and throw it into the deep blue sea, in its deepest and darkest place.

No one, no one must ever find it! Otherwise, even from beyond the grave, the cunning and bloodthirsty Old Man Cook will lure you, or one of your closest friends, to set out in search of infinite treasures, surviving which would require nothing less than a miracle...

Never Skip Ahead While Reading a Book

"he clock on the city tower struck two and a half minutes past ten. The brass hum of the bell still hung suspended in the warm air, just as the most distinguished members of the court, raising gingerly the hems of their long, dark robes, were climbing up its dust-covered stone steps, their heads drooping low, as though weighed down by worldly concerns. Their black hoods, entirely covering their foreheads, draped down almost to their eyelashes, hiding even their gazes from the prying eyes of the crowd.

The somewhat befuddled members of the jury and a sea of the curious faces of the unlookers, flowing together like columns of ants, were already filling the great hall of the courtroom. The sun's rays were trying to tickle their serious faces, but the thick, pale yellow, stone walls barely admitted them through the narrow slits of the tall oval windows.

The iron-clad sentries with their tall and pointy spears, their faces covered by masks with only a slit for the eyes, carried in the heavy cage. Huddling inside it, like a hunted animal, quivering in fear in its furthest corner, was the body of a small child.

"Your Majesty, the Laws of our Grandest of States were violated in the most horrible manner and, moreover, deliberately and cold-bloodedly, by this wayward child! I call upon you to declare the boy guilty of all of the seventeen charges of the indictment!" the speaker for the prosecution pronounced.

Brandishing above his head the thick stack of pages covered in a microscopic script, the prosecutor triumphantly pointed with it into the corner where the iron cage rested.

"Taking into consideration the uncertain origins of the foreigner boy, *who does not possess knowledge of the Laws of our Most Sacred of States, I ask the court to be lenient in its sentence. And to substitute the public quartering on the city's main square with an execution by hanging on the smaller square, behind City Hall," the defense interceded.*

Bang! A slap resounded, and the small, persistent fly that had only just been squashed by the scroll of papers in the strong hand of the public defendant ended its all too brief life, expiring right there, on the table in the hall of justice.

The youthful head with its unruly mop of curly hair was raised up for one second, as though in an attempt to swallow the long-awaited breath of fresh air, and immediately faltered back down to its knees, tightly bound together in the grasp of the child's thin arms. The cold iron bars of the cage once again came into contact with his spine, hunched, as though it too were a weapon of accusation that stood at the ready, with lightning speed, at the beck and call of an order, to pierce his body.

Reading out the new counts of the charges resoundingly and unanimously passing the indisputable sentence, the judges and the jury departed from the hall. Despairing of ever getting a peek at the assembled, if even only with one eye, the rays of the sun sluggishly and disappointedly slid across the western windows as the third day of the trial came to an end.

The sentries heaved the cage upon their backs and the heavy, forged doors, awakening, instead of yawning, barked in irritation, angered that their peace had been disturbed.

A wave of light, brazenly and life-reaffirmingly, burst into the hall, as though impatient to overhear the sentence. The child's eyes, squinting tightly under their long bangs, were not delighted, but frightened by the light, as by everything and everyone that surrounded him.

"Criminal! Bandit!" the throng in the market hooted.

"Villain! Evil doer!" exhorted the street vendors.

Someone grabbed a tomato out of a basket and with a running start hurtled it with all their might at the cage. The tomato made a squishing sound and splattered on the massive iron grating of the bars. The cage on the broad shoulders of the iron-clad goons rocked slightly to and fro and, slowly but surely, like an icebreaker wedging its way through the crowd, split it into parts, scattering the curious, maliciously gloating, riled up throng to the left and to the right like pieces of shattered ice.

The morning of the execution was slightly chilly, fragrant, and piercingly silent. The child's bare feet, bound in shackles, barely surmounted the damp and cold steps of the dungeon. The early morning breeze fluttered the heap of the child's hair, and it seemed that for the breeze alone, the crude iron grating was no obstacle in this. The cart kept bouncing over and over on the pavement cobblestones, and the guards, sensing the importance of the impending hour of retribution, stretched to their full height as though on a string, as though it were an entire enemy army and not a single lonesome, little boy, that was being led to its execution."

"Ray! Are you awake yet?" a woman's voice burst into the room.

"No! I'm still asleep!" Ray replied immediately, slamming shut the book.

He knew that what he was doing now was something that ought never to be done: first of all, he was reading, instead of getting up and quickly getting ready for school. And secondly, he was reading the book not from the beginning, but opening it at random and butting in in the middle of the narrative. He had decided he wanted to know nothing more about the execution of a child! And if he were ever to open this book again, then it would be from the very beginning, and he would read it all the way through, in the order that it was written, without even being tempted by the thought of looking several chapters ahead.

Something under his pillow made a crunching sound, and Ray, plunging his hand behind it, fished out his notebook of drawings, and a pencil. His fingers did not obey any prohibition and, gliding along the surface of the paper, made the following appear: the spear of the guard, his steely, pointy-nosed boot, the cone-shaped hats of the judges... The pencil hurried and, suddenly, for a split moment, it came to a full stop: the rays of the sun and the wind, only they had been sympathetic to the boy; how should he depict them? The hair, that's it! His hair had fluttered in the wind! One stroke, and yet another stroke and, above his squinting gaze, the wind was now already ruffling the boyish bangs.

"Ray! Are you dressed yet?" his mother, rushing by, asked from beyond the door.

"Yes!" Ray shouted, hurling the notebook with the pencil into the corner where his school bag rested. Precisely there, where it had no business being.

"Yeah, yeah, yeahhh," Ray sang along with the familiar, catchy tune playing on the radio, while at the same time brushing his teeth.

Putting on a fresh t-shirt, he noticed in the mirror the reflection of his naked, childish torso, and it, yet again, disappointed him.

Why is it that ten-year-olds don't develop muscles right away? And how much longer is he going to have to wait until his body too will become strong, and manly? Ray tousled his hair and stuck out his tongue at his reflection. Having pulled on his favorite jeans that had by now become much too short on him, he ran to the kitchen. Running by, he accidentally knocked his elbow against the framed portrait of his father, and then immediately adjusted it back in its place. In another second, he was hanging suspended from the crossbar in the kitchen doorway.

"Ray! Now is not the time to be hanging. Will you please eat faster!" his mother pleaded with him. Her ruffled, ginger-colored tresses were especially unmanageable when she was in a hurry. Buddy, reveling in his owner's caresses, was already standing on his hind legs, his muzzle buried between Ray's knees.

"Buddy, how many times have I told you, dogs don't have jam for breakfast!" Ray's mother smiled, fixing a wayward curl behind her ear. The kitchen smelled of burned toast, the first piece of which would always burn while his mother was trying to do ten things at once, and of raspberry jam, which Ray adored.

"Ray, I have something to tell you. Mr. Barnes had expressed to me his dissatisfaction, with the fact that you were drawing during his physics lesson. And Mrs. Rose scolded me about you drawing during her math class. And Mr. Joyce..."

"Yes, I know! I know," Ray jumped in. "Complained that I was drawing during his chemistry class..."

"It's not funny! You don't pay attention in school, Ray! Your father wouldn't have liked it one bit," mother remarked sadly.

Since his father had passed away, his mother had quite often resorted to such a tactical threat. From time to time, it began to seem to Ray that, were his father still alive, there would be nothing he would like about Ray. At times, he would secretly bring the portrait of his father to bed and speak with him, especially when he was faced with having to make an important decision and had no one to consult with. For example, what does he think about the following: which of the two school baseball teams would win this Saturday? And how should he reply to that hulk-of-boy Murray if he, in front of everybody, calls him "snot-nosed shorty" again? When would he finally get taller, if even by just a couple of inches? Right about now, it seems that he's the shortest boy in his class. And when is it exactly that boys begin to grow mustaches? Should he go out and buy himself a razor blade now? You know, just in case, if it were suddenly to happen to him all at once sooner rather than later. And how should he ask Jane if she might go out with him to the movies? Or, just in general, what question could he ask Jane so that she would, finally, take notice of his existence?

"Ray! Do you hear me? You're again off somewhere with your head in the clouds. I would like to know what it is that you're constantly thinking about?" his mother confided to him.

"I'm going to have to stay late at the hospital. Could I ask you to bring my work over to Mr. Fox after school today?"

They were constantly running short of money and so, that she could buy Ray a new pair of shoes, his mother agreed to iron and darn the laundry of their strange, elderly next-door neighbor. Ray would feel weird every time he saw the basket with this strange clothing in their house. The man's clothes were generally strange, resembling no one else's, and not because it was simply out of fashion, but as though it existed altogether outside of time. Old man Fox himself seemed to exist outside of time. People said that he was almost a hundred years old, or even older, and that he was in possession of numerous recipes for magic potions that could extend his life forever. Ray did not believe any of these rumors, but he sincerely regretted only one thing, that not a single one of Mr. Fox's potions, not even had they covered every surface of his entire house, could give Ray his father back.

"No, Buddy! No!" mother exclaimed, and the chastised Buddy, who had just been blocked from snatching the piece of bread with jam from his distracted owner's plate, quickly sulked off into his corner, thereby having escaped, ironically, that very punishment just in time.

"Ray Taylor, do you know the answer to my question?" Mr. Barnes shouted, trying to drown out with his own voice the noise of the voices of the entire class.

"Yes, you, Taylor!" Mr. Barnes repeated as though issuing a challenge, and he pointed with his beloved long ruler in Ray's direction.

"Me?" Ray mumbled, having been startled from his daydream.

"Why me?" Ray ventured in reply.

"Mr. Barnes! Taylor was not listening to you again. He was probably drawing during the entire lesson," inserted the beanpole Murray.

"Nobody asked you," Mr. Barnes parried, without even turning to look at Murray.

"If he wasn't drawing, Mr. Barnes, then he was probably gawking at Jane the whole time, like he was smitten or something!" Murray added, reveling in the laughter of the entire class, as though it were a round of applause.

Jane, blushing and entirely innocent, loudly slammed shut her textbook. What she really wanted to do was to run out of the classroom.

"Taylor, there are students, I will not call them out by name now, who may as well not show up in my classes because they will not take anything away from them anyway. But you, Taylor, could grow up to be a smart young man, if physics were to draw even a part of the attention that art seems to represent for you. You are all free to go now, for today," Mr. Barnes concluded, and tossed his beloved long ruler into his open briefcase.

Ray's eyes slid across the pages of the book...

"That can't be! It simply can't be! Did you hear about it already?"

"What exactly do you mean?"

"Bloodthirsty Cook had croaked on the Island of Saint Mary Magdalene!"

"No way! That very same Bloodthirsty Cook? It can't be!"

"Can too! That's what it is!"

"So, what's gonna happen to his fabulous treasure now?"

"The crafty old man hid it! Yes, and he hid it, they say, so cunningly that neither in this nor in the other world will you ever find a daredevil capable of finding it!"

"Yes, may his pirate soul be damned to hell, the old devil's got so many ships and men's lives on his conscience! I wager that whoever finds his treasure will become richer than a dozen kings. What am I saying a dozen, perhaps richer than a whole hundred kings!"

"They say that his Secret Book is making the rounds of our city!"

"What's in it?"

"What, you say? That's where it's all described, where and how he hid his treasure! But only someone who is suicidal would set out in search of it. If anyone knew how to protect his plunder, it was he... Whoever sets out to find this treasure will surely die no less than seven tortured deaths!"

Ray suddenly heard Ms. Rose's voice coming from somewhere far away.

"Ray Taylor, what is that on your table? It doesn't look like a math textbook. If you've completed the assignment, hand in your notebook!" Mrs. Rose proposed.

"That's it, that's it, everyone who has completed their assignment must immediately hand in their notebooks for a check-up!" Mrs. Rose continued, trying to drown out the din of the entire classroom.

Everyone jumped up all at once, flung themselves toward Mrs. Rose's table, and in a split second piled it with a heap of their notebooks, some with correctly, some with incorrectly completed, and others with completely uncompleted assignments.

Someone shoved Brandon, who stumbled and fell into Bruce, Bruce collided with Darren, and together they tumbled onto Ray's table, who immediately knocked foreheads with Gary, while trying to pick up his book that had spilled on the floor.

"Is this yours?" Jane asked, handing the book to Ray, who was now scratching his smarting forehead in annoyance.

"Nn-o..." Ray replied indecisively, as though he had been asked the question not by Jane, but by Mrs. Rose.

"But, thank you anyway..." clearly agitated, Ray added out of turn, and froze still for more than a second.

Jane smiled at him. Well, of course, the sun rises each new day and sets that evening. Summer arrives, winter departs, one may make a wish, or wish something for oneself for Christmas, and to receive precisely the gift he had wished for himself. But to receive something like this, not even having had time to wish for it?! Jane had smiled at him. Jane had smiled at him. Jane had smiled at him. She had smiled at him...

"Get out of my way, shorty!" yelled Murray, knocking Ray off his feet while elbowing his way to the exit, to be, as always, the first out the door.

Jane was still smiling, while Ray was already feeling as though, out of shame and frustration, he wasn't simply falling to the floor, but collapsing through the ground.

"Well, what do you say, wharf rats? Are there any daredevils and conquerors of the watery distances among you? Or are you afraid of water and squeal even when just your mama squirts in your face while bathing you on Sunday evenings?"

Ray was dragging his feet, his eye's glued to the pages of the book.

"Who is this one-eyed goon?"

"He is a minion of The Black Devil"

"The Black Devil? The owner of the Black Galleon?"

"That very same!"

"So, what does he want?"

"Fools to go in search of Bloodthirsty Cook's treasures. Shark feed, that's what!"

"Whoever's got rum flowing through their veins instead of blood, whoever still dreams of becoming fabulously wealthy, come today to The Mangy Cat tavern!"

"And we just might, you one-eyed thug, if you're serving rum!"

"Archie, you're raving! Setting out in search of Bloodthirsty Cook's treasures, that's the same as just letting the sharks devour you right away!"

"Who is this? Who is this guy, squealing something about rum?"

"I am Archie White, you one-eyed pirate!"

"But can your spindly legs take another mug? Or will you collapse right away at The Mangy Cat, while the other lucky devils are waving goodbye to you from the ship?"

"Well, may I be torn to pieces by a hundred sea devils if you do not meet me today at seven at The Mangy Cat"! Archie growled and grabbed the one-eyed goon by the throat.

"Let me go, captain… I am willing to wager, you'll find so much of Cook's gold that a whole dozen strong hands won't be enough to drag all of it aboard your schooner…," the one-eyed sea dog gasped.

"Ray, you're getting the usual, right, a half a loaf of black bread?" Mrs. Spoke asked and immediately held out a paper bag with the bread.

"Ray, instead of having your face stuck inside a book all of the time, why don't you look where you're going or you'll trip and fall, you oddball!" Mrs. Spoke smiled and raised her double chin, as though wanting to show Ray how to hold up his head correctly.

The bus was moving slowly, as if it was in no hurry to get anywhere, and it was groaning monotonously, as though complaining about its advanced age.

The faded, wooden, single-story little houses drifted slowly by, accompanying Ray with their familiar, pensive gazes. His fingers, tightly gripping the pencil, proceeded to glide along the surface of the paper. The fluttering hair, eyebrows, eyes, smile… No… No, that's not her smile … Her smile is completely different… Irritated with himself, Ray redrew everything over and over again. One page replaced another: the fluttering hair, one more lock of hair, yet another, eyebrows, eyes... No! That's not her either... Ray was disheartened, but Jane's smile refused to yield itself to his pencil.

"Music was blaring at The Mangy Cat, and the fumes, smoke, and stench hung suspended in the air, along with the cackling and salty language of sailor talk.

Ray's eyes raced across the pages of the book.

"Hey, missus, shake a leg, will you, and serve our table already, we're dying of thirst!"

"Where you going?! Bring it over here, our throats are parched too!"

"Did the cook fall asleep in the kitchen, or is he not awake yet from yesterday's jag?"

"And where did you find these lousy musicians? Dispatch them to feed the sharks, if they don't start playing a bit livelier!"

"Where is that one-eyed punk? Who's seen him? Let him find me, Bandy Jack! I know the sea like the back of my hand, may I be torn to pieces by a hundred sharks if I don't come back with Cook's treasure, if only he'd give me a ship, and some money!"

"Bandy Jack, you're clearly cockeyed from yesterday's grog! You would soil your pants at the sight of the first shark; the second one wouldn't even go near you, squeamish of the stench!"

"The one-eyed ninny doesn't even have a map. How would he know how to find Cook's gold?"

"Cook would have been more likely to put his other eye out than to entrust him with protecting the secret of his treasure!""

"Hey, Taylor, what is that in your school bag?"

Right above Ray's ear, someone's roar mingled with the sounds of the sailors' squabble.

The bus groaned, as though cursing, and the schoolchildren spilled out of it as though unburdening an old nag of their weight.

"Hey, Taylor, are your ears stuffed with cotton or something?"

Another moment and the school backpack was knocked off Ray's shoulder.

"Didn't you hear what Mr. Barnes told you today? You're not interested in his physics lessons! And I, Taylor, don't give a damn, and not just about physics, but about Mr. Barnes himself!" the bully Murray guffawed and tossed Ray's bag into the spread arms of the pudgy Brandon.

"Give it back to me!" Ray yelled.

"And what did Mrs. Rose tell him today? That's not a math textbook on Taylor's table, but the hell knows what!" the pudgy Brandon giggled and flipped the bag over to skinny Dalton.

"Give it to me, do you hear me!" Ray grunted angrily.

"And I, Taylor, don't give a damn what Mrs. Rose said! Don't put your shabby bag in the aisle or my new sneakers will be too disgusted to stomp on it!" skinny Dylan gloated and tossed Ray's bag high up into the sky.

The sky began to cry with all of Jane's likenesses. The torn out pages of Ray's notebook spun around in the air, as though performing a mysterious dance in which the dancing girl hid neither her eyes, nor her hair, but only her smile, as though shielding it from the tasteless and intrusive gaze of the public behind a thick, impenetrable veil.

Chapter Two

Never Take Anything that Doesn't Belong to You

"Buddy, Buddy, leave me alone, not now," Ray nudged the dog's muzzle aside in irritation when, thrilled by the long-awaited arrival of his owner, Buddy started licking his hands and, now and then, jumping up on his hind legs and ceaselessly whipping the air with his tail.

"Listen Buddy, Mom is still at work, giving little children their shots, or putting compresses on their foreheads, or changing the bandaging on their arms, or their legs. You know, she is doing everything she can so that they get well soon and be able to go home. And I, Buddy, for starters, am going to have something to eat. If Mom left me some pea soup, then, I'm not going to eat it. I'd rather have some bread with jam. Only promise not to tell on me, my pal! If you don't, I will trust you with one of my secrets..."

Buddy squealed impatiently, as though expressing his agreement.

"When I grow up, Buddy, I will start earning a lot of money and buy for us – for myself, for Mom, and, of course, for you, Buddy – a big house. Oh, yes, I forgot to tell you. I'll become the tallest man on our street, and maybe even in our whole city."

The wooden floorboards made a creaking sound, but Buddy remained silent, only pricking up his ears even more, as though he were afraid to miss a word of this curious description of the future.

"When I become the tallest man, Buddy, well and, of course, the strongest, I fill finally wallop that bully Murray!" Ray's eyes shone at this triumph of justice.

"Buddy, if I'm not able to earn a lot of money, or no money at all, then I'll set out in search of Bloodthirsty Cook's treasures! They say that he had so much of it, it would be enough for ten kings, and maybe even for a whole one hundred!"

Buddy suddenly squealed again.

"So, you don't believe me, you say that I made it all up," Ray became disheartened.

"But you must understand, Buddy, that if I find the treasures, then mother won't have to work at the hospital anymore, well, unless the sick children miss her so much that she will come to visit them. And she won't have to earn extra by sewing and ironing old man Fox's clothes anymore. Oh, Buddy! Mr. Fox's clothes!" Ray yelped and hit himself on the forehead.

Ray's bicycle was bouncing over the bumps, so that the basket with the clothes, perched on the back rack, must have felt itself less than safe and secure.

"Where are we rushing to, Ray?" shouted Mr. Hansen in his wake.

"Hey, Ray, watch out so that your load doesn't end up in a pothole!" yelled Mrs. Smith with a wave of her hand.

Mr. Fox lived in isolation, in seclusion even. He had arrived in the city not so long ago and no one knew where he had come from or ever saw him out in public. Ray hit the brakes sharply, climbed down from his bike, leaned it against a tree and, as best as he could, carefully got the basket with the clothes off its perch.

Having approached the door, he knocked quietly. No one opened it. Ray knocked once again. Again, there came no reply. Ray put the basket down and knocked with both hands.

"Mr. Fox!" Ray screamed at the top of his voice.

No reply disturbed the silence of the strange house. No way was Ray going to drag the basket with the clothes back to his house. Besides, it would upset his mother very much if Mr. Fox were to accuse her of being irresponsible. The after-dinner rays were caressing the old wooden porch. Ray tilted his head back to face the sun and scrunched up his eyes, and then pulled the schoolbag that he usually carried slung across one shoulder off himself and tossed it down on the steps. The thought even crossed his mind to stretch himself out on them while waiting for Mr. Fox. The book slid all by itself out of his bag.

"The Mangy Cat absolutely reeked of a squabble.

"If the Black Devil gives me the map and some money, I will pilot the schooner!" tipsy Bandy Jack roared, hammering with his fist on the tabletop.

"I swear by the whale I'd stuck full of holes that Cook's treasures will be mine!" Jack barked and proceeded to burp loudly.

"Don' pour out any more today for Bandy Jack, mamasan! Or the one-eyed fellow will believe him and give him a schooner! Then, it will be the whale that sticks our Jack full of holes!" the sailors guffawed.

"I, Archie White, will pilot the schooner," Archie replied calmly and stretched out his feet shod in heavy boots across the chair next to him.

"Who's this Archie White?"

The tavern sunk into total silence.

"Aren't you the Captain White who sunk that brigantine last year? And your entire crew went down with the ship to feed the fishes so that you alone survived, escaping like the last rat?" drunken Jack screeched

drunkenly and turned around.

"It's none of your business, what happened with the brigantine, you sissy! Have you ever struggled to stay afloat to know what it was like, you wharf rat?!" Archie howled, grabbing Bandy Jack by his lapels.

In a split second, Jack escaped his grasp and landed a solid right to Archie's jaw. Skinny Wilson whiffed and took a punch from the sailor drenched in sweat to his left. Hulking Bill caught someone by the throat, but in the same moment was walloped in the kidneys. Nimble Larry, barely managing to escape the blow from his right, landed between someone's knees, which immediately began squeezing the life out of him, so that he howled in pain. Pudgy Ike sunk his hands into someone's beard with a howl. The three-legged stools flew into the wall and the tables were flipped upside down on the floor. The chandelier began rocking from side to side, as though this was all happening not inside a tavern but on the deck of a ship that was being tossed and pitched on the waves. Cook Duke loudly smacked his favorite frying pan against someone's cast iron head. Suddenly, a shot was fired, and the drunken brawl came to a complete standstill.

"Who among you here hungers to possess Bloodthirsty Cook's gold? Or do only drunken mama's boys gather here for fisticuffs?!" the one-eyed man, who had just appeared in the doorway, croaked in a hoarse voice.

And he intimidatingly raised his arm and pointed with the still smoking barrel of the gun at the ceiling.

In the tiny room, set off to the side from the large hall that had been demolished in the fracas, the dim light of oil lamps fell on a bulky table.

"This is The Secret Book of Cook himself," the one-eyed man hissed and placed the captain's log bound in dark leather down in the very center

of the table.

Archie and Skinny Wilson, incapable of suppressing their curiosity, immediately stretched out their hands towards it. Slap! And the one-eyed man took a whack at Wilson's wrist that had already been busted in the skirmish.

Wilson wailed and recoiled backwards.

"You'll get your schooner and money for the journey. You'll sail under the white flag. Steer hard by Bloodthirsty Cook's own chart. Do not diverge from the course and don't make any unnecessary stops," *he continued, scanning all those present with his one good eye.*

"Something doesn't smell right here... Why wouldn't the Black Devil set sail on the course and find Cook's treasures himself?" *Archie suddenly stared straight at the one-eyed bandit.*

"If it were that easy to let oneself become shark feed! That's the bargain, captain! You and your crew are risking your lives and will receive one half of the treasure for it. The Black Devil will wait for you to return. He'll be happy with the one half of such a haul!" *the one-eye man replied, winking cunningly with his one good eye.*

"If Duke is in on this, then I will sail also!" *Pudgy Ike offered.*

"I reckon I'll take the risk!" *the cook replied and passed the palm of his hand over his hair in excitement.*

"I'll join you, if Bill too doesn't say no!" *Nimble Larry raised himself up slightly without rising from his seat.*

"Sure, and why not?" *Hulking Bill smiled and cracked his knuckles.*

"So now, together with the captain, we are six! When will you give us the money?" *Skinny Wilson rubbed his hands together impatiently.*

"So, there's only six of you? That's not going to work," the one-eyed man raised his eyebrow in displeasure.

"Why?" Wilson wondered aloud.

"This Secret Book is magical, there must be seven of you, just as in Cook's crew. Otherwise, you will not find the treasure! You idiot!" the one-eyed man got mad and smacked the table with his palm.

"Don't you get worked up," Archie interceded. "We'll find a seventh. Better you explain to us what the The Black Devil is paying us for? And where and what are we to search for?"

"Everyone knows that Bloodthirsty Cook was on friendly terms with the Dark Powers," the one-eyed man began reluctantly. "Cook's treasures are hidden in an underground grotto. The map will tell you exactly where to look and where to dig. It lies now underground on the island of Tuki-tuki, torn into seven parts in seven different chests. In order to open them and assemble the map together, instead of keys, you will have to insert seven shining magical stones into the seven keyholes."

The one-eyed man caught his breath and resumed.

"In order to acquire the stones, you will have to visit seven distant nations."

Skinny Wilson began to wiggle around in his seat. Nimble Larry began nervously tugging at his shirt tails.

"Where the stones are hidden, nobody knows. Each stone will be found if you are able to decipher Cook's own riddles," the one-eyed man concluded and rubbed the handle of his pistol.

The entire crew, that had just been assembled, froze in place and all together they stared at Archie.

"It shall be done," the captain replied concisely and clicked his tongue against the roof of his mouth.

"And one more thing…" the one-eyed man added and placed two canvas bundles on the table.

"This is Cook's own spyglass and compass. Here, you see them for yourself now?" he asked Archie, who was unwrapping the bundle.

"B. C." glinted the letters on the blindingly shining copper.

The quiet creak of departing steps could be heard beyond the door.

Archie jumped up and swung it open. A woman's skirt flashed in the darkness.

"Tomorrow morning, we will be seven. We will load up the schooner and set sail. You have Archie White's word on it," Archie cut the conversation short, slamming the door shut."

Ray slammed the book in his hands shut. To his complete amazement, the door to Mr. Fox's house came slightly ajar, as though it had never been locked.

"Mr. Fox?" Ray called out, carefully peeking inside.

Some sort of strange noises were coming from the kitchen and, stepping carefully and slowly, Ray proceeded in their direction.

What came into his view was not just Mr. Fox's kitchen, but an entire factory for processing grains, flower petals, enormous roots and little rootlets, long branches and little twigs, huge mushrooms and small berries. Hanging from the ceiling were bouquets of dried grasses and stumps, strange and elaborate in form, like squirming snakes that had been caught by their tails. Gurgling on the stove top stood huge cauldrons and little saucepans, from which, boiling over, flowed a viscous crimson-colored brew.

Nearby, as though pickling that had been canned and vacuum sealed for the winter, stood little glass jars with tightly sealed lids. Hot steam was rising only above the last one, as though it had been forgotten and left unsealed by its owner. Ray took a step forward, turned around, and stretched out his hand. The sticky sweet substance, which was the color of his favorite raspberry jam, was begging to be taken into his mouth. Ray launched his tongue into the jar and licked his chops... And then he swallowed it all in one big gulp.

A strange scroll of old paper, standing on a shelf directly before him, seized his attention. It was tied up not with a piece of string, not with a lace ribbon, not with a bow, but with some dark cord, tied together with tight knots from dozens of shorter ones into a single long one. Ray had an incredibly eerie sensation when it began to seem to him that this long cord was nothing other than a single huge old mouse tail, tied together out of smaller old, dried up mouse tails.

"Mr. Fox?" Ray turned around.

Suddenly, he heard strange voices, arguing, and quarreling.

There was nothing for Ray to do other than make his way toward the door into the living room. He swung it open, and the quarreling voices neither vanished nor became clearer, because beyond the open door there turned out to be another, shuttered one. Ray opened this one also, and the voices grew louder, but in front of him, yet another closed door beckoned.

Ray raced through a labyrinth of doors, running around in a circle, swinging them open and immediately coming face to face with the next one. Darkness, a doorknob, a jerk, and again a shuttered door. Darkness, a doorknob, a jerk – and again, a door. "M-i-s-t-e-r Fo-o-o-o-x!" Ray screamed, drenched in sweat now. He seemed to himself to be a small, trapped, racing squirrel in a strange, gigantic spinning wheel. The voices kept getting louder and louder.

"A-a-a-a-a-a-a!" Ray screamed again and suddenly sensed that he was spilling out of a rolling barrel whose lid had finally become unsealed.

Without opening his tightly clenched eyes, he heard the cries of the seagulls and sensed the aromatic odor of the sea.

"May I be torn to pieces by a hundred drunken sharks! Where did this boy come from?!" Archie White howled and picked Ray up by the scruff of his neck off the ground as though he were a newborn kitten.

The port had awakened and come to life a long time ago. Cook Duke was rushing Pudgy Ike, whose back was laden with two heavy sacks of flour, Skinny Wilson was spurring on Nimble Larry, who was barely keeping up with the wheels of his water cart, Hulking Bill was trying to roll two barrels simultaneously with two hands. Everything around them was running, rolling, being dragged, and being tossed from one set of skinny hands into another, strong one, out of cracked palms into bruised ones, from weak, hunched shoulders onto strong, broad ones. And rising behind all their backs was a two-masted schooner, proudly and approvingly inspecting its cargo, as though it were its long-ago promised dowry.

"Archie!" someone shouted. "The Black Devil!"

Everything that had only just been in motion now froze and came to a standstill in piercing expectation. A quickly approaching carriage came into distant view. A muscular sailor was pulling a closed rickshaw with drawn black curtains. Barely keeping up, jogging along its right side, was the one-eyed man.

The sailor, drenched in sweat, having come to a stop right across from Archie, carefully lowered the front end of the carriage to the ground. No one came out of the rickshaw, but out from behind the previously tightly drawn black curtains appeared a hand adorned in a black leather glove and a ring.

The gloved hand with a skull ring on its middle finger, handed a heavy, tightly wrapped, little purse bag over to the one-eyed man.

The one-eyed man, bowing, accepted the burden and turned toward Archie:

"Here is the promised gold for the voyage. Cherish each coin, you will not get anything more!" he uttered threateningly.

"And should you happen to go down to the bottom of the sea before your time, tie this little bag to the mainmast. The Black Devil will find and collect it!" the one-eyed man burst into a bout of laughter.

"And where is your seventh?" he suddenly remembered and severely glowered with his eye.

Archie, who was still holding Ray by the scruff of his neck, slightly raised him up.

"A boy?!" the one-eyed man roared.

"He'll stand on guard at the entrance, when we descend into the grotto after Cook's gold!" Archie winked cunningly.

The one-eyed man froze still in indecision.

The hand in the black leather glove again appeared though the gap, rising and falling in an apparent show of approval.

The one-eyed man one more time respectfully bowed before the carriage and, having nudged the muscular sailor on the shoulder, barked out: "Get going!"

The rickshaw with the fluttering black curtains, along with the one-eyed man barely managing to keep up with it, were still visible off in the distance when a youthful woman's voice whispered hard by:

"Archie! I sewed these for you last night..."

Archie turned around. Behind him stood the willowy and dark-eyed daughter of the tavern keeper, handing him a bundle. Displayed inside the broad, woven strip of fabric embroidered with meticulously hand-sewn stitches were seven perfectly formed, empty pouches.

"I will wait for you to come back, Archie," she added shyly and ran off, flashing her nearly childlike heels and holding up the unruly hem of her long skirt, which, that night, had become exactly one strip shorter.

"So, what shall we call her?" Skinny Wilson called out suddenly.

"Who?" Archie shot back in confusion.

"Our schooner!" Wilson replied and threw his head back to gaze up at the masts.

"Ce-les-tine!" Archie announced and smiled, squinting his eyes against the bright sun.

Chapter Three

The Dead Never Forgive

"Cast off the stern line! Anchors aweigh!"

Two masts, like arms stretching out toward the sky, and angular sails, like the sleeves of a pirate's shirt, inflated by the intrepid wind, slit the sea's stilled surface. Like a callow youth driven by a passionate desire for distant voyages, unconcerned with whether he'll be able to return home triumphant (or whether he'll return home at all,) the Celestine was leaving port to the cheering acclaim of the curious crowd that had come to see it off. The sea beckoned, it enticed, promised, tempted, and not a single one of the seven ecstatic pairs of eyes on her deck saw in it any ill omen at all, but only providence and an unshakable faith in their success.

On the first day of the journey, it seemed to Ray that they had already been at sea for an entire month. For some reason, each member of the crew assumed that, because Ray was not a fully-fledged pirate, but only one half of one, then that pirate half can be, without any hesitation, be detailed to assist them. So decided the Pudgy Ike, when he was moving the barrels of provisions in the cargo hold and repeatedly calling Ray over to take a look at them: was there any space left unutilized, there, in the corner: that needs to be urgently repacked, so that the cargo not shift. So thought Cook Duke, when he was peeling potatoes and tossing them haphazardly into the pot, often missing, so that Ray was forced to crawl around on the poorly lit floor of the galley kitchen collecting them. So thought Nimble Larry, who got it into his head to swab the deck now, so that Ray was called upon to check whether it was, finally, shinning like a mirror, and he kept slipping and falling on his backside. So thought Hulking Bill, who first threw himself into securing the lifeboats, then into sundry carpentry work, all the time misplacing his tools around the deck, so that Ray had to first run and then clean up after him. Shuffling endlessly back and forth, Ray was literally working his butt off.

Only two crew members did not require Ray's assistance, and they didn't ask for it, either. This was Skinny Wilson, who, it seemed, simply didn't do anything, but was secretly seething instead: "Could this brat be really thinking he'll get the same share of Cook's gold as all of us?"And Captain Archie, who, almost without interruption, was looking inside the Secret Book.

"Hey, captain! I can't imagine how on earth you were able to manage it, but in your hands is the genuine article, the very same Cook's Secret Book!'

Archie read the very beginning.

"Yes, that very same Bloodthirsty Cook. In all likelihood, it's not difficult for you to figure out what rightfully earned me the title of Bloodthirsty!

Do you really think that you, a blunderer and perpetual looser, having gathered a bunch of good-for-nothings, fools, and mama's boys, will get your hands on the gold of Cook himself?! You will never manage to either solve my riddles, or reach the seven distant lands, or find the seven magical stones! Perhaps you've already heard something about the grotto with the seven chests that contain enough gold for ten kings, and perhaps even for a whole hundred? I laugh at you from the pit of hell! And laugh so loudly that the ears of the devils who are roasting me this moment ache! Turn back while it's not too late, you wharf rat! If you haven't already done so, set your course onward to the southwest. That is enough for today. We will meet again. And, I hope, it will be for the last time!"

Here, the text broke off, and Archie's eyes were now impotently staring at the empty pages.

By no means could Cook Duke's first night have been called restful, because Pudgy Ike, who shared his cabin, was laughing loudly in his sleep. And when Duke poked him, so that he, finally, woke up and stopped laughing, he began snoring so loudly instead that Duke immediately regretted Pudgy Ike was no longer laughing. Nimble Larry was having a nightmare and squealing, so that Skinny Wilson, who was lying beside him and dreaming of his share of gold, also didn't have a moment's peace. But in the most interesting moment, when his turn came to claim his share, Larry kept waking him up with his idiotic girlish squeals and all of Wilson's attempts to count the coins in his sleep kept being interrupted. Hulking Bill neither laughed loudly, nor snored, nor did he squeal. He slept as might a huge whale, only exhaling a long whistle from time to time, like a departing train. None of this bothered Ray one bit, because, having stretched a thin blanket over his head, with his eyes closed, he was thinking, the entire time he couldn't fall asleep, of home, about mother and Buddy. Just as soon as sleep finally overcame him, he dreamed of the bully Murray, who was forcing him to drink the small jars of the sweet raspberry mixture in Mr. Fox's house, all of them down to the very last one. And of Jane, who was simply looking reproachfully at Ray in silence, and then waving her head in disappointment.

Captain Archie could not shut his eyes and kept returning endlessly to Cook's Secret Book. But no matter how hard he stared at it its pages remained empty...

The sun had already burned Ray's nose, but, having tied his pirate bandanna around his head, he continued to refuse to come down from the mast. In its crow's nest, he felt himself free as a bird, unbound by any circumstances, entirely free to choose, where and how to live, and how high or how low, and, most importantly, where to fly. Ray thought, if he were a bird, the first thing he would do is fly to all the seven lands, and find all the seven magical stones and, no doubt, he would reach the grotto that held Cook's gold. And then, also without a doubt, he would return home.

"Hey, Ray! How are you going to spend your gold?" Pudgy Ike, whom Ray could not hear at all, screamed up to him from down on the deck.

"I will buy myself a whole slew of new skillets, and then, just maybe, an entire island! I swear, by the devil of the seas!" Cook Duke answered in his place and stared off dreamily into the distance.

"And I, well I'll be darned, I'll open my own tavern in some quiet harbor," said Ike, slipping off into some reverie.

"And I will come visit you every day, just to see your pirate mug!" Hulking Bill burst out laughing.

"Maybe I'll get married and have myself a couple of kiddies," Ike smiled crookedly.

"And I will probably open my own store and sell such weird and wonderful goods from foreign lands that everyone will flock to me just to see for themselves what new things Larry has. I swear, I really will! May I be fed to an entire school of sharks if I don't!" Nimble

Larry added and looked up at Wilson.

Wilson had stretched himself out on the deck, shielding his eyes from the sun with his tricorn hat.

"And you, Wilson?"

"I will buy white shoosies for my floozies!" Wilson yakked hoarsely and burst out in a fit of crude laughter.

Ray was still dreaming of bird flight when his gaze hit upon something approaching in the distance. It was neither another ship, nor land, nor a mountain, nor a cliff side, but a huge wave, the size of a mountain, that was rapidly rolling in directly over him. The sky turned black in a split second and began to thunder, and this enormous wave, like a giant rising from his knees, rose up as though it were gathering up its strength to come down crashing upon him with all of its terrible force. And in its path lay not a thing, except for the unfortunate Celestine.

"A-a-a-a-a-a!" Ray began screaming at the top of his lungs.

That very second, the schooner was tossed up high into the sky, but instead of being liberated, like a bird, it was once again swatted back down into the water.

"A-a-a-a-a!" screamed Pudgy Ike, grabbing a hold of Cook Duke.

"A-a-a-a-a!" screamed Nimble Larry, barely managing to grip onto Wilson.

"A-a-a-a-a!" screamed Wilson, clutching at the ladder on deck.

Captain Archie kept a firm hold of the steering wheel.

"All hands on..." Archie was screaming, but no one could hear him, for the sea smothered his voice in its deafening roar.

Suddenly, a human face burst out with great force out of this enormous, as tall as a mountain wave. This monstrous face seemed pirate-like, bearded, and disfigured by a groan.

"A-a-a-archi-ie-ie-ie!" the distorted face began to howl.

"How could you-u-u-? How could you-u-u- a-baaan-don us?" shrieked Bearded Howard.

"A-a-a-archi-ie-ie-ie!" a voice suddenly erupted from the other end of the ship, and out of the cliff of sea foam appeared another set of lips, twisted with pain and despair. Another second, and a second monstrous face emerged out of the water and stared directly at the Celestine.

One second, another second, and a third second, and more gargantuan pirate faces heaved up and out of the water, one after another, issuing groans of pain and despair and screams of terror. The Celestine was tossed from side to side, into the sky and again driven under the water, with a raging, terrifying force, as though being dragged forever to the sea's bottom. Gigantic pirate heads, bursting out of the sea foam, howled and rolled up in pain their foam-covered, waterlogged eyes.

All of them, Bearded Howard, and Jolly Jerry, and Bald Lorenz, and Toothless Mickey, all the pirates of his sunk brigantine, cried out to Archie and, bawling and moaning, begged for help.

"I did not abandon you-u-u! I-i-i was washed overboard by a waaaave!" Archie screamed with all his strength.

Were the sea not flogging him, in that moment, with its merciless, salty slaps on the cheek, it would have been able to witness the rare sight of his manly tears.

Ray came to, lying on the deck. He opened his eyes and saw Duke cowering beside him, Bill, with his arms spread outwards, Larry, curled up in a corner, Ike, lying silently on his back, and Archie, sprawled helplessly beneath the ship's helm. The Celestine was gently rocking on the stilled surface of the sea. The entire next day, she was licking her wounds, like a young tigress who had tangled in her first grown up skirmish.

Hulking Bill dashed about in the cargo hold, salvaging the remains of the provisions. Cook Duke was trying to restore some semblance of order in the kitchen, or whatever was left of it. Nimble Larry and Pudgy Ike performed their black magic on the sails. Wilson holed himself up in a corner, his teeth still chattering. And Ray, out of joy that he was still alive, was offering his assistance to one and all.

Captain Archie mustered the nerve and opened Cook's Secret Book again. It seemed that, even if the Celestine had perished in this storm, the only thing that would have floated back up to the surface is the unsinkable Secret Book.

"Well, may I be bitten by the Sea Devil! Are you still there, Captain? Your lousy leaky tub didn't withstand even the first sea quake, and you dared think that you would succeed in finding the first stone?

Well, go ahead and try, you miserable pirate soul! If you wish to reach the gold of Cook himself, then you will, first of all, need to go and find the blood-red Credisford.

And, one more thing:

DO NOT BELIEVE YOUR OWN EYES AND HEED THE CRIES OF SEAGULLS.

Farewell, captain! If only you knew, how much fun it is on the far side of paradise! The devils, just now, lost to me at cards. For this, I now have the privilege of frying one of the new arrivals on one of their frying pans! Ho-ho-ho-ho!"

"Do not believe your own eyes and heed the cries of seagulls?! Cook be damned! Is there anyone at all in this world who will succeed in solving this riddle?!" Archie became furious. "Only don't believe for a second that I will ever back down! Don't even think that I can be broken! I will see it to the end, even if I'm the last man standing. Do you hear me, you, old sea devil!?"

CREDISFORD

Chapter Four

The Lost City of Sacro-Luxe, or The Hidden World

s it had done consistently, Cook's compass guided their way. Archie nervously clambered up the mast and saw the outline of a huge cliff on the horizon, suddenly rising up before them as though out of nowhere. Its stony height grew so quickly that one no longer had to climb up the mast in order to see it.

"There's a cliff right in our path! The devil take me!" screamed Nimble Larry, who had taken Archie's place at the helm.

"Captain, right in our path is a cliff! May the devil take me!" Hulking Bill repeated.

"That's what it is. Well, kill me now! We're changing course, Captain!" affirmed Skinny Wilson.

Ray ran out on deck.

"Captain! We're heading right for the cliff!" Cook Duke and Chubby Ike cried out in unison.

"We cannot change course! The compass points exactly here!" Archie screamed.

In quick leaps and bounds, he climbed down, grabbed Cook's spyglass, and again clambered up, his eyes now peeled to the spyglass.

Looked at through Cook's spyglass, there was not a hint of the cliff face, as though it had never existed. Instead, what he saw was the long awaited-for land!

"Land! Stay the course! Land!" Archie screamed at the top of his lungs. "Do not change course, straight ahead!"

"Idiot! You'll kill us all!" hollered Skinny Wilson.

"Archie, change course, while it's not too late!" squawked Ike and Duke.

"Archie, come to your senses!" begged Nimble Larry.

"Change course, Captain!" thundered Hulking Bill.

"Stay the course! La-a-a-and!" Archie kept screaming, shoving Larry aside and gripping tightly onto the helm.

The huge black cliffside sprouted quickly, like a black iceberg, and the Celestine was hurtling right for it, now irrevocably, like a stupid, tiny moth at a flame blazing nearby.

"A-a-a-a-a-a-a!" the entire crew screamed in a choir.

"La-a-a-and!" Archie croaked out, losing his voice.

"Ba-a-a-ang!' the black cliff thundered, crashing into the Celestine.

The Celestine struck into the cliff and went right through it, gliding gently into a dock at an alien shore. Chubby Ike, Cook Duke, Hulking Bill, Wilson, Larry, Archie, and Ray all turned around: there was not a trace of the cliff left, only the sea's stilled surface being caressed by the waves. And spread out before them was a new, unexplored world, where the red magical Credisford lay hidden....

The Celestine came to moor in a strange port, but something here was amiss. Ike and Duke came ashore, Nimble Larry was taking quick, short steps in front of them, Wilson was cautiously glancing about, Hulking Bill, having offered him his strong hand, helped Ray get down, Archie turned around and shrugged his shoulders in bewilderment. This was indeed a port, but besides their Celestine, that had just docked there, there was not a single other ship. And only the malevolent creak of the shabby door of a seaside dive bar ruptured the dreary, dead silence.

The crew reluctantly trudged ahead, passing a strip of abandoned buildings. Suddenly, the silence was pierced by music, the lively, joyful music of the jubilant cheers of a crowd. Ike and Duke exchanged glances, Skinny Wilson listened intently, tilting his head, Larry and Archie quickened their pace, and Ray, barely managing to retrace with his feet Bill's gigantic footsteps, almost started skipping and jumping. One more street, and the sounds grew louder, one more, and they were lifted up by a wave of a human throng, quickly and warmly plunging them into its crush, as though squeezing them in its tight, welcoming embraces.

"Hey! Who are you?" Ray was nudged by a redheaded girl with a funny looking gap between her front two teeth.

"Ray!" having turned around, Ray replied immediately.

"Are you here by yourself? " she looked at him, puzzled.

"No," Ray replied. "We are seven," and he nodded his head in the direction of the crew, who, just as he, were drowning in a sea of people.

"But you aren't dressed?" the girl said, surprised.

"In what?" Ray asked, at a loss for what she meant.

"All in white! Don't you see, today is a holiday?"

Ray looked around and confirmed that only the seven from the Celestine weren't dressed in a white and spacious robe, like each and everyone else in this cheering crowd.

"This isn't permitted. If they see you, they will immediately take you away!" the girl wouldn't leave him alone.

"Who?" Now it was Ray's turn to be surprised.

"The Ruler's people," she replied and whispered something to the woman who was walking beside her. The woman leaned over, looked attentively at Ray, and whispered something to the man on her right. The chain of whispering people turned to look at the crew of the Celestine and suddenly parted for a moment, but only in order to immediately merge even tighter together again.

"Take this," the girl whispered to Ray, handing him a white robe.

"Put it on, I'm telling you, if you don't want any trouble," she said, threateningly.

Ray definitely did not want to have even worse trouble than what they've already had, and so he pulled the broad, white robe on over his own clothing almost eagerly.

Duke dove into a robe, pressured to do so by the woman to his right. Ike reluctantly squeezed himself into the white sheet, after the man on his right gave him a severe look. Larry scuttled inside a robe, glancing over at Archie, who was already wearing white. Dressed in a white robe, Wilson resembled a ghost, and the white sleeves of someone else's robe had only just burst on Hulking Bill's arms.

"I am Gwyneth!" the girl with the funny-looking gap between her teeth smiled. "And this is my mother, Terra," she nodded in the direction of the woman standing beside her.

"Hold this!" Gwyneth yelled, trying to drown out the loud music and singing, and stuck a thick pole into Ray's hand.

Ray threw his head back and saw that above him, fluttering on the wind, was an enormous white seagull, flying, or more precisely, floating on the poles in the dozens of hands hiked upwards.

"We are the seagulls!" Gwyneth smiled joyfully.

Ray turned around: above the human throng, soared some dozen similarly enormous, white, airborne seagulls.

"On the even-numbered streets – the second, the fourth, and the sixth – are the seagulls. On the odd – the first, the third, and the fifth – the fish. The fish must not allow themselves to be caught by the gulls, or the gulls will eat them!' Gwyneth explained proudly.

The festival of the seagulls and the hunt for the fish seemed enviable to Ray, and he regretted that in his world and in his city, people did not get dressed up all in white and pursue and hunt down, with the huge seagulls held up on poles, the enormous fish from the odd-numbered streets.

"And have you had it a long time?" Ray asked.

"What?" Gwyneth asked back.

"This festival," clarified Ray.

"Ever since all the seagulls in our parts vanished. Or haven't you noticed?"

"Of course!" it occurred to Ray. An isolated, old, neglected port and not a single cry of a seagull!

"And what about the port?" asked Ray.

"It had been abandoned long ago. Ships no longer visit us. My father too went to sea and did not return," Gwyneth replied, and gazed over at her mother, who was looking at her reproachfully.

"They say that before our shore stands an enormous rock. That is why the entrance to our harbor is blocked," Gwyneth whispered directly in Ray's ear, fearfully gazing back at her mother.

And she added, "But it is visible only from the sea, we're fated never to see it, this cursed bewitched rock!"

"Gwyneth!" her mother restrained her. "Better you ask the foreigners if they have a place to stay tonight?"

"No, mother. There are seven of them and they all have no place to stay tonight!" Gwyneth pronounced with distinct pleasure.

"We rent rooms, but because no one ever sails here, they are always standing empty," Gwyneth added, tugging at Ray's sleeve.

"Fi-i-i-i-ish!" the throng of seagulls screamed, and the two streams of humanity dressed in white robes merged together, stretching the poles higher in suspense. And the hungry, soaring seagulls collided with the airborne fish happily prepared to offer themselves in sacrifice for the sake of the long-awaited return.

Like all the houses in the city of Sacro-Luxe, Gwyneth's house was built out of light stone and had a quiet, winding lane leading to it. Here and there, the way was decorated with mosaics made of light- and dark-shaded smooth cobblestones. The mosaics spelled out strange words, apparently in an ancient tongue long-ago forgotten here, in which, once upon a time, Gwyneth's ancestors spoke. Beside the entrance to every house, a slight niche for a lamp resembling a stone nest was built into the wall. And, as soon as twilight fell on the city, every inhabitant lit her lamp, and the entire city of Sacro-Luxe was transformed into a single, large, flickering firefly. According to local legend, it was the widows of sailors who had never returned who were the first ones to leave their light on for the whole night, refusing to believe that their husbands and grooms would never again return. Lighting these lamps, they tried, even at night, to show the way to their houses for the vanished vessels in hopes of a miracle. It was precisely this night light that performed a miracle and helped a lost ship return home many hundreds of years ago.

Ike and Duke, sharing a single room in Terra's and Gwyneth's house, having turned red after a hot bath, devoured their hostess' soup in the common kitchen on the first floor. Skinny Wilson kept making Larry run to the hostess for the local wine and loudly knocked with his spoon, greedily gathering up the last drops in his bowl. Hulking Bill asked for a third serving, and Ray was so famished he wouldn't have minded a fourth. Archie sat, deeply immersed in thought, his arms crossed and his legs stretched out.

Gwyneth, having moved even closer to Ray at the common table, whispered in his ear: "Today, I will knock exactly three times on your window. Then, you must come out and quietly close the door behind yourself."

"What for?" asked Ray.

"We will go for a walk on the nighttime roofs!" Gwyneth replied mysteriously, her eyes ablaze with excitement.

Someone knocked three times, but on the ledge and not the window. Terra immediately got up and came out, closing the door tight behind herself, as though wary that someone who ought not know what was going on overhear their evening conversation.

"Why are they here?"

"They are not bothering anyone."

"We don't need them. They might spoil everything."

"And what if they could help us instead?"

"It could turn out to be a question of life and death... But why should they risk their lives if, just as strangely as they appeared here, they might vanish tomorrow into thin air. And we will remain alone to rot here. We will remain alone, cut off from the world just as before, and your husband will never succeed in returning. No matter how many lamps you might light for him!"

"I must go, come back tomorrow" Terra replied, and slipped back inside the house.

Terra's heavy hair was pulled together tightly in a bun on the back of her head, as though their owner did not wish to display their beauty to the world. Her long, modest dress served as though it were a defense against prying eyes, which were seeking to appraise her figure. And her large, dark eyes, framed by thick, black eyelashes, more often than not looked downward than into someone's eyes, so that their flame wouldn't give away her thoughts to anyone.

"Terra!" Archie called her. "Would you bring me more wine," he asked, following her with a long and pensive gaze.

"Knock. Knock. Knock," came a crisp, loud sound in the window. Still sleepy, Ray got up reluctantly, barely found his clothing in the dark by feel, pulled it over himself and, without even being afraid to awaken Hulking Bill, loudly trudged across the length of the entire room, the silence of which was broken anyway by a resounding, nocturnal snoring resembling the whistle of a train engine.

"Take it, it's for you!" Gwyneth Ray slipped him a small lantern on a crook-shaped handle.

"Give me your hand!" she hurried him, lighting the way with a similar small lantern.

Ray jumped up, clambered up a ladder and, supporting Gwyneth with his strong hand, in a heartbeat, found himself on the roof.

"And now, come here!" Gwyneth rushed him again and, without drawing their hands apart, pulled him along after herself.

The houses along the narrow, convoluted lanes of Sacro-Luxe descended the island's slopes and climbed up its hills.

"We go only higher!" Gwyneth commanded, and pulled Ray along from one roof to another.

In some places, the distance between the roofs was sufficiently wide that one wouldn't even dare think of jumping over to the neighboring roof in the daytime, but quite narrow enough to clear the gap in a couple of seconds, in one jump, at night.

With the small lantern in one hand and Gwyneth's daring and indomitable strong hand in the other, Ray was pulled further and further.

"Loo-ook o-o-over the-e-ere!" said Gwyneth, smiling at Ray, who was out of breath.

Ray got up, straightened himself, caught his breath, and... He felt himself to be free as a night bird, soaring somewhere high upon high in the dark night sky. And beneath him, as though pointing the way home, flickering like an enormous firefly, was the dreaming, but never sleeping, lit up town of Sacro-Luxe.

In the morning, after Ray had finally fallen asleep and Gwyneth had left for school, he was left to his own devices. Wandering along the narrow lanes of the early morning Sacro-Luxe, it was difficult for him to imagine that last night he had been flying across its roofs. All the window displays of the little shops were decorated with the small-, medium- and large-sized statuettes of a short, balding, fat little man. The short, fat, balding little man sleeping. The short, fat, balding little man eating. The short, fat, balding little man thinking. This seemed amusing to Ray, and he went inside one of the stores. In this stuffy shop, where he was at once welcomed by the ring of a little door bell, all the walls, from floor to ceiling, were filled and hung with the drawn, hand-sewn, embroidered, blown out of glass, sculpted out of clay, and burned into wood images of a short, fat, balding little man. One could use the bar of soap with the face of the short, fat, balding little man to wash one's hands, then use a towel with the face of the short, fat, balding little man embroidered on it to wipe them, put on a shirt and hat, and wear on your back a canvas backpack with a portrait of the short, fat, balding little man. One could eat from a plate, severely looking at you from the bottom of which was a short, fat, balding little man. Then, you could wash down your meal from a goblet, smiling magnanimously from the wall of which was the short, fat, balding little man. Then you could wipe your mouth with a woven napkin decorated with the face of the short, fat, balding little man. Generally speaking, if one wished to, one could spend an entire day without ever parting from the short, fat, balding little man. And perhaps, even not your entire life.

"Are you interested in any souvenirs? Which of the Rulers did you like the most?" asked the stringy little old man leaning over across his counter.

"I have some new wares! Embroidered bed sheets, a nightshirt with a nightcap. Oh, of course, you probably need something for school instead... Yes? Quills, notebooks? Or is it a school bag?"

"And all of it comes with the face of the little man? Hmm. The Ruler?" said Ray in a tone of surprise.

"Well of course! I always have the latest goods!" the shop owner assured him.

The little doorbell forced him to turn around once again. A man, his face wearing an expression of alarm, entered the shop, stooping to pass under the low doorway. At his appearance, the shop owner became alarmed himself and quickly squeezed through the narrow passageway behind the counter, as though he had been expecting exactly this visitor a while ago.

"Are you interested in clay figures of the Ruler? I have all the latest goods: twelve statuettes symbolizing the months of the year, and they fit quite nicely in any flowerbed. They are modest in height, from fifteen to forty inches. If you order both the summer collection, "The Ruler in his summer dress," and the winter version, "The Ruler in his long robe," I will definitely give you a discount!"

That moment, the shop owner nervously stretched out his neck, looked out of the window, and suddenly, not finding anyone there, quickly nodded to his visitor.

"Well? Did you bring it?"

"I did," the visitor replied.

"We must still discuss the final version. But, meanwhile, this will do. Mr. Hill's print shop is closed today. It's being searched."

"Let me have it!" the shop owner whispered impatiently and grabbed a neatly rolled up sheet from the visitor's hand.

Unexpectedly, the little doorbell rang one more time and two men, dressed identically in gray, entered the shop, cursing that they had to stoop to do so.

"Hello, Mr. Howard!"

"Hello!" replied the shop owner.

"How is business?" the men in gray asked.

"I can't complain," the owner replied again.

"We have a suspicion of your insincerity, Mr. Howard... The year is already long in the tooth and you haven't yet ordered the new portraits of our Ruler. That's not good, Mr. Howard," the men in gray expressed their dissatisfaction, casting disparaging glances in all directions.

"You're absolutely right! I must urgently, urgently update my wares!" the owner immediately agreed and took a single step back.

Stepping backwards, he dropped the sheet neatly rolled into a scroll, that he was hiding the entire time behind his back, on the floor. The scrolled-up sheet rolled on the floor and landed right at Ray's feet.

"Perhaps I'll come another time," the visitor who had just been mysteriously exchanging whispers with the owner suddenly bid farewell. He quickly ascended the stairs and exited the shop.

"Well, I too will come another time then," added Ray, bending down, as though to tie his shoelaces and, again straightening out, ran up the stairs and slammed the door shut behind himself.

As soon as Ray found himself out in the street, he immediately turned the corner, looked around fearfully, and unscrolled the rolled-up sheet.

"Dear inhabitants of the town of Sacro-Luxe! If you are not yet despairing entirely, if you still believe that the cursed barrier rock blocking us off from the rest of the world may one day vanish, if you still hold on to the hope that your brothers, fathers, and husbands will find their way home and return to Sacro-Luxe, if you still pause to listen for the voices of the seagulls returning to our shores, unite! Having heard the cry of the seagulls, follow it. We are already many, but, if you join us, we will be yet even more numerous!"

Ray neatly rolled the sheet back into a scroll and shoved it inside his pocket.

They were sitting on a steep precipice, the wind ruffling Ray's hair and shirt, and Gwyneth, offering her face to the brazen breeze, closed her eyes.

"I would also like to fly away, like a bird!" she confessed to him and spread her arms wide open.

"But this is where I was born and I am waiting for my father, because he can only return here." "Otherwise, he would be unable to find us..."

"And where is your home?" she suddenly asked Ray and looked directly into his eyes.

"Very far away..." Ray answered, looking with a sorrowful expression off into the distance.

"Your family lives there?" Gwyneth would not let it drop.

"Mother and Buddy," Ray affirmed.

"And your father?"

"He will never return again," Ray replied.

"Did he also go out to sea?" Gwyneth said, surprised.

"No. He's dead," Ray replied, and lowered his eyes.

"And I don't believe that my father is dead!" Gwyneth suddenly yelled out, jumping up from where she was sitting.

Ray stretched his hand out to her, as though inviting her to sit back down again.

"Who do you think blocked the entrance to your world? And will the ships return once again to your port, if the cliff disappears? And why does the short, fat, balding little man have so much power?"

"I-I-I-I! Is it me?" Gwyneth asked with excitement, having caught a glimpse of the drawing in the notebook she had only just given Ray as a gift.

"Nnno," Ray had no choice but to admit.

And Jane's proud, girlish eyes shot a triumphant gaze from the newly completed drawing at Gwyneth's disappointed face.

A strange-looking man who was rapidly shuffling his feet and continuously looking around himself side to side ran across Archie's and Wilson's path. Having crossed to the opposite side of the street, he immediately collided with Duke and Ike. In another split second, awkwardly stepping on Larry's foot, he accidentally buried his nose in Hulking Bill's stomach, because instead of looking where he was going, he was constantly fearfully wagging his head from side to side. Turning around for the last time, he suddenly cried out like a seagull and disappeared behind a door. Archie nodded to Bill, Bill nudged Larry, Larry stumbled and fell onto Ike, who nearly dragged Duke down after himself. Duke was able to stay on his feet, but accidentally stepped on Wilson's foot. Wilson, having burst out in a howl, immediately stopped himself, seeing Archie's fist threatening his face. Biting down on his lip, he bent forward and shoved the door beyond which the stranger had vanished with his shoulder.

"What's the password?" he was asked in the dark.

Archie moaned like a seagull.

"Enter. Down the stairs, first turn to the left," an answer came out of the darkness and the doors were hospitably flung open.

Having ran quickly down the stairs, turned left, and promenaded down a long and dark corridor and having once again found himself facing a closed door, Archie tugged at it. The door immediately gave way and in the poorly lit cellar, he saw a group of men standing bent over two large tables that had been moved together. On the single large table thus formed, there lay a massive, chessboard-like playing field, set up with the black and white figures of the short, fat, balding little man, for playing a game between two large teams. Out of breath, Wilson came to a complete stop behind Archie's back. Larry and Ike had their gazes pealed to all sides, Duke was struggling for breath, Hulking Bill was exhausted from craning his neck in these low crawl spaces, and Ray could barely contain himself from jumping up and down so that he could see what was going on over everyone's backs.

"Who are you?" the men who had just been playing froze still in incomprehension and, all to a man, turned their heads around to stare at the unexpected visitors.

In the darkest and most distant corner of the cellar space, suddenly, the creak and squeak of a rocking chair could be heard, and an elder with a long beard, a wrinkled (like an old, dried out apple) face, and closed eyes took the pipe out of his mouth and, without batting an eyelash, said in a hoarse voice: "It's the outlanders. Let them in. They've come for the red stone..."

"But, prophet!" one of the men objected.

"Let them in!" declared another.

Someone, standing behind the door, stepped back, opened it wider and, for some reason, respectfully bowed his head.

In the blink of an eye, the black and white figures of the short, fat, balding little man, swatted at by the players like pesky flies, flew in a jumble to the floor, knocking their bald spots against each other. With the coordinated swinging of a dozen arms, the over-sized board for the game played by the Ruler's faithful subjects was flung into the air and landed back on the table with its back side up. Tall toothed and low arched gates, grand entryways and tiny secret portals, broad main and narrow parallel lanes, large buildings and minute barns, all this was revealed to the public eye on this huge, scrupulously composed model of the Ruler's lands.

"Precisely here, in this small room, both day and night, the walls are illuminated by a red light," one of the men pronounced emphatically, sticking his finger in the very center of the map.

"So that's where you are, magical Credisford!" Archie thought to himself and, smiling indistinguishably, for one moment, closed his eyes.

Terra was doing the wash. Her ruddied face was framed by disarrayed jet-black curls. The bodice of her sleeveless dress revealed her long arms, and her tucked-in skirt accentuated her strong, shapely legs.

"Well, what do you say, mistress, is it hard for you? Have you been here alone a long time now?"

"I-I-I!" Terra was frightened and out of breath.

Wilson popped up in front of her as though out of nowhere. He leaned in closer and placed his hand on her shoulder.

"Leave me alone!" Terra tried to cut him off.

"Really, I am not even allowed to help you?" Wilson wouldn't drop it; his face was twisted into a grimace.

"I'm telling you, drop it already!" Terra answered sharply, trying to free her shoulder the entire time.

"Take your hands off her!" someone said behind them.

"A-a-ah... We've got ourselves a knight in shining armor!" Wilson bared his teeth at Archie. "The Captain has already set his sights on his booty, and here, I jumped the line in front of him!" he said, breaking into crude laughter.

"Shut up!" Archie snapped and walloped Wilson in the jaw with everything he had.

"Damn it!" Wilson wiped his bloodied lip and immediately landed a right on Archie's jaw.

"Aaah!" Terra shrieked.

"Stop it! Cut it out!" she hollered.

The two men were rolling around on the floor of the laundry room in each other's bitter embraces, upsetting the tubs of laundry and the vats of scolding hot water. Like the seaside waves, the soapy white foam flooded the entire floor, on the slick surface of which the freshly laundered wash set sail.

"It's the outlanders again!" the sentry at the door announced and, for the third evening already, the entire crew of the Celestine, bending their heads to pass beneath the low-hanging arched ceiling, skittered into the dim cellar. The map of the Ruler's possessions was prickling with markers and with secret, abbreviated inscriptions.

"Tomorrow, we will be bringing his favorite three-layered nut torte to the Ruler's estate," the caterer launched into an explanation.

"I will sneak inside along with the caterers," Nimble Larry proposed.

"And then what?" Archie didn't quite catch his train of thought.

"Once in the kitchen, I will quietly steal over to the fireplace and climb through it up to the roof. And once on the roof, I will make my way to the chamber with the red stone!" Larry explained.

"And how will you recognize from the roof, you idiot, what room you must crawl into?" Wilson barked out, nursing his swollen lip and black eye.

"I'll wait until it's dark, crawl carefully across the roof, and see for myself what window glows with a red glimmer!" Larry winked cunningly to all those listening to him attentively.

"Who else will be going to the Ruler's estate tomorrow?" Archie inquired.

"Our coachman, who usually takes us to deliver the order to the Ruler," the caterer replied.

"And what if tomorrow this will be Duke?" Archie proposed.

"And also his wife, who always sits next to him, and each time tells the sentry: "Good day! It's the caterers with an order for the Ruler!"" the caterer recalled.

Archie, barely suppressing a smile, stared at Wilson.

"Don't joke like that, Captain!" Skinny Wilson snapped back.

"And the wife will turn up as well!" Archie blurted out, incapable of holding back a fit of laughter.

"And where do we go?" Chubby Ike and Hulking Bill intoned, sagging in disappointment on the backs of their chairs.

"The three of us, like all the Ruler's faithful subjects, will be parading beyond the stony gates awaiting the signal," Archie commanded.

"And what about me?" Ray chimed in resentfully.

"Here, by the stone wall, grows an ancient tree," one of the conspirators interceded, sticking his finger into the map.

"If you're not just short, but also agile and nimble, you will be able to send us signals about what is going on beyond the gates," he proposed, and bored into Ray with his gaze.

"Let it be so," Archie agreed.

"Prophet! And you? Do you give us your blessings?" one of the men threw himself at the feet of the bearded elder seated on the rocking chair in the room's furthest and darkest corner.

"His feet are always cold... The Ruler's feet freeze easily," the bearded man intoned slowly without ever opening his old, wrinkled eyelids and once again sunk into his interrupted dream.

The twilight glided like spilled ink down the hillsides, slowly but surely coming to embrace each and every stone house of the town of Sacro-Luxe, curiously taking a peek into its windows. As though finding this shameless intrusion unbearable, the windows immediately slammed shut, guarding their secrets with their unyielding shutters.

"If we succeed, tomorrow evening we will already be on our way," Archie said and looked attentively into Terra's eyes.

"I must go. But I could return, for someone like you," he suddenly added.

Terra froze still for a split second.

"I could wait my entire life for someone like you. But I am already waiting for another... and I still believe that he will return," Terra answered, lowering her head.

"Who are you? What are you here for?" the sentry uttered in his steely timbre.

"Catering, with an order for the Ruler!" a woman's odious squeal came in reply.

"And a good day to you too!" having caught an elbow under his ribs, the squeaky voice added, as though having just remembered that detail.

"Proceed, but only straight ahead! No gawking around! And come to a full stop at the intersections!" the sentry roared, letting Duke's and Wilson's wagon through, the latter man attired in Terra's scarf and long dress.

Archie sat on a terrace near the stone gates, playing against one of the conspirators, the game resembling chess with the figurines of the short, balding, fat little man. Hulking Bill was dawdling around in the street with another of the plotters. Chubby Ike was helping the owner of the little grocery stand with the awnings arrange her fruit display. Six pairs of sharp eyes were casting anxious gazes in Ray's direction. Ray, having quickly clambered up and nimbly hidden in the crown of the mighty tree, waved his arm downward, which they had agreed meant: "They let them through".

"We're bringing the Ruler his favorite torte!" Duke answered the sentry at the next intersection without waiting for a reply.

The sentry stared at Duke peevishly, then circled around the cart laden with confections and the tall, nut torte, carefully inspecting each item.

Everyone froze still in indecisiveness, so that it seemed that even the horse had lost its bearings. Ray, as though sensing the boring, worried gazes of the impatiently awaiting men, traced a horizontal line in the air with his hand, which meant: "They've been stopped."

"Achoo!" Skinny Wilson couldn't withstand the tickling of the tassels of Terra's scarf with which he was covering one half of his face.

"My wife has caught a cold," Duke immediately apologized.

"Then leave her with me!" grunted the sentry.

In anger, Duke zapped Skinny Wilson with his elbow even harder, and Wilson readied himself to give him back the change but remembered in time the sentry who was reducing him to ashes with his gaze. Reluctantly, he turned around and, covering himself with the scarf and cursing under his breath, climbed down from the cart.

Ray, spreading the foliage apart and not believing his own eyes, immediately crossed his arms above his head, which in Archie's code meant: "Only the devil himself knows what is going on. But something out of the ordinary and not according to plan is happening, may God help us!"

Archie chopped down his own figurine of the short, fat, balding man instead of that of his opponent. Hulking Bill inexplicably pushed the trash back to the clean side of the street which he had only just swept clean. Chubby Ike dropped a box of apples and they quickly scattered in all directions in the street, as though each of them had wished to return to the tree they had come from.

Duke drew on the reins and the horse once again started pulling the cart. The "caterers" lowered their eyes, afraid to once again anger the guards.

Having come to a full stop, they quickly jumped down and, like a ship entering harbor, the tall, three-layered nut torte, borne on four pairs of stretched out, strong arms, came into its kitchen dock. Nimble Larry quickly scurried inside after them.

"Well, finally! What took you so long?" the caterers, dressed all in white, and the chefs, wearing the tallest, white toque hats, were rudely greeted.

"The guard was in a bad mood today! He took the lid off each pot and looked inside every box! Soon enough, he'll demand that we repackage the bags of flour under his watchful eyes!"

"Where is he?"

"He's here already!" the caterer replied and pointed at Larry.

"Hurry up! Over here!" somebody waved his arm and pointed out to Larry the way to the fireplace.

Larry looked around and, without giving it much thought, slipped off into the dark.

The catering cart with Duke, but now without Wilson, Larry and the three-layered torte, barely had time to leave the Ruler's stony estate, when the alarm raised by the guard forced the kitchen to shudder.

"Hey! This ain't no dame! It's a man! Grab the bandit!!!" the sentry screamed and poked with his spear, tearing Terra's dress on Wilson's back.

Nimble Larry lay still on the roof until twilight. When his dreams of the red magical stone, the Credisford, ceased to be merely thoughts, but threatened to haunt him even in his deep sleep, he shook his head vigorously from side to side, trying to wake himself up, and carefully set off for his destination. Each lit room shed an eerie light, just as he had thought. Here, it was yellow. Larry crawled on, grasping on with his hands, like a cat with its claws, and pulling his feet behind himself. Here, no light of any kind was being emitted, and Larry again resumed crawling forward. Here, it was yellow again, then again nothing, suddenly again yellow, yellow, yellow, yellow, yellow. And then – red! Eureka! From the room below him shone a perfectly red light!

"So here it is, the Credisford! May the devil take me!" Larry said to himself ecstatically. Crawling carefully, he lowered himself down to the ledge and, clinging on to it with his fingers trembling from the tension, swung his feet inside the window.

His feet immediately felt the tight embrace of strange arms, and his mouth, not having had time for even a pipsqueak, a strange, broad palm silencing it.

"And here's the second!" the sentry erupted with laughter, squeezing Nimble Larry even more tightly.

In the cellar dim, above the map of the Ruler's possessions, in the stuffy, locked up air, the atmosphere was one of despair.

"He had to have descended with the magical red stone through the chimney down to the kitchen and got out along with the shift change of the cooks!" Archie shook his head indecisively.

"The guards are ranting and raging! As soon as they arrested the two, entrance to the Ruler's estate was forbidden to everyone! Even the servants weren't allowed to go home!" the plotter added anxiously.

"What should we do, Captain? We will never reach the stone now!

And how are we going to get Larry and Wilson back?" said Ike, scratching the back of his head.

"Tomorrow is the Ruler's birthday. But due to the incident, celebrants will not be permitted to enter in the usual manner... They will only make an exception for children. Tomorrow, Gwyneth's class will pass beyond the stone fence and sing to the Ruler in his honor in his private chambers," the plotter concluded, sinking into his chair.

"I will go too!" Ray jumped out of his chair.

"Can I go to the Ruler's estate tomorrow together with Gwyneth's class?" Ray shouted and, unable to contain himself, jumped up and down.

"I am afraid you simply have no other option..." the conspirator seconded him and stared pleadingly over at Archie.

"Prophet! Is it worth the risk for us to try again?" the plotters flung themselves towards the rocking armchair in the room's darkest corner.

"The stone. The magical red stone. It alone holds the Ruler's power. His feet. His feet get cold easily," the elder said hoarsely without awakening, supporting his beard the entire time with his hand, as though his power of prophecy resided in it alone.

Terra entered Ray's room carefully and quietly: filled with excitement, he could not fall asleep for even a minute, and Hulking Bill's train engine-like snore was shaking and rattling the night air.

"Hey, Ray!" Terra called out.

Ray immediately jumped up.

"Don't get up," she asked and sat down next to him.

"You have a big day ahead of you. You can save your crew. And rid all of Sacro-Luxe of the tyrant. You will succeed, if you will be brave, and if you are fortunate," Terra whispered to him.

"All the children will bear their lit lanterns to the Ruler tomorrow, as they always do to celebrate state holidays. This is my father's old lantern; in our family, we assign a mystical force to it... Take it with you tomorrow, let it bring you and all of us luck!" Terra concluded, raising the little lantern upwards.

Ray carefully accepted it into his hands and nodded, as though promising to try his best.

The door to Archie's room was wide open; passing by it, Terra saw him sitting on his bed, immersed in thought and cradling his head in his arms. She stopped, dawdled and, as though prohibiting herself from some frivolity, quickly, so as not to have time to reconsider, stole quietly down the stairs.

The gigantic iron gates swung open reluctantly, the guard having nodded approvingly, and the caravan of children bearing lit lanterns flowed like a swarm of tiny fireflies into the Ruler's estate. Seized with anxiety, Gwyneth kept on shaking her head, and Ray had to tug her by the sleeve to bring her back to her senses. Bypassing all the checkpoints and without any questions from the infuriated guards, the caravan glided to the main building along the broad central street. The children began to slowly climb the endless steps leading to the main entrance. And only a single lantern, like a mettlesome firefly departing its flock, flickered and was extinguished, disappearing behind the little side door.

From all the time he had spent huddled above the plotters' map in the dim cellar, it already seemed to Ray that he had all the entrances and exits, chimneys, storerooms, staircases, back doors, and secret passages on the Ruler's estate memorized. He raced to the servants' changing room down a narrow, hidden, dark corridor, opened the door, stretched out his hand and, precisely where the cooks promised it would be, he found a white chef's jacket and hat, both of them the right size for a cook's apprentice. Skipping and hopping on the track of odors emanating from so many exquisite dishes, Ray, kicking the swinging door with his foot, flew headlong into the kitchen, and, having floated over to the serving counter, ordered: "Two of yesterday's portions for the newly arrived prisoners!" Having grabbed the platter with the two tin bowls, having barely glanced at the dishes, Ray raced downstairs toward the entrance to the dungeon.

"What is going on here?" the sentry stared at him inquisitively.

"Gruel for the prisoners!" Ray reported military style.

"Have you gone crazy over there in the kitchen? You want to fatten them up or something?"

Ray shrugged his shoulders.

"They've been fed already!" the sentry barked out, but nevertheless, reluctantly opened the prison bar door to let Ray in.

Ray, trying to scurry past the gate, collided with the sentry, stepping on his painful foot callus, and was then off to the races down the long staircase, almost dropping and spilling the tin bowls.

"Hey-y-y! Shorty! Look where you're going!" the sentry muttered in irritation, gingerly raising his aching foot.

"Don't move and don't make a noise!" Ray commanded, having reached the deflated Larry and Wilson. "As soon as you hear the clock strike seven, open the lock, run up the staircase, and turn into the tunnel to your right. The changing of the guard begins exactly at seven; they will be arriving by the tunnel on the right. And the departing shift will leave through the left one!"

"And how are we going to get this lock open, you joker, may the devil take you?!" Wilson snapped back.

"Here's the key for you. We have the painful calluses of that gorilla by the dungeon entrance to thank for this!" Ray winked cunningly and tossed the key through the bars into Larry's open arms.

Having darted upstairs, Ray raced along three narrow and convoluted corridors to the chimney sweep's storeroom. Quickly shedding the apprentice chef's white apron for the dirty and dark jacket of an apprentice chimney sweep, smearing his cheeks with coal and grabbing a broom, Ray ran up to the roof. Having carefully climbed out through a small, narrow window, he found himself under the cupola of the black sky. Once his eyesight adjusted, he counted off the sixth chimney, stretched himself tall and, spreading his arms in the air like a tight rope walker, set off on his way. He was trembling with fear and

excitement and his feet were barely listening to him, but the sixth chimney was rapidly approaching! Just another step, just one more step, now the next to the last one, now the very last, and the very very last one, and the la-a-a-ast! Grabbing onto the gutter pipe, Ray shimmied along its edge and swung himself inside.

"You, what are you doing here?" the sentry barked, seeing black-faced Ray come tumbling right under his feet.

"I am cleaning the chimneys!" Ray came up with an answer.

"It is the Ruler's birthday and the chimneys have not been swept clean yet!" Ray did not let up.

"Are you the son of the chimney sweep?" the sentry bent his head off to one side in an expression of distrust.

"And who else might I be?" Ray frowned.

"Alright, well then go ahead and clean them!" the sentry consented, fearing the ire of the birthday celebrant, and punishment for not having had the chimneys cleaned for the holiday.

Ray slipped inside the slightly ajar door and froze dumbstruck... On its little pillow on the pedestal, shining with all the shadings of red, was the magical red Credisford.

"All right, shorty! Make it quick already," the sentry grunted and shook his fist at Ray.

The warm evening breeze was fanning the curtains of the open window. Like sails, craving freedom and not having seen the sunset for a long time, flaring out above their hanging rod, they were now observing the outside world with curiosity. The magical Credisford no longer lit the room; it was now pleasantly warming Ray's chest inside his shirt. He raced down the secret staircase to where his long-ago extinguished lantern was patiently awaiting him.

"Ma-a-a–ay o-u-ur w-o-o-rld be-e-e li-i-i-ight a-and pu-u-ure!"

The children's choir was finishing its hymn. In a giant armchair raised high above them, his eyelids folded in a pose of affection and nodding his head in tempo, the Ruler sat enthroned, wearing his light, ceremonial dress, with his ever freezing feet covered up to his belt with a brightly colored, warm blanket. Single file, to the applause of their one and only listener, the children exited the hall and, under the severe gaze of the guard, quickly descended the staircase. Ray joined in at the very end of the line, where Gwyneth, who had long been awaiting him, shone with joy no less intensely than the Credisford.

"Where is it?" Gwyneth jumped up and down in anticipation.

"Here I am!" Ray replied smiling broadly, and he carefully transferred the magic Credisford from under his shirt inside his extinguished lantern.

The single red lantern, shining with a magical red color in a sea of yellow flames, was reflected in Gwyneth's ecstatic eyes. When the children had passed the main street and were already approaching the large, wide open gates, the voices of the guards shook the evening air like thunder.

"He-e-e-y! Sto-o-o-o-p! They have the Cre-dis-ford!" screamed the guard.

The children, obeying the order, came to a full stop and sharply turned backwards. The lantern on Ray's stick, burning bright red, suddenly collided in the air with Gwyneth's lantern and, in that very instant, miraculously lit it red. Gwyneth, frightened, turned around and accidentally knocked her red lantern against Rachel's yellow one. Rachel, turning around, pushed Pete, holding his lantern, knocking it against her own, and both of them now also turning a bright red. What had only just been a sea of yellow flames, like a kite writhing and wriggling on the wind or like a chain of falling dominoes, suddenly changed its color. When each and every lantern in a moment shone red, the guard thundered: "Gra-a-a-a-b them a-a-a-a-l!!!"

And the children came tumbling out of the gates like a flock of glowing red fireflies, each one of them scattering in their own direction.

The entire crew of the Celestine and half of the members of the conspiracy had gathered in Terra's house; it would not have been able to hold any more of them.

"We don't know what will happen next! But it would be best for you to be on your way as soon as possible!" one of the plotters begged them.

"It would be good to somehow hold out for the night. But with the morning breeze, you must set sail!" warned another.

"They are searching the entire city! They're looking for the red stone and turning every house upside down for it!" said someone who had just burst in from the street.

"Open the window!" one of the men suggested excitedly.

Everyone threw themselves to the window and, swinging it sharply open, saw the hills of Sacro-Luxe glowing, but not with the usual yellow light of their lanterns, as it had always done, but with a red one, as it had happened for the first time that very night.

"They don't even know which house to begin their search with! All the city's inhabitants have painted the lanterns beside the entrances to their houses red!" one of the plotters broke into a triumphant laughter, still not believing his own eyes.

"Goodbye!" Archie said at daybreak.

"Goodbye" Terra answered him.

"He will definitely return," Archie added.

"I know," Terra nodded.

"Men always return when they are waited for," Archie smiled and ran down the slope over the cobblestones toward the crew of the Celestine awaiting him.

"Cast off the stern line! Set sail!" The air on deck of the long dormant Celestine vibrated with activity.

"Goodby-y-ye, Ra-a-ay! I will wa-a-ait for you-u-u!" Gwyneth yelled from the precipice, waving her arm, unable to keep up with wiping away her running tears.

"Goodby-y-ye Gwy-y-y-neth!" Ray yelled from atop the mast.

And awaiting her, on the pillow in her room, was a portrait, smiling from which was a ginger-haired, exuberant little girl with the funny-looking gap between her two front teeth.

Archie carefully deposited the magical Credisford into the first pocket sewn out of the hem of Celestine's skirt.

The schooner was departing the old port, driven by a stiff tailwind. And, if one of the crew were to turn around then, he would have seen behind himself, instead of the rock that had previously hidden this small but proud world, the flickering with all the shades of red city of Sacro-Luxe, forever bidding farewell to them. And, if one of them, even for a moment, stopped to listen carefully, he would have heard the cries of the first seagulls returning to their birthplace. But the crew of the Celestine did not look back; they were being beckoned on by as yet unexplored worlds. Oblivious to the cries of the seagulls behind their backs, they were now being lured by the fresh sea breeze lashing their faces, the music of which was the only thing that their deep heart's core could hear.

Chapter Five

The Devil's Smirk, or Death's Empty Eye Sockets

n its first days at sea, the Celestine, like a fish that had finally found its way home – in water – relished each minute of its freedom. She climbed the waves, effortlessly and smoothly falling back down, as though admiring herself from all sides. She allowed the sails to billow so tight that it seemed it wasn't the wind that ordered it about, but that they were intractably dictating its course to the wind. But when the Celestine had scoured the sea for two weeks already, her reserves of drinking water dwindled, and for dinners, Duke now could barely manage to scrape together respectable rations for the entire seven-headed crew. The Celestine, like everyone on board, seemed to fade and weaken, like an empty-headed, young hound that had exhausted itself running around and now dreamed only of food and a good nap.

Cook's compass steadfastly pointed the way. In possession of the Credisford now, Archie already felt himself to be almost the conquering hero and had prepared himself for the next skirmish with Bloodthirsty Cook, but the latter's Secret Book remained silent, and its blank pages angered Archie, who felt himself powerless, as though Cook had prepared unexpected surprises for him which he was never fated to know.

Just as Archie had drank the last drop of his ration of fresh water and felt that, not only had he not quenched his thirst, but that he had only teased his parched throat, Larry's voice coming from atop the mast, compelled him to grab a hold of Cook's spyglass and run up and out on deck.

"Captain! A bri-gan-tine on the horizon! We're saved, Captain!" Nimble Larry screamed, triumphantly waving his arm above his head.

"We're saved!" Hulking Bill chimed in with all the remaining strength of his parched from thirst throat.

"Flour! We'll have flour again!" yelled Chubby Ike.

"Water! We'll have water to drink, you idiots!" Cook Duke burst into hysterical laughter out of such sudden relieve from despair.

"Where is it?" Skinny Wilson hollered and stared off into the distance.

"Over there! Off in the distance! I see it too!" screamed Ray.

Archie glued himself to Cook's spyglass and was dumbstruck. The strange brigantine, rocking helplessly on the waves, greeted him with a vision of dozens of corpses that had been mutilated in a fierce skirmish. They were swinging, limply suspended from the horizontal spars on the masts, spilling overboard, with the short blade swords still sticking in their backs, and gawking into the water with their empty, long-ago pecked out eye sockets. The earth could not have covered over this bloody inhuman slaughter. Like a sea devil's sneer, not having swallowed up the brigantine into the watery abyss, the sea's stilled surface remained its final refuge. For one moment, it seemed to Archie that someone's empty eye sockets were glaring at him, while aiming the barrel of a gun with its lifeless hand right at his head. He shuddered with disgust, lowered the spyglass, and yelled with all his might:

"Enemy starboard! Prepare to board her!"

"Well, I'll be damned! I'm not climbing aboard!" Chubby Ike exclaimed, when the Celestine collided with the starboard of the "dead brigantine".

"To hell with it, Captain!" squealed Skinny Wilson.

"Yes, may the earth swallow you all up!" Cook Duke groaned.

"Yes, I would rather be torn to pieces by sharks!" protested Hulking Bill.

"All I wanted to do was to quench my hunger and thirst, Captain! Not to cuddle up against corpses!" howled Nimble Larry.

Ray remained silent, hunching up like a hedgehog out of horror.

All of a sudden, the explosion of Archie's gun shook the air.

"You're all going! Each and every one of you! Everyone who doesn't want to croak from hunger and thirst!" Archie roared.

"Only the boy will stay behind, to handle the goods we'll pass back to him!" the Captain commanded, and quickly ran up the gangplank that had only just been slung across to the "dead brigantine".

"Hey, take away your paws!" Hulking Bill grunted to Larry, flailing around before him, while stepping over the dead bodies of strangers.

The barrel of water leaving the "dead brigantine" on his shoulders did not seem at all huge, as though there was easily at least room for a couple more on his back. Chubby Ike was trying to squeeze himself between two pirates who were permanently united in mortal combat, their faces forever frozen in an expression of horror. Skinny Wilson, having grabbed someone by their feet and struggling to drag him off to the side in order to free up passage, suddenly let out another squeal. A stranger's pirate boot remained in his hand, and the wooden leg, that had been hidden inside it loudly smacked against the deck with a thud. Duke was lugging a sack of grain, when he suddenly ran into a pair of a stranger's glassy eyes and the stone-like grimace of death. Ray, who was dragging a sack of flour that had just been tossed over to the Celestine, tried to keep himself from looking backwards.

"A-a-a!" Duke screamed.

"A-a-a-a!" squealed Skinny Wilson.

"A-a-a-a-a!" roared Hulking Bill.

The corpses, as though on command, suddenly fell, rolled down, turned right side up, came crashing down, slipped off, toppled over, or turned around, as though to greet them, fixing their fearful frozen grimaces and glassy gazes on the faces of the crew of the Celestine.

"A-a-a-a-a-a-a-a!!!" all of them screamed in unison and broke into a dash.

Archie, now sated and sitting with a full mug of rum, for the umpteenth time opened the Secret Book in unconcealed and agitated expectation. Bloodthirsty Cook did not force him to wait.

"Well, well, Captain! Are you expecting praise from me? You've got your hands on only one single magical stone and you already reckon yourself the rightful owner of Cook's entire treasure? You've overcome the obstacles of one single world and decided that the remaining six will give themselves up to you without a fight? You little snot-nosed brat! You're a nothing, with a bunch of good-for-nothing loafers! Turn back for home and run to your mama. No one! Remember this, no one! No one will ever fathom my six remaining riddles and find the six remaining magical stones! And who gave you this book, anyway? May he go to hell, or may he be forced to tussle with Cook himself! And now, get lost! The devils are calling me to dinner. Oh yes, such is my punishment:

EAT WELL, SLEEP TIGHT, STEP LIGHTLY.

If you manage to solve my riddle, then you will find the orange magical Plorangestone! Ho-ho-ho!"

PLORANGESTONE

Chapter Six

The Gentle Tread of Evil Intent, or the Meowling Wind of San Felis

"-a-a-chie-e! Ca-ap-tain! Ma-an o-over-bo-o-oard po-ort-si-ide!" someone on deck shouted, and Archie immediately took off running.

Glued to Cook's monocular now, as though striving this very minute, having looked into its glass, to unravel all of his riddles, the Captain saw an emaciated man, in old, tattered clothing, helplessly swaying on a raft and, resting obediently in his arms, a short-hair calico cat.

"Ma-an o-over-bo-o-oard!" screamed Chubby Ike!

"Someone's in the wa-a-ater!" yelled Duke!

"I see a ra-a-ft!" barked Hulking Bill.

It wasn't even ten minutes later that on the deck of the Celestine, Quentin, his teeth chattering under the blanket they had tossed over him, greedily swallowing rum, some of it dribbling down his short beard, was petting his darling, who was ogling all the crew members with rapt curiosity.

"If you are bobbing up and down here on a raft, then land is already not far away?" Duke glanced at the stranger with hope.

"I think we have been on our way for a couple of days already," Quentin, who was still soaked to the bone, replied.

"What the hell are you doing out at sea with this cat?" Nimble Larry raised his eyebrows.

"You won't believe me, but the inhabitants of our city of San Felis are forbidden to own cats!" Quentin sighed. "Kitty and I escaped, so that we're not parted from each other forever!" he added in obvious distress.

"What could the cats have done to challenge your authorities, if they have now fallen into such disfavor?" Chubby Ike asked with genuine curiosity.

"The beauty Margo is to blame for it all... Once upon a time, a very long time ago, the Duchess owned a cat herself, her beloved Margo. But she died. And, since then, the Duchess is so miserable that the sight of any cat would upset her terribly, reminding her of her untimely departed darling. For this reason, all the cats, it would seem through the intercession of the Duchess's faithful servants, the Priests, have vanished from our city."

"Do you blindly obey all of your Duchess's whims? Didn't a single one of you think to ask her: why should you be prohibited from owning cats? What the hell is wrong with you?!" Duke was indignantly surprised.

"Only the Head First Priest is permitted access into the Duchess's private chambers! We, simple mortals, would not know on our own how to live, what next year's harvest will be like, or whether sufficient rain will fall! All of this, all of it, is known only to the Duchess. The Head Priest asks her about everything, transmits her highness' answers to the other priests, and it is they who enlighten all of us, the inhabitants of San Felis," Quentin explained.

The crew of the Celestine looked at each other in incomprehension.

"So where did all of your cats go?" Larry sounded bewildered.

"No one knows! But sometimes, at night, it seems to us that we can hear their plaintive feline moans, somewhere far-far off, where only the wind can reach and carry back to us their call," Quentin answered pensively, gazing off into the distance.

"And how did your Kitty manage to survive?" Ray stared at him inquisitively.

"I found her when she was but a kitten, hiding under a stone on a large meadow, as though she had only just escaped. I immediately hid her under my shirt and brought her home. At first, I would take her out into the street, hiding her in my pocket, and when she grew a little, we started taking walks with her at night. I call to her in the dark oh so very quietly: "Kitty!" And I can already see how her shinning cat eyes are racing towards me through the nocturnal gloom."

Kitty rubbed herself against her master's foot, as though affirming that all of what he had said was the unvarnished truth.

"How does the Duchess feel today?" the Second Priest knitted his eyebrows together in concern.

"She was sleepless last night. She is tormented by migraines," the Head First Priest replied, rolling his eyes up, as though imitating a migraine headache.

"Despite all this, she once again granted upon you tenure over a multitude of servants. When does she even manage, despite her feeling unwell, to think so much of you?" the Second Priest raised his eyebrow in amazement.

"My friend, my loyalty is to blame for it all. I am devoted to the Duchess, and she is only letting me understand that my most sincere faithfulness and deepest loyalty are worthy of recompense," the Head First Priest confessed.

"I am also devoted to the Duchess, but despite this, it has been a long time since she had admitted me into her private chambers... Not to speak already of the fact that I had never received from her property as a gift," the Second Priest remarked in a tone of acrimony.

"My friend, envy blackens your sterling reputation. I suppose that the success of another blinds your eyes so that they no longer see the big things at a distance, and all the time pay more attention to the petty things close at hand... Be more humble in your thoughts and more modest in your expression and you too will likely be recompensed," the Head First Priest suggested.

"And for starters, my friend, transmit to the people the Duchess's decree: all celebrations on this Friday must be canceled, in avoidance of noise that so oppresses the Duchess's head that is already so burdened by migraine," the Head First Priest bowed his head, depicting her sufferings.

"On Saturday mornings, noise is permitted and even welcome! I, the Duchess's obedient servant, have the honor of being awarded the Order of Allegiance in the First Degree. And now, with your permission, my friend, I must take my leave; my functions on the occasion of this celebration require heaps of my already nonexistent free time," the Head First Priest made a slight bow and departed the grand hall.

"Land! Land on the horizon!" Ray screamed from atop the mast, waving his hand in pure joy.

The entire crew of the Celestine ran out on deck.

"Kitty, my tiny one! We are once again in our place of birth, San Felis!" the emaciated and haggard Quentin smiled, affectionately petting his darling.

San Felis stood on a hilltop, and all the roofs of its houses were topped with hat-like crowns, painted in a stripped pattern of alternating white, blue, and turquoise color. The wide trim framing these crowns flickered with a golden glimmer in the rays of the sun. The large buildings rising up above the town's center, proudly stretched their large stripped crowns decorated with pure gilding toward the sun and, at first sight, appeared to everyone as nothing less than the domain of the Empress of the Realm that it was.

Little, miniature, and tiny houses were scattered around and were similarly stretching their crowns towards the sky, as though standing on their tip toes, measuring their heights against the majestic gilded cupolas, despite the fact that their crowns were framed not with gilded, but only pale white trims.

"Look Kitty, there, in the distance, is our home!" Quentin, overjoyed, was kissing Kitty on her spotted forehead.

"Cast off the stern line!" the command was given on the Celestine and the entire crew, having moored at an alien shore, spilled onto dry land with impatience, their heads tilted back in amazement.

A thousand narrow stone steps of a footpath zigzagging to the right and the left carved the seashore and cleaved to the sky with the town's stripped crowns.

"To hell with all of you!" Duke cursed, soaked through with sweat, climbing the second hundred of the narrow stone steps.

"What have I done to deserve the sea devil's scourge?" complained Hulking Bill.

"I am willing to wager that it would be easier to survive your average sea battle!" wailed Skinny Wilson.

"Do not lose heart, we have almost reached goal!" Archie commanded.

"Three hundred and forty-two, three hundred forty-three, three hundred and forty-four," Ray muttered under his nose, hoping and skipping in front of all of them.

Chubby Ike, wiping the sweat from his forehead, followed behind

Larry, and Quentin, carrying Kitty, who was nestled in his arms, was already waving to them with his free arm from the crest, as though climbing it were no big deal for him.

"I will settle you at my sister Betty's! She and her husband own a small tavern with a couple of guest rooms," Quentin offered.

"Only don't be afraid of Norwood, her husband. He can be strange and even harsh at times... But, on the whole, he is no ruffian," he warned them.

The people of San Felis were dressed strangely: almost all of them wore either off-white or pale, cloudy blue clothing. Some of them wore cloak-like capes edged with silver piping over their shoulders.

"These are the more affluent gentlemen," Quentin explained.

And only once, in the road, did they meet a man whose cloak was edged with piping radiant with a golden luster.

"It's the Eight Priest!" Quentin whispered, respectfully bowing before the patrician passing him by and gazing with indifference above Quentin's head. The crew of the Celestine ogled at the inhabitants of San Felis, the inhabitants of San Felis were, likewise, examining the outlanders following behind Quentin with curiosity, while the striped, hat-like crowns of the roofs of San Felis, craning their necks, stared in astonishment at the seven-headed crew of strangers.

"Do they have any money? What will they pay for their lodging with?" barked thickset Norwood, wearing a sleeveless shirt that revealed his thick forearms. And then he loudly banged his overfilled mug on the tabletop for emphasis.

"I think so," Quentin whispered awkwardly. "Please, quieter," he asked them.

"Yes, come in then, come in!" the jolly and plump Betty invited them in. Wondering at her girth, one could hardly imagine how she might possibly be the sister of the emaciated Quentin.

Ray swung his window wide open and felt himself to be flying, but not along the surface of the sea, in a schooner with a mast towering above mid-deck, but across the sky, in a ship adorned with large, medium-sized, and miniature white and turquoise caps, shining here and there with a golden sheen.

"Hey, you, get down from my window!" somebody commanded.

Ray turned around in incomprehension.

A heavyset boy, who looked like an exact miniature copy of Norwood, had entered the room.

He immediately tossed his bag on the floor and flopped down, hiking his feet up on the only bed standing in the room.

"Richie, be more polite!" his mother asked him.

"These are our new guests; all the rooms are taken, and this boy will have to stay with you for some time," she smiled artificially, hoping for understanding from the uncooperative Richie.

"Fat chance!" Richie lashed out.

"Ri-chie!" the mother exclaimed in a threatening tone, knitting her eyebrows.

"There's no place to sleep here!" Richie defended himself.

"We'll bring in an old, little couch for him," his mother looked at him beseechingly.

"He probably snores!" Richie once again defended his personal space.

"Richie, children don't snore!" his mother pushed back.

"And what if he steals something from me?" Richie wouldn't let it go.

"Richie, stop it!" his mother pleaded.

"If you're going to continue behaving this way, I won't sew your cape for the celebration this Saturday!" his mother admonished him.

"Alright, let him stay... Only not too long!" Richie warned and, turning his back to his mother, immediately stuck his tongue out at Ray.

"My friend! I have an urgent matter!" the Fifth Priest made his appeal, hastily bowing as a sign of his deference.

"What is it? I must confess that every surface of my table is covered with urgent matters," the Fourth Priest replied with indifference.

"It's about my nephew... He's a good boy. He's no fool and dreams of becoming priest!" the Fifth Priest launched into his explanation in a roundabout way.

"And who doesn't dream of becoming a priest?" the Fourth Priest smirked.

"Yes, but it is not just anyone who is given the chance to enter our line of work," the Fifth Priest ventured.

"But if only the Duchess were to give him a chance to serve her. There would be no equal to him in obedience and loyalty!" the Fifth Priest reassured him.

"Are you asking me to add him to the list of future Priests, who undergo training with us?" the Fourth Priest asked in bewilderment.

"At least that, if it were only possible?" the Fifth Priest bent his entire body into the shape of a crook resembling a question mark.

"That is absolutely impossible," the Fourth Priest replied. "The lists are full for the next four years."

"If you, however, were to try your luck and speak to the Head First Priest. Year after year, he places his signature under the lists," the Fourth Priest added.

"How can you! May God preserve me were I to trouble the Head First Priest with such stupidities!" the Fifth Priest recoiled in horror.

"And what if we get lucky? On Saturday, there is a celebration in his honor. The Duchess is awarding him yet another Order of Allegiance. If you were to succeed in making your way through the crowds of well-wishers and gawkers, then his mood, on such an occasion, will more than likely be propitious," the Fourth Priest suggested, bowing slightly in a farewell regard.

All of Richie's school supplies were a pale white and blue color. His white and blue striped fountain pen was adorned with a white little dome-like- cap and his striped pencil with a little blue dome-like cap.

"Don't touch it!" Richie barked and Ray immediately placed it back on the table.

"How are you going to go to the celebration? You don't even have a cape!" Richie said scathingly.

"If you won't tell anyone, I'll show you something interesting now!" he smiled cunningly.

Swirling the edges of his short cape and throwing it over his shoulders turned inside out, he proudly paraded back and forth in front of Ray.

"What, you don't see it?" Richie couldn't hide his disappointment.

"See what?" Ray still didn't get his secret message.

"Mom secretly sewed golden piping on my cape that only Priests are allowed to wear! But only on the inside, so that no one will see it!" Richie burst out laughing.

"When I grow up, I will become a Priest," he suddenly grew serious, as though it were a matter of great solemnity.

"And perhaps even a First, Head Priest!" Richie's eyes lit up.

"Do you have any idea how he lives? Only he is permitted entrance into the Duchess's private chambers! She always bestows gifts and awards on him! And only he knows how we ought to live and whether there will be a harvest this year. The Duchess tells him this, and he transmits it to us," Richie explained all this with excitement, as though he were already preparing himself to assume that position of responsibility.

Cook Duke, Nimble Larry, and Chubby Ike were devouring white and blue meringue candy shaped like little dome caps. Hulking Bill was wiping with his hand his white and blue mouth, into which a dozen little meringue domed caps had just disappeared. Ray was hopping on one foot and licking the melting edges of his white and blue dome-shaped ice cream. Archie and Skinny Wilson were ogling the window displays of the local shops. For any new arrival, this would seem strange: in a world where cats were forbidden, and great reverence, even veneration from birth, was lavished upon the Duchess, the inhabitants were permitted relations with only one, single cat, and namely, the Duchess's favorite who had died in an untimely fashion. Framed portraits of Margo, haughtily reposing on the lap of the rail-thin, long-nosed Duchess, with her knotty fingers frozen in the act of petting it, graced each and every shop window.

"May I be torn to pieces by a thousand devils!!!" Archie exclaimed and sat down on his haunches, slapping his knees and struck dumb in amazement.

The entire crew of the Celestine flung themselves towards him and, shoving each other, thronged at the window display. The cunning feline muzzle, with a handsome, star shaped spot above its left ear, was staring at them from the imperial lap, and sticking out for show, as though issuing a challenge, her collar, adorned with a large, multifaceted, orange stone, shining with a magical luster...

"I have had it up to here with this arrogant hypocrite!" the Second Priest confessed.

"I beg you, quieter please!" the Third Priest asked him and lowered his own voice. "But what are we going to do about it?"

"How many more of his orders and medals will we have to endure like some slaps in the face? All of us dream of being elevated too!" the Second Priest added, without lowering his volume.

"Yes, my friend, but your elevation would signify the removal of the Head First Priest from his post! And then, what is he going to do about that?" the Third Priest replied quietly.

"He is awarded medals, acquires possessions, directs the guards, hands down verdicts, and gives orders! And she's just laid up with migraines! We can never manage to even get close enough to her so that we may get our own one and only chance!" the Second Priest seethed.

"My friend, let's write to her, there is such a thing as mail, after all," the Third Priest proposed.

"How naive you are, my friend. There's not a single piece of mail to the Empress that does not pass through his hands!" the Second Priest burst out laughing.

"And the doctor? What if we were to transmit a letter through him?" the

Third Priest's face lit up.

"That is an idea. But she's stupid! The Duchess has not allowed doctors to come near her for quite some time!" the Second Priest replied even louder.

"That Margo just had to croak... Since then, once she was no more, everything has gone to seed!" the Third Priest raised his voice.

"Quieter! I think somebody's coming!" the Second Priest now too took fright.

"What, what qualities must a future Priest possess?" the teacher asked a question and gazed at the class above his pince-nez.

The schoolchildren of San Felis raised a forest of arms and were impatiently jumping up from their seats.

"Humility!"

"Obedience!"

"Loyalty!"

"Who, who is worthy of receiving a place for training to become a Priest?" the teacher knitted his brow.

"Only the very best!"

"Only the A students!"

"Only the most obedient!"

"Only the most diligent!"

"To what and to whom does a priest dedicate his life?" the teacher continued his examination, drilling through the class with his beady little eyes.

"Service to the Duchess!"

"Fulfilling her will!"

"Executing her decrees!"

On the same day, Ray was sent off to the San Felis school despite the loud protestations of Pudgy Richie, who begrudged lending Ray even his old, too-short, pale blue, washed out, student cloak. Having been handed a notebook, Ray's fingers, starving a long time now for a pencil, immediately grabbed it, and the pencil began sliding quickly across the surface of the paper. On the first page, employing densely packed strokes, hundreds of steps, and perhaps even an entire thousand, were now flying upwards. There was no more room on this page, and Ray flipped the page and turned his attention to the domed caps. Almost touching the closely packed clouds, from the top of their stone cliff, large, medium-sized, small, and miniature domes were stretching toward the sky.

Along the narrow little lanes winding around the little houses with their dome peaked roofs, people wearing short cloaks were beginning to rush about their business. The proud and rail-thin Margo was majestically casting her guileful feline gaze from the portraits decorating the large and small merchant shops. And prominently displayed on her feline neck, spoiled by the petting of an imperial hand, was the multi-faceted, orange Plorangestone, resplendent with a magical luster.

"What, what ought we be grateful to our Duchess for?" the teacher finally got around to his principal question.

"For everything!" the children answered in a choir.

"That's right!" the teacher was overjoyed.

"How would we be able to live without our Duchess?" the teacher was tireless in his prodding.

"We would not know how to live!"

"We would not know what the harvest would be this year!"

"We would not know what characteristics we ought to possess in order to be accepted for training at the school for priests'!"

"Who among you has studied the biography of our Duchess well?" the teacher now asked his most important question.

"Me!" freckled Dave raised his hand.

The teacher nodded approvingly.

Dave rose from his seat and coughed to clear his throat, as though preparing to sing.

"The Duchess was born into the family of the Duke, her father, and the Duchess, her mother..."

"All of us know that," the teacher bowed his head in disappointment.

"From her early childhood, she has often been ill!" freckled Dave immediately inserted, afraid to disappoint the teacher once again.

"That's right!" the teacher beamed with delight.

"In order to avoid getting sick often, she was no longer able to go to school. The teachers began to visit her at home," Dave added with obvious satisfaction.

"Well done, Dave, sit down. Beverly, continue!" the teacher redirected.

Beverly, who had just been whispering back and forth while trading miniature portraits of Margo under the table with the girl sitting next to her, jumped up from her seat.

"Only the most obedient! The most diligent, and the best of the best! Only the top students!" Beverly blurted out.

The class burst out laughing.

"We have already covered all of that!" the teacher replied with obvious irritation.

"Sit down, Beverly, you are reprimanded! No recess for you! And your parents must come to school this Saturday!" the teacher retorted, scanning with his eyes the sea of hands impatiently stretched out and up.

"Richie!" the teacher made his selection.

Pudgy Richie rose up proudly from his seat and undid the top button of his tightly fitting collar.

"Because she was forbidden to play with other children, afraid that she may again get sick, her parents decided to give her a kitten. And so, from her earliest childhood, Margo became her friend and companion, until she herself became ill and died, leaving our poor Duchess all by herself!" Pudgy Richie loftily scanned the entire class, as though he had just disclosed to them a dark mystery.

"Hey, Ray!" fair-haired Claire called out to him from the neighboring desk. "Are you a coward or a daredevil?"

Ray raised his eyebrow in surprise, hesitating to respond one way or another.

"After school, we're going to have a race, climbing the stone steps, first down towards the water and then back up again! Come with us, if you aren't going to be afraid!" Claire smiled cockily.

This idea did not seem to Ray at all adequate as a test of bravery, but he nodded his head, having rejoiced at the fact that in this world, there is someone else who, unlike the mean-spirited Pudgy Richie, was glad about his presence.

"Beverly will stay behind. Everyone else is free for the rest of the day!" the teacher barked out and the schoolchildren of San Felis – stepping on each other's feet, hurling their writing implements, and using their textbooks to wallop each other, flipping their neighbors' short capes against their wishes from their shoulders over their heads – spilled out of the classroom.

Ray, Pudgy Richie, the bully Dustin, and fair-haired Claire were standing by the stone steps, which Ray had climbed with difficulty only a couple of days ago, and looking downward. Ray shed Pudgy Richie's short, pale blue cape, and prepared himself to go first.

"Hold on!" the bully Dustin yelled.

"Stop!" commanded fair-haired Claire.

"Did you really think that on a dare we would be racing these baby steps?" she broke out laughing, shaking her wild tresses.

"Let's go! We will show you another path, but it's not for weaklings!" Claire added, and all of them set off after her.

"For the dare, we will be racing here!" the bully Dustin yelled and pointed downward.

Terrified, Ray and Pudgy Richie approached the edge of the precipice and both of their heads immediately began to spin.

"I'm not running this!" Pudgy Richie protested.

"Nobody invited any scaredy cats over here!" fair-haired Claire taunted him.

"Ray can run down the right side, because Dustin is going to race down the left!" Claire declared.

Ray looked down: this rugged stony, precipice had probably once been an old, shorter ascent into town. Here and there one could make out the dilapidated forms of old stone steps, or rather, that which, a century later, remained of them.

"Are you going to race? Or are you too afraid?" the bully Dustin stared at him with a searching look.

"Three, two, one...Go!" the countdown rang in Ray's ears and he plunged downhill.

Like an agile rock climber, Dustin, carefully placing each foot on the stair, was already, immediately, searching out a place for the second, as though he had known this footpath from childhood.

"Let's go! Let's go!! Let's go!!" fair-haired Claire and Pudgy Richie chanted.

Ray placed the sole of his lead foot on a rock, dragging the hind foot behind, and the rock, that had only just seemed solid and stable to him, was already crumbling underfoot into a dozen finer pebbles, immediately scattering like stone fireworks from the cliff. Drenched in sweat, Dustin slid down the final fragments of steps and, in another second, was scrambling up with the help of his hands, grasping tightly at any protrusions, crevices, hollows, and depressions of the crumbling, stony, hundred-year-old footpath, which, it seemed, he knew by heart.

Ray placed his foot on the step, yet another crevice, yet another rock, yet another uncertainly placed stone flew, instead of Ray, downwards, and he turned around and with all his strength, grabbing with both hands onto a ledge, pulled himself up, and headed like a banshee up the cliff.

"Dus-tin! Dus-tin! Dus-tin!" Pudgy Richie and fair-haired Claire were chanting Dustin's name, even though he was several meters ahead of Ray anyway.

Ray clambered uphill as hard as he could, grasping at anything that had once been a solid stone but, in another second, crumbled into sand under his sole. His maimed fingers felt no pain, his hands the scrapes, or his knees the bruises. He forged ahead, like an undervalued player,

on whom no one was willing to wager, who was yet possessed by the promise of victory. One more thrust, though far from the winning one, and the opponent is still far ahead, but suddenly, they exchange glances... fair-haired Claire and Pudgy Richie for some reason have grown silent and staring at the two human figures suspended from the stony precipice.

The narrow crevice of the hundred-year-old stony descent would not release its grasp on Dustin's heel and he, truly frightened perhaps for the first time in his life, was staring at Ray with an imploring expression.

"If you give me your left hand and shift your left foot to the stone over there, then try to free your right one!" Ray gave the command.

Dustin hesitated for a moment and then carefully stretched out his shaking left hand to Ray, clenching his so tightly, as though he was expecting never to loosen his grip on it again. Just as carefully shifting his left foot on the indicated stone, he tugged and pulled out his left one, freeing his heel from the narrow crack in which, now, his boot would remain stuck forever. They both lowered their heads and gazed down: beneath them, the calm surface of the sea stretched out as far as the eye could see, and above them, the suspended remnants of the stony descent that had disintegrated centuries ago. One of the cobblestones groaned under someone's heel, and Ray and Dustin exchanged glances one more time and started running with all their might up the hill, gripping tightly onto the steep slopes, unsteady stones, and sheer precipices.

On the way back to the city everyone was silent, and Dustin dragged his right leg, missing its boot and shod with only a torn sock, behind himself.

San Felis was getting dressed up for dinner, and the little houses with their cap-like domes, here and there, were lighting their night lights that reminded one from a distance of a birthday cake with its just lighted fifty candles.

In the morning, Betty brewed strong tea. Her white and blue tea kettle, shaped like a portly cat, was cozily situated on a large round table.

"Where on earth did you get so beat up, Ray?" she was smearing Ray bruises with a malodorously smelling blue ointment from which all his cuts burned only more, but he sat still, tightly clenching his lips and bravely arching his back.

"I fell," Ray replied tersely, parrying Pudgy Richie's searching glance, who was afraid he would have to face punishment.

Larry and Duke were playing cards with images of cats on them, and Duke, who was, time and again, losing every hand was scratching his forehead aching from Larry's endless noogies that were the victor's prerogative. Ike and Hulking Bill were devouring Betty's freshly baked buns, white, puffed up, and chubby like herself. Wilson stretched himself out on a bench under a window, picking his teeth with something resembling a toothpick that ended in a tiny wooden cat paw. Archie, who was mixing his tea with a little spoon with a feline muzzle on its tip, immersed deeply in his own thoughts, did not even notice that he had long ago spilled more over the cup's edge than he had drank from it.

Inasmuch as Ray could no longer stand to look at his scrapes and scratches burning from the blue ointment, he stared at the portrait of the Duchess that seemed to occupy a place of honor on Betty's wall. The long-nosed Duchess with her smoothly slicked back hair, wearing a dress with a white and blue striped bodice and white and blue rhombuses on its skirt, patterned, it would seem, like the floor of her royal majesty's chambers, was observing her loyal subjects from on high. The stick-thin, like her mistress, Margo, was squinting her little cat eyes just as haughtily, as though very deliberately displaying the source of her secret power adorning her collar with a magical orange sheen.

"Our poor, our oh so poor protectress... Our poor Duchess!" plump Betty sighed most sincerely, noticing Ray gazing at the Duchess's portrait.

"She isn't so poor, you know, your poor Duchess!" Nimble Larry chuckled, slapping the table with yet another winning card.

"Say what you will, but the death of her favorite really devastated her," Betty defended the Duchess, for a moment turning to face the portrait.

"I don't remember already the last time we saw our poor Duchess. After such a loss, she became completely shut in," Betty sighed and once again applied herself to Ray's bruises, who didn't even have time to enjoy the short break from his ordeal.

"And who is this?" Ray asked, hoping that Betty would turn around and proceed to tell him a long story about her cousin, thereby freeing Ray from his burning torments.

"That's me!" Betty burst out laughing.

Beside the portrait of the Duchess, a sweet, young, rosy-cheeked young woman was petting what was likely her own beloved little cat, nestled in her lap covered with a festive white and blue dress, poorly imitating with her stiff pose the Duchess's majestic bearing.

"And is this your cat? Did she also die?" Chubby Ike interjected, hoping that Nimble Larry, distracted by the conversation, would forget to administer him yet another loss-deserved noogie.

"Yes, she is my little cat! My tiny little Daisy!" Betty purred out.

"Yes, she too was doomed after Margo's death," Betty almost burst into tears.

"But I will tell you this; I do not believe. I most certainly don't believe that our kind Duchess ordered the extermination of all our cats! I will never believe it! It is all due to the machinations of the Head First Priest!" Betty lowered her voice, "Who only sleeps and looks for ways to please her!"

"But I swear on my late favorite, she could not have given him such an order!" Betty closed her defense on an exclamation point.

"And where did they bury this Margo?" Wilson interjected suddenly.

"Oh, the funeral had such pomp! She was buried by the entire people, all together. I remember it like it was yesterday, although a couple of years have passed already," Betty added, and sighed.

"So, where is she now?" it was Archie's turn to interject.

"And she lies in a grand casket, the poor one, in the crypt of the Dukes, where to the left and the right of her repose the bones of the Old Duke and the Old Duchess. The Old Duke had suffered so much when the Old Duchess passed before him," Betty remembered, and was about to tell him this story with its tragic ending, when suddenly, turning around, she noticed that her listeners had a long time ago sneaked out of the room. Only the tea kettle, shaped like a corpulent cat, pricked up its ears and, having no other choice, resigned itself to listening to the fate of the suffering Duke for exactly the one hundred and seventeenth time.

San Felis was dressed up for the day of celebration, and all the children put on their white and blue little dome-like caps. Their short blue capes, which were traditionally worn, and their white and blue clothes had been freshly laundered and hung on hangers for the night, having also been ironed the previous evening. Capes without piping and the capes of the proud owners of silver piping, as material evidence of their more prosperous social standing, mingled in the crowd, ecstatically united by their shared happiness, leveling all, those with and without property or income, making the haves and the have nots equal. And only the gold piping of the priests' short capes never mingled with anyone, and would always remain standing apart, greeting the jubilant people with venerable restraint while reverently bowing before the Duchess's carriage.

"People of San Felis! I, your faithful servant and a humble subject of our Grand Duchess, make haste to announce the good news: the generous and just Duchess has once again given an order to bestow on me the Order of Allegiance in the First Degree, which I had the honor to be awarded today from her own most resplendent hands!" the Head First Priest proclaimed and bowed in a genuflection of gratitude.

"On this occasion, I propose we should mark this day of the calendar as a day of celebration and declare it free from work!" the Head First Priest intoned and bowed yet once again.

The musicians began playing a grandiose march, and their music soared up and, filled with joy, embraced and showered with kisses all the domed roofs framing the central square. The people began to raise a racket, rejoice, cheer, and their dome-like caps flew upwards among the general din and landed back on other people's heads. The crew of the Celestine ogled in all directions, pressed in on from all sides by the jubilant, festive delirium. Betty put on her very best white and blue dress, Plump Norwood barely squeezed into his holiday costume, Ray, wearing Richie's old cape, caught someone else's dome-like cap and immediately stuck it on his head. Skinny Quentin was not dressed up and, as always, he wrapped the left flap of his roomy jacket over the right one, supporting it with both hands, as though he had only recently gotten drenched to the bone and was still freezing cold.

"Good Lord, what astounding hypocrisy! What lack of restraint! He was decorated with yet another medal and the day must immediately become a national holiday? Let's see, so this is now the second most important day in our state, after our Duchess's birthday?" the Second Priest erupted in a scathing tone on the high tribunal erected especially for the Priests.

"Though truth be told, I don't recall any such resolutions passed at our Council?" the Third Priest added, expressing his dissatisfaction.

"What Council? Perhaps you might recall, my friend, the last time that any resolutions were issued by our General Council? And the Council can be easily dissolved! There is no one and nothing for us any longer to council! He is constantly exchanging whispers with the Duchess and we learn of the news, standing on the public square, as though you and I are not Priests, but a baker and a shepherd!" the Second Priest, now seriously irate, tightly clenched his fists, hidden under his blue cape, edged with golden piping.

The rows on the Priests' tribunal, no better than the jubilant crowd on the square, lost their orderliness.

"My friend, we have such a festive commotion now, I doubt that this would be the appropriate place and time to put in a word about my nephew?" the Fifth Priest, occupying his rightful fifth place on the tribunal, expressed his doubts.

"An appropriate place and time to ask something of someone does not exist anywhere or ever, I think. Taking into consideration as well, that our colleague is not disposed to burden himself with the requests of strangers," the Fourth Priest replied from his own rightful fourth place.

"Hurrah to the Duchess!" the Head First Priest proclaimed.

"Hurrah to our wise Duchess!" the crowd on the left shouted.

"Hurrah to our generous Duchess!" the crowd standing to the right picked up the chant.

"Hurrah to our kind Duchess!" the people in the center shouted.

Everyone's dome-like caps again flew up towards the sky.

Boooom! Someone's firecracker cracked.

"Me-e-e-eo-ow!" the frightened and almost deafened Kitty roared and broke free from under Quentin's jacket, leaping up his neighbor's back.

"A-a-a-a!" the plump lady screamed and, sensing feline claws on her plump, hunched shoulders draped in a festive dress, vigorously shook her back.

"A-a-a-a-a!" a little boy onto whose dome-like cap Kitty had just jumped squealed.

The crowd scrambled and began to spin chaotically.

"Me-e-e-eo-ow!!" Kitty was now even more frightened.

"A cat?! Who dared bring a cat here on this day?" the Head First Priest roared from the tribunal.

"Who dared, on such a day of celebration for everyone, to upset our otherwise sad Duchess?!" he almost growled.

"She's mine!" Quentin, who had already grabbed back his pet, saving her from the commotion, and tightly clenched her to himself, suddenly spoke out.

The crowd around him parted and Skinny Quentin, clenching Kitty in his arms, as though time had come for him to defend everything that he had, remained standing all alone in the center.

"Good Lord!" the Second Priest was dumbstruck. "Look at this poor wretch! Does he not remind you of someone?" he turned to face the Third Priest, barely suppressing a smile.

The Third Priest was staring at the rail-thin, helpless Quentin, abandoned by the throng.

"If he had a bit more meat on his bones... and if he didn't have his goatee... He'd be an exact copy of the Head First Priest! So much that it would be impossible to tell them apart!" the Third Priest almost squealed with pleasure.

"Let's grab the criminal?" the Second Priest whispered, smiling.

"We're grabbing the bandit!" the Third Priest replied, almost bursting into laughter, in his joyous impatience rubbing together his hands, hidden in the folds of his short, blue cape with the gold piping.

"Guard! Seize the hooligan!" the Second and Third Priests screamed in unison from the tribune.

The guards did not force them to wait and, confidently marching to the front and center, dragged off the helpless and non-resisting Quentin in the direction of the Duchess's estate. Huddling in Quentin's arms, Kitty, gawked in all directions, not feeling herself to blame for any of this. The Head First Priest bent forward in a slight bow, turning around to face the bleachers, as though expressing his gratitude for the instantly restored rule of justice. The Second and Third Priests, hiding away their cunning smiles, replied to him in kind with a slight bow, as though affirming their loyalty and zeal.

"Again, this Quentin! How could he have done that? And what's going to happen to him now, the poor wretch?" Betty impotently wiped away her tears, clutching tightly onto Pudgy Richie's frightened hand.

"Didn't I tell you! His secrets would not end up well!" fleshy Norwood grunted.

"And to boot, he has led to us God knows whom! God forbid that we will have problems!" he hissed out and glared malignantly in Ray's direction.

The warm, dark night enveloped the agitated city of San Felis in hope that today she would no longer dream of anything nightmarish, for the worst that could possibly happen had already happened. The crew of the Celestine, armed with pickaxes, short handheld axes, and ropes, quietly made their way toward the town cemetery, lighting their way with lamps.

"A-chu!" Wilson's sneeze had demolished the night's silence, and he immediately had to avert his eyes from the light of the six lamp lights aimed in his direction in great annoyance. Some or other wild animal began to howl somewhere off in the distance, the goggle-eyed moon and the stars, full of their usual curiosity, were unceasingly observing their nightly rounds, and the cap-like domes of the roofs pretended to be asleep.

The tall cemetery gates began to creak, admitting the unexpected visitors. The crew of the Celestine slipped inside single file. Ray felt like his legs had turned to cotton and, any second now, would refuse to carry him any further. The light of the lamps slid across the strange graves. He saw a heavy stone nail carved on a tombstone with the inscription "Veterinarian Smith". Two broad stone boots of different heights, one of them, distinguished by the absence of a heel, rose on top of a stone inscribed with the name of "Cobbler Williams". The light of Ray's lamp skidded across a tombstone without any decoration and, overcoming his fright, he got down on his haunches. "A lover of ladybugs, Ms. Murphy" Ray read and only then noticed the tiny, stone-carved ladybug, stilled forever on the grave of her mistress.

"H-e-e-ey!" Archie called out to everyone under his breath and pointed upwards.

The moon light, illuminating the gilt of the domes, set apart the family crypt of the Dukes from an entire forest of other dark tombstones.

All of them flung themselves in its direction, as though the exhumation of the grave of a cat that had only been dead a couple of years was a more pleasant undertaking than the ogling of the gravestones of strangers under the cover of night.

The damp stone steps of the crypt receded into its depths. Chubby Ike almost knocked down two of the candles that lit the entrance way. Wilson stumbled, but didn't fall. Nimble Larry coughed quietly under his breath, and Ray cringed, and scrunched himself up even more, like a hedgehog, as the light of the seven lamps fell upon three identical tombstones. Hulking Bill looked around and placed the no longer needed pickaxe on the ground. He strained with all his might and, grunting, heaved the heavy stone lid of the third tombstone carrying the inscription: "To my beloved Margo". Ray clenched his eyes shut. But because everyone had suddenly gone silent in indecisiveness, after some wavering, he finally decided to open one eye. The young, rail-thin, Duchess, all dressed up in a festive white and blue dress with gold piping, little silk slippers with little gold buttons sewn on them, and a magnificent dome-like hat, lay there in the crypt, strangled with a ribbon-thin white and blue scarf....

"Who's there?" the sentry barked.

"It's me, Betty! I have come to see my imprisoned brother!" Betty shouted into the tiny window of the steel door, raising herself on her tip toes.

A key made several turns in the keyhole and the heavy door swung wide open. Plump Betty and Ray wearing Richie's cape and little hat slipped inside.

"You won't believe me!" Quentin, his eyes lit up, was telling his story. "It's been a week already since they forced me to shave my beard. They bathe and dress me, and stuff me with food!"

"Me-eow!" Kitty purred, confirming his words, and brushed against Quentin's leg with her furry back.

Steps could be heard outside, the door swung open one more time, and two men wearing blue capes fringed with a gold piping entered Quentin's cell. In their hands was a man's tunic and a similar blue cape, embroidered with gold.

"Leave us alone!" they ordered, and Betty rose obediently and slipped out.

Ray tarried, slipped off into the dark, hid outside and, finding the right moment, immediately pressed his ear to the door.

"You will put these on tomorrow morning. Your door will remain unlocked tonight. You will be allowed to pass through her estates and will reach the Duchess's private chambers," the first man explained excitedly.

"Having seen the Duchess, you will admit to her that you are no longer able to bear on your shoulders the heavy burden of responsibility of your high position. And you will ask her to release you to your well-deserved rest," the second one ordered, barely containing his heavy breathing.

Having swallowed hard and listened in for a moment, he resumed: "If, after having expressed her surprise, she still refuses you, do not relent! Don't even allow her time to think! Here is your resignation letter; do not leave her chambers until she signs it! No matter what happens there!"

The rays of the morning sun set to pleasantly tickling his eyes. The False First Priest rose from his bed, robed himself in a long dress, threw on a cape trimmed with a gold piping, and left the damp cell. He walked down numerous corridors, halls, and stairways, and everywhere he went, people greeted him, bowing respectfully and flinging open doors before him. Carefully knocking at the Duchess's private chambers, he did not receive a reply. He then knocked even louder, and louder, and louder still.

Steps could be heard beyond the door.

"Who dares this?! The Duchess requested that she not be disturbed, she has a migraine!" an irritated voice rang out and the Head First Priest flung open the door.

For a second, he was struck dumb, as though he had seen his own reflection in a mirror. Suddenly, Nimble Larry jumped out from around a corner and shoved him inside. The False First Priest, followed both of them, and the entire crew of the Celestine after them, looking around from side to side.

"And where is Margo now?" Archie asked and stared at the Head First Priest.

Hulking Bill, as was his habit, rolled up his sleeves. The Head First Priest sat there, impotently sunk into his armchair and didn't say a word in reply.

"To the devil with all of you!" he suddenly screamed.

The inner door of a hall as long as a public square swung wide open opposite them and a woman's figure appeared in the distance wearing the Duchess's dress and seated on her throne.

"Why did you do it, First Priest? How could you do this to me?" she pleaded, petting a cat resting on her lap.

"A-a-a-a-a-a-a!" the First Priest screamed, grabbing his head.

Noises were heard from outside, followed by the clanging of weapons, and the Second and Third Priest immediately burst into the Duchess's private chambers, accompanied by the infuriated guards.

"Seize the demon!" Quentin screamed commandingly, immediately pointing at the First Priest.

The guards wagged their heads from side to side, uncertain about which one of them they ought to grab first.

"Where is she? Where is Margo? And all the cats in this city? Where are they?" Betty, wearing a dress resembling the Duchess's, and petting Kitty on her knees, pleaded.

"A-a-a-a-a!" the First Priest howled once again. "They are in the cellar of the abandoned old estate of the Duke! May the devil take her, the dead as a door nail, foolish, bonny woman who wanted to dismiss me!" the no longer Head First Priest howled, trying in vain to escape the steely grips of the guards.

Archie blew away the cat hair from the multifaceted orange Plorangestone, iridescent with a magical sheen, and carefully lowered it into the second little pocket sewn from the hem of Celestine's skirt. Having come to miss her crew, the schooner was raring for the sea.

"Sto-o-o-op!"

"Sto-o-o-op!" someone shouted from the top of the precipice.

"Ray, this is for you!" Pudgy Richie, all out of breath now, passed to him his worn, short,

blue robe.

"Farewell, Ra-a-ay! Co-o-ome ba-a-ack to-o-o se-ee u-u-us, Ra-a-ay!" the bully Dustin and fair-haired Claire were waving their arms from the top of the stone steps.

"Me-e-e-eow!" the wind carried the yowls of all the cats that had returned home.

The Celestine was swallowing up the waves beneath herself, and behind her back, on a high promontory, remained the white and blue city of San Felis, framed by its dome-like roofs, which towards evening will again light up and, from a distance, remind one of a birthday cake, on which fifty candles had just been lit.

Chapter Seven

The Turquoise Lagoon

he Celestine, like an animal that had been let out of its cage, rejoiced in its freedom, splitting the waves, rising on their crests and gently descending through their troughs. The entire crew was pining for the salty smell of the sea and the wind's audacity, fluttering the ship's tightly stretched sails. Cook's compass continued to show the way, but his book remained silent. Archie, feeling himself victorious, patiently waited for a new challenge that would surely be issued to him.

Pudgy Ike and Nimble Larry were playing dice with noogies doled out to the loser.

Counter to the established tradition, it was Larry who was unlucky today.

Cook Duke, seated Indian style on top of a wooden box while trying to remember some long-ago forgotten melody, was torturing his tin whistle. Wilson had drunk too much rum and was irritating everyone with his burping.

"Cap-tain! Look!" Nimble Larry called out from the deck, interrupting the game that had long ago lost its appeal to him.

"Captain! Just look at this!" screamed Pudgy Ike.

"What the hell? That's a fine kettle of fish!" Hulking Bill inserted his two cents worth.

Archie leaned out over the stern, the sea water suddenly turned neither black, nor a dark blue, but a sky-like azure, and in places, a pale turquoise, as though the Celestine had been furrowing not the open sea, but had now found itself in a fairy tale turquoise lagoon.

"Captain! We are adrift! We're all jumping overboard!" Nimble Larry yelled out, spotting Archie's nod of approval.

Larry quickly pulled off his shirt and pants and took a swan dive overboard.

"E-e-e-k!" Pudgy Ike squealed and tumbled over the stern.

"Wait for me!" screamed Duke, and finally letting his tin whistle have some peace, hurriedly stripped down to his tidy whities.

Hulking Bill and Skinny Wilson, who was barely able to stand on his wobbly legs, undressed as though they were racing each other to do it and leaped, after the rest, into the water.

"The water's not warm, Captain, it's almost hot!" Larry yelled out of the water, plunging beneath the waves.

"The water's as warm as soup in a pot!" Cook Duke laughed his head off, trashing in the water.

Wilson was swimming backstroke in silence, seemingly enjoying himself with his eyes closed and from a distance reminding one of a sleeping crocodile. Hulking Bill and Pudgy Ike were competing in sending up spouts of water from their mouths and resembled two white whales. Ray was laughing his head off on deck and regretting that he didn't have a pencil at hand, so that he could sketch all this piratical tomfoolery.

"He-ey, sailor!" Larry heard a woman's silky-smooth voice right near his ear and immediately turned around.

Looking at him were the turquoise eyes of a young woman of heavenly beauty. She suddenly jumped out of the water, as though to display her lithesome young body covered only with the thick, long hair streaming down from her head. Her willowy arms were wrapped around the neck of a trained dolphin, which, it seemed, repeated after her her every movement.

"May a hundred devils tear me to pieces!" Larry said in shock.

"He-ey, sailor!" the young woman embracing the dolphin again jumped out of the water behind Duke's back.

"He-ey, sailor!" the long-haired beauty whispered right in the ear of napping Wilson.

"He-ey, sailor!" yet another beauty let out a spout of water out of her mouth next to Hulking Bill.

"He-ey, sailor!" another beauty called out to Pudgy Ike.

The dolphins, as though on command, jumped out of the water, as though competing with the shapely, long-haired beauties with turquoise eyes.

"Well, this is really something!" Ike said, stunned.

"Well, I'll be damned!" Hulking Bill said, shaking his head as though he were trying to wake up.

Archie flew over to the bow, having ran up on deck, and again greedily glued

himself to Cook's spyglass. Hideous monsters, covered with huge warts and sticky spittle oozing from their yellow-toothed maws, riding atop half-fish, half-tortoises with huge floppy gills, heaved out of the warm, turquoise water beside the crew of the Celestine.

"Ra-a-ay!" Archie barely had time to shout, tossing the spyglass into his hands.

The arrow of Cook's compass in Archie's palm was rotating madly around its axis as though it had gone insane.

"The musket, Ray!" Archie screamed over to Ray, who was glued in astonishment to the spyglass. Obeying his order, Ray flung himself toward the musket and with all his might tossed it right into Archie's stretched out arms. Archie took aim. Booom! And he hit one of the creatures right in the eye. The half-naked, long-haired beauty, contorting in horror right before Larry's face, suddenly turned into a drooling, yellow-toothed, dead ogre, slowly sliding down into the water from her grunting half-fish, half-tortoise.

Booom! This time, Archie missed. Booom! Booom! Again, a miss.

Booom! and the second drooling chimera toppled from its turtle into the water beside Pudgy Ike.

Booom! and the third ogre loudly flopped down beside Hulking Bill.

Baaang! Baaang!

The yellow-toothed monsters, as though fighting for their lives, were flailing the water full-force with their half-paws, half-flippers and, becoming inert, emitted a gooey, green slime out of their mouths as they slowly sank under the water.

"A-a-a-a-a-a-h!" the crew of the Celestine was screaming at the top of their lungs and, squeezing their way among the bodies of the dying, groaning monstrosities, lashed the water in a race to get back to their lifesaving schooner.

"Are you still alive, Captain?" The pages of Cook's Secret Book finally came to life and spoke.

"And your nitwits as well? I'll wager the five yet to be found magical stones against your two that you don't have much longer to live in this world, you fool! Drop your scheming, you nincompoop! One didn't have to go to school in order to figure out that five is greater than and trumps two! What? You again want my riddle?

You'll die happier with my riddle? Then, here you have it:

RISE LATE, GO TO BED EARLY,
SQUINT FROM THE MOON LIGHT,
AND SAY FAREWELL AT SUNRISE.

And then you will find the magical yellow Prelloubridge! I've stuck around here too long with you. Some soft-hearted old woman knitted stockings for me over here. Could it be that she's your grandma? Well, OK then, I'll take pity and toss her in the cauldron to the devils third today! Ho-ho-ho!"

"La-a-and, caaap-tain! La-a-a-and ahoy!" Ray shouted from the mast.

"La-a-a-and!" Pudgy Ike rejoiced.

"I see, I see land!" Wilson confirmed their opinion.

Archie ran out on deck; the new trial was already awaiting him, and he squeezed his eyes shut and yelled out: "I see-ee-ee-ee it! I see-ee-ee-ee!"

PRELLOUBRIDGE

Chapter Eight

San Stella Diurna, or the City Where Lives Not a Soul

"ast off mooring lines! Drop anchor!" the command was heard on the deck of the pirate schooner and everyone spilled out onto the strange shore.

Having wondered around the gently sloping shoreline and not meeting with anyone, the crew of the Celestine set off for the town. The round-shaped little stone houses with thick roofs resembling thatched ones and tightly sealed shutters silently escorted the new arrivals with their glances. Large, broad avenues and small, narrow alleyways, squares and little yards between the houses, terraces and little porches, everything was frozen still in lifeless silence. You could tell that, only a short time ago, someone had still lived here, but, apparently, they were forced to leave this city forever.

"Archie, the city's empty!" Larry yelled out.

"Empty!" the echo on the square replied.

"He-e-ey! To hell with all of you!" screamed Bill.

"You-u-u!" replied the echo.

"Does anyone live here or have all of you been eaten by sharks?" screamed Pudgy Ike.

"Arks!" the echo replied.

"Is there anyone here?" Ray's voice rung out.

"He-e-e-e-re!" the echo answered.

"Damned Cook! We're not going to find any stone here!" screamed Archie.

"Here!" answered the echo.

Having walked the place backwards and forwards and finding everywhere only tightly locked shutters and doors, with the coming of night, the crew of the Celestine collapsed on the square in exhaustion.

Archie placed his tricorn hat under his head and covered himself with his raincoat. Wilson pulled off his boots and stretched out his tired legs. Duke and Larry curled up in the fetal position besides Pudgy Ike. Hulking Bill spread his arms and legs in all directions and immediately began to snore like a train engine. Ray, not having anything to stuff his ears with, slung his jacket over his head and immediately started snorting. The yellow moon, like a pancake flattened against the bottom of a huge, black celestial frying pan, stared at the outlanders with indifference. And the stars, taken aback in bewilderment, did not know what to say.

"Just look at that, there are people here!"

"They are outlanders!"

"What are they doing here?"

"And why are they sleeping on our square?"

"And where did they all come from, anyway?"

"Hey, Pierce, look at that one over there, how fat his stomach is! And, boy, how he snores!"

"Hey Sue! Look here! This hulk of a man wouldn't even fit through our door!"

The crew of the Celestine was awakened by light, not the light of day, but that of an oil lamp directed at them, and the noise, but one heard not in the midst of blue day, but in the deep of night. Archie, Hulking Bill, Pudgy Ike, Nimble Larry, Cook Duke, Skinny Wilson, and Ray opened their sleepy eyes and indecisively raised themselves up. A crowd of the curious had gathered around them, the shutters of each and every one of the windows were wide open, the doors were being opened and closed like revolving windmills, everything was brightly lit, all the shops were open, and a ton of people were scurrying about in the streets. In general, the city lived its normal, turbulent life, but only reversing day for night.

"Hey! Who are you?" a girl dressed like a boy asked Ray.

"Ray," Ray answered sleepily.

"I am Pierce!" the boy took the lead. "And this is my sister Sue!"

"Why are you all sitting here?" the girl persisted.

"We're not sitting," Ray replied. "We're sleeping... It's the dead of night out..."

"Wha-a-at?! How could you possibly not know that you're supposed to sleep in the daytime. And the night is the time for waking!"

"We, for example, are just on our way to school!" Pierce explained.

"Mr. Choice will ring his little bell at exactly midnight and we're not permitted to be late!" Sue added.

"If you have nowhere to stay, go down that narrow street over there! And, as soon as you see a brass turkey hanging by the door, there will be a sign: "Rooms available at Mr. and Mrs. Bristley's," Sue suggested.

"Let's run, Pierce! It's already a quarter to twelve! Mr. Choice will ring the bell any minute now!" she tugged at her brother's sleeve and they both broke into a trot.

"He-ey! Sue!" Ray called to them in their wake.

"Your note-boook!" he was waving in the air with the notebook that had fallen out of her bag, but their trace had already gone cold on the brightly lit night street.

Bearded and well-slept Mr. Bristley, with a large, meaty nose and a pencil stuck behind his ear, settled the crew of the Celestine in their rooms at one o'clock past midnight. Mrs. Bristley, her ponytails rolled up into funny looking pretzels, as though she were not a lady of advanced age, but a first grader, invited everyone to the table.

"What a rigmarole, the devil take me!" Larry was dumbfounded.

"Have they been bitten all over by a sea devil?" Hulking Bill, yawning, expressed his indignation.

"What nutty little people!" Pudgy Ike complained.

"I feel as groggy as a drunk ship rat. I'm so sleepy!" Skinny Wilson barked out.

"Did all of you together confuse day for night?" Archie stared at Mr. Bristley in incomprehension, reluctantly swirling his spoon in a bowl of Mrs. Bristley's unappetizing gruel.

"O-o-oh, outlander... For many, many years, we have not seen a hint of daylight. The moon is our sun. Night is our day. And as soon as there is a hint of sunrise, we tightly close our shutters," Mr. Bristley replied and smiled guiltily.

The starcounter Articus, wearing a tall conical hat and a long cape embroidered with a starry pattern whose hem slid along the floor, sat down at the small table, bent over it and, with barely noticeable nervous excitement, without which he never approached this table, looked into his telescope. The stars greeted him in their usual way, winking with their beaming flames. But still absent among them was that one, which he had been searching for already the past several years.

"Articus! No sign of it yet?" the starcounter Emines called out to him.

"Will there ever come a time when you will come to your senses? You are chasing a mirage and are forcing the entire city to suffer for it!" he implored.

"Be silent! It exists! I will definitely find it and call it after myself! Because no one besides myself believed in it!" Articus took umbrage.

"But you can continue searching for it by night, and still allow the people to lead their lives by day, and not under the cover of night!" Emines added, raising his voice.

"Be quiet! How naive you are, Emines, do you really think that we will then no longer be needed by our people? And what will become of our Planetarium? All of us, you and I and Veritus, will then become unnecessary! And our Sovereign? You genuinely suppose that, having discovered his secret, anyone will continue to obey his will? He will seem weak and useless to them! His days, and ours along

with him, will be numbered! Is that what you want, Emines?" Articus was really irate now.

"Our authority lies solely with our Sovereign. Only under the cover of night will he be able to retain his power. You can choose for yourself, the best way to act," Articus lowered his eyes and turned toward his telescope.

Emines forcefully bent the thin, wooden pointer and it cracked loudly in his hands. He threw it down on the floor and departed the round hall of the Planetarium.

"Fresh fruit! Fresh fruit!" a plump saleswoman was soliciting customers, her arms akimbo, adjusting her apron.

The city market, lit by portable lanterns and oil lamps of various sizes, was leading its usual life on the central square, making noise and haggling, bickering and brawling, arguing and making peace. The only unusual thing about it was that all this was taking place not under the scorching seaside sun, but under the cover of the starry night.

"So, what kind of fruit do you have over here?" Duke said in a tone of surprise, when the crew of the Celestine had set off to explore the city's bustling night life.

"Try these, stranger, you won't regret it!" the saleswoman invited him to partake, slicing off a fleshy piece of the fruit.

"And how do you grow these, if you live only at night?" Duke pressed her, by the time that Hulking Bill and Pudgy Ike were already heartily chewing the juicy wedges.

"How do we grow them? The usual way: we sow, water, and fertilize them, and they grow all by themselves during the day, the fortunate ones! Only we are not permitted to be out in the light, as though we'd been cursed for some wickedness," the saleswoman sighed.

"But they say that, if Articus, our starcounter, discovers his new star, then this curse will be lifted from us," she whispered confidentially.

"You can't imagine how hard he's been trying and trying! If it weren't for him, there would be no one to save us from this wretched curse," the kind-hearted saleswoman recounted and gratefully raised her eyes towards the round cupola of the Planetarium, rising above the town on its mountaintop.

"Emines! Did you speak with him?" Veritus stared at him with fervent hope, seizing the starcounter by his sleeve.

"It's all useless... He is unrelenting," Emines replied and guiltily lowered his eyes.

"But it can't continue in this way any longer! Our children are growing up without the light of day! Our entire lives will pass under the cover of night! Someone must put an end to this protracted madness!" Veritus's voice rang out under the high, rounded cupola.

"But if they believe that they will go blind at sunrise, if they do not hide themselves in time? They believe it and hide themselves! It means that they are not so miserable," Emines shrugged his shoulders.

"You're going out of your mind, just like Articus! He is seeking his Star! And what is it that possesses you?" Veritus screamed.

"I am a starcounter. and there is no happier fate then that for me. The starry sky is my life. If the people's eyes are opened to our Sovereign's secret, then they will never again follow his will. And not just Articus, but you and I and the Planetarium will become unnecessary!" Emines shouted in reply.

"And what if the people punish us for the years they had spent in the darkness?" Emines suddenly whispered.

"It is far too late to speak the truth... The dark night is our truth. You will be alone against us... You will lead all three of us to the gallows... The protection of an impotent ruler will not be worth a penny!" Emines hissed out and yanked away his sleeve, which Veritus had been clenching tightly the entire time.

Ray could not restrain himself and, sitting down under a lamp by the roadside, opened Sue's notebook.

"A composition on the theme: Who do I want to be when I grow up," he read from the very beginning and leaved through a couple of pages of the long text written in an accurate, tiny handwriting.

"...Yes, I'm a girl, but it is unfair that only men may become starcounters! When I grow up, I will definitely become a starcounter. And I will discover that one and only, magical Star, which will save my people from the darkness. And we will once again begin to live under the sun. To greet the sunrise and sunset, and we will never again have to hide by closing our shutters. We will never go blind from the light!"

"Hey, Ray!" Nimble Larry called him over.

"Just look over there!" he pointed.

Above the entrance to one of the shops hung a wooden sign: "Mr. Harris's Miscellany".

In a city where life in daylight did not at all exist, it was strange to see a shop that sold umbrellas from the sun.

"There's nothing unusual about this!" Mr. Harris greeted them.

"Hannah, these are the outlanders that were found today on our square! If you only knew all the sorts of things I have!" he shut his eyes in an expression of humility.

"People bring me things that had long ago become unnecessary. And it's not just umbrellas from the sun. Children's swings, also! Once upon time, they hung from the tree and Mrs. Mason's sons fought over who would go on the swing first. But children don't want to ride the swings under the cover of night, the tall, sprawling tree frightens them, and no one seeks the protective shadow under it any longer, hiding from the sun. And the chair! Just look at this wonderful chair with a reclining back!" Mr. Harris stretched out his long index finger.

"Yes, once upon a time, Mrs. Davis would warm herself in the sun in it. And it's not simply that the old woman Davis is long dead, but is there anyone still alive who sunbathes these days? We are forbidden to go outside in daylight; the authorities assure us that we are cursed and will immediately go blind. And why is it that in the entire city, you will not find a daring man who would brave testing this curse for themselves?" Mr. Harris lowered his voice and winked at Ray conspirationally.

"Don't talk nonsense!" the rail-thin Mrs. Harris inserted from her furthest corner.

"You will probably ask me why I don't test the power of the curse myself?" Mr. Harris raised his brow.

"I am already far too old to contradict the authorities. And what if I really do go blind a day later, having come out into the light? I will no longer be able to work in my shop. What's going to become of Mrs. Harris then? I cannot do that to her," Mr. Harris concluded and sighed heavily.

"So that's how it is! I am always to blame for everything," Mrs. Harris smiled in gratitude and fixed her hair.

"Articus! What did you see today?" the Sovereign asked impatiently.

"I saw Ursa Major and Ursa Minor, the Dipper, and full moon, Sovereign," Articus replied and bowed reverently.

"What do you think; when will you find HER?" the Sovereign asked suddenly.

"I will discover HER, as soon as she shows me her trail, or casts a shadow, not having had time to hide from my gaze. I will find HER, even if she hides behind a thousand other planets, or a million other stars. I will search for HER my entire life and there is nowhere for her hide from me. Because the sky gave her birth exactly for that purpose, that I discover HER!" Articus replied, holding the Sovereign's hand while bending down on his knee before him in reverence.

"Go with God, Articus! I believe you!" the Sovereign replied and rose up from his armchair.

A group of children wearing dark capes embroidered with a starry pattern, glimmering in the darkness, with the teacher at their head, carrying a lantern in his raised arm, were stealthily pussyfooting single-file through the nocturnal dim. The school for future starcounters was climbing the mountain in order to test how well they knew the lessons they had recently learned.

"Hey, Sue!" Ray called out to her.

"Your notebook!" he shouted, catching up with the group and waving the notebook in the air.

"So that's where it went! And I had already tormented poor Pierce about where he had hidden it!" shaggy-haired Sue smiled.

"Where are you going?" Ray persisted

"We're climbing up the mountain. To study the constellations!" Sue reported proudly, hiking her head up to the star-filled sky.

"Can I go with you?" Ray asked, hoping she would say yes.

"Find a place at the end. And don't stick out too much!" Skinny Pierce replied and winked at Ray.

"Alright, let us continue... To which constellation does the brightest star in the sky belong to?" the teacher posed the question, scanning with his gaze the children, who were all trying to make themselves more comfortable in the darkness.

"To the constellation of Canis Major!" Balder jumped up immediately from his place.

"That's right!" the teacher nodded with satisfaction.

"Teacher's pet," Sue whispered into Ray's ear.

"The son of the starcounter Emines thinks that when he grows up, he will take his father's place," she explained.

"And what is this star called?" the teacher inquired, scratching his nose in anticipation.

"It's Sirius!" Austin was the first to raise his hand.

"And this one's just like him," Sue grunted.

"The son of starcounter Veritus. Thanks to his daddy, he is secretly allowed into the Planetarium more often than the rest of us," Sue wrinkled her face in aggravation.

"Well, and what about the second star of the triangle?" the teacher pursued his line of questioning.

Everyone suddenly became silent and contemplative.

"That's Procyon!" Sue raised her hand.

"You're right," the teacher agreed.

"And what constellation does it belong to?" he questioned the students once again.

"To the constellation of Canis Minor!" Sue once again jumped up from her seat.

"Yes, that's right, also," the teacher nodded.

"And the third star of the triangle, is..."

"Betelgeuse!" Skinny Pierce raised his hand.

"And it..." the teacher pronounced his words slowly.

"Belongs to the constellation of Orion!" Pierce inserted once again, catching the

abrasive gazes of the annoyed Balder and Austin trained on himself.

"Today, we will be talking about Bellatrix, Rigel, and Saiph. Of the bright giant stars of the constellation of Orion!" the teacher pronounced solemnly.

Mimicking their teacher's gesture, the twenty five children raised their little heads towards the starry cupola, which, like a huge, black, upside-down tub filled with shimmering lights, covered the future starcounters, together with the towering mountain that seemed now laughably tiny in comparison.

"Hey, Pierce," Balder whispered.

"Don't jump ahead of me when you're not asked the question directly!" he hissed out irately.

"Why do you bother talking to him! If he thinks he's smarter than the rest of us, then let him also prove that he is the bravest!" Austin suggested, grabbing Pierce by his sleeve.

"Leave him alone!" Sue snapped.

"Just because you are the children of starcounters doesn't mean that you can do anything you want!" she confronted them.

"More of the same from you! Then, why don't we all go to the old tree to jump on a dare!" Balder proposed combatively.

"If you think you scared me because I'm a girl, you're sadly mistaken," Sue pronounced deliberately.

"Break off from the group and wait until Mr. Choice turns the corner with the rest of the class. We will follow after you, you cowardly upstarts!" Sue snarled.

"Come with us Ray, you will be the judge!" she proposed, grabbing Ray by his hand.

Skinny Pierce, Sue, dressed like a boy, with her tousled hair, the sons of the starcounters, and Ray walked in the darkness without exchanging a word on their way. The broad avenue turned into a narrow road, the road into a path, the path into a trail, where after their every step, the pebbles would scatter in all directions, and the trail itself then broke up into a gravelly swamp. Drowning in pebbles and barely able to pull his feet out of the gravel, Ray came out to an old, sprawling tree, towering on the precipice and illuminated by the moonlight. A rope with a short, thick branch secured to it was attached to a black, long, curved bough.

"Well, what do you say? Let's see who jumps the farthest! Two against two! The losers...," Balder paused to think.

"Are cowardly upstarts, once and for all!" Sue shouted out, stuffing the hem of her shirt deeper inside her slacks.

"Yes! Once and for all!" Austin agreed.

Balder took off his cape, embroidered with stars, his pants and shirt, and stood there wearing only his underwear. Having jumped up and grabbed the short rope tied to the branch, he took several steps backwards, made a thrust forward, took a few mincing steps and, rocking back and forth on the rope as though on a pendulum, jumped into the water, barely missing one of the four huge boulders, rising with their sharp points out of the dark water. Having swam away from the rocks and climbed up onto dry land, he immediately wrapped himself in his starry cape and squatted down on his haunches, his teeth chattering loudly.

"To the second stone! He jumped as far as the second stone!" Austin, already getting undressed, yelled threateningly in the direction of Sue and Pierce.

Skinny Pierce, Sue, and Ray nodded silently.

Austin grabbed the rope and took a running start; the bough began to squeak under his weight, but bore his weight and hurled him, with the full force of its pendulum, into the water.

"The third stone!" Austin screamed triumphantly, popping out of the black water and surveying his surroundings.

Skinny Pierce undressed slowly, to all appearances not believing in his chance of being victorious. He took a running start with the rope in his hands, slowed down, as though aiming, jumped and plopped down in the water without having reached even the first stone. The sons of the starcounters burst out laughing, for a moment interrupting the chattering of their teeth. Sue, once again, checked that her shirt was tucked in deep enough into her pants, hopped up, grabbed the rope, took a running start, tucked her legs under herself, flew pendulum-like, and jumped into the water, barely missing the sharp point of the second stone.

The sons of the starcounters, still trembling under their starry capes, immediately gave each other a high five, celebrating their victory.

"Co-ward-ly up-staaarts!" Balder and Austin guffawed, when in her wet clothes, Sue, her hair now no longer disheveled, but sticking to her forehead, jumped, shivering, out of the water.

"Three against two!" Ray suddenly shouted, issuing a challenge.

He quickly shed his clothes, hopped up and, exerting himself to his absolute limit, with difficulty, grabbed onto the rope that was dangling above him. With all his

strength, he took a running start and dove from the pendulum rope into the water. The desiccated tree he swung from emitted a loud crack.

"The fourth! The fourth stone!" Skinny Pierce and Sue, with her sticky hair, started jumping up and down on the shore when Ray was still bobbing up and down in the black water, trying to disentangle himself from the rope and the old branch that had fallen in the water together with him.

The goggle-eyed moon was gawking at all this disgraceful risk-taking and decided that in this, as in all other silly altercations, there must be no victors.

"Ray, look, the morning star! When it rises, we go off to sleep!" Sue yelled out.

"We must immediately head home! Let's run, or they will start searching for us!" Pierce affirmed.

"The guards begin their rounds towards morning! There must not be a living soul in the city!" Sue added hurriedly.

And all four of them, on the run grabbing their clothing and capes sewn with stars, their heels flashing, flung themselves in the direction of the city of San Stella Diurna, soundly falling asleep at the break of dawn.

Ray was so tired that Hulking Bill's train engine snoring didn't bother him one bit, and he slept soundly the day through. Nimble

Larry, exhausted after his nocturnal revelry, was not at all bothered by Skinny Wilson's nervous tossing and turning. Cook Duke slept like a dead man. Pudgy Ike dreamed of a hot day and was squinting his eyes from the sun in his sleep. Archie slept on his back, as though he wasn't at all asleep, but had lay down and closed his eyes to think. A wise thought came to him in his sleep: if all of this weren't true and the inhabitants of the San Stella Diurna were not cursed by anyone and would not go blind from seeing the daylight, then this could be proven if one of them braved to look at the magical Prelloubridge stone that shone brighter than the light of day.

Opening his eyes and, having considered his dream, he understood that only one small thing remained to be done: to find the yellow, shinning magical stone.

At breakfast and during dinner time in Mr. and Mrs. Bristley's tavern, the crew of the Celestine was joined by one other guest. His slovenly appearance, exhausted face, and crumpled clothing spoke of the fact that he didn't live according to the local schedule and the sunset is not sunrise for him, as it was for all the others. It seemed that he lived his own, separate life. Mrs. Bristley's insipid tea and her similarly tasteless, colorless chowder, unburdened by culinary talents, was left standing untouched. Instead of having breakfast, he was taking some sort of notes and making some sort of drawings, having barely found room for them on the table in front of himself by pushing his plate aside.

"What, you don't sleep in the daytime?" unable to restrain himself, Archie asked him, sitting down besides the unshaven stranger.

"I never sleep at all," he replied, something that his entire disheveled, sickly appearance affirmed.

For some reason, Archie was delighted with this response, as though only he spoke the same language as this odd stranger.

"We are seeking a magical yellow stone," Archie suddenly confided in him.

"It is stored in a casket under Articus's telescope," the exhausted sufferer replied as though it were nothing unusual.

"How do you know that?" Archie went numb.

"I saw it there three years ago," the stranger affirmed.

"And you never sought to possess it?" Archie expressed his surprise.

"What do I need it for?" the man replied in incomprehension.

"I am searching for Stella di Tolle! My new star! And I will most definitely find it! Even if you or any other of this city's ignoramuses do not believe in me!" he suddenly shouted out, quickly rolling up his drawings and, wrapping himself in his old, tattered cape, hurriedly left the room.

Mrs. Bristley wagged her head in a gesture of disapproval in his wake.

"That was the former fourth starcounter, Iritus. A couple of years have passed already since he and Articus quarreled over which star they should be looking for! After their mighty falling-out, Articus won out, and the man was banned from the Planetarium. Since then, he wanders like a ghost around the city, almost entirely deprived of sleep," Mrs. Bristley nodded in the direction of the door that had just been slammed shut, still reproachfully shaking her head with its ponytails wound up like pretzels.

"Hey, Ray! Draw the light of day and the sun for me!" Sue asked, handing Ray her notebook.

Ray thought for a second. and after another moment, shrouded in the nocturnal gloom, his pencil began sliding across the paper. On the notebook's page, there arose a little stone house, with a roof resembling a thatched one, a girl wearing funny-looking pants running toward the water, rushing after whom was a a skinny boy. Children standing by the shore were ratcheting back their arms and flinging flat stones into the water. Under the obedient strokes of Ray's pencil, the house with the thick thatched roof, and the girl wearing pants and the skinny boy, and the children standing on the shore, everything was casting long and short shadows, under the hot sun that was standing at its zenith.

"Keep it down!" Mr. Choice asked them.

"Has everyone paired off with someone?" he scanned the group of children with his gaze.

"Everyone!" Sue replied, tightly clenching Ray's hand.

With Mr. Choice in the lead, carrying, as he always did, a lamp in his outstretched hand, the group of children from the school of future starcounters set out this night for that holy of holies, the Planetarium,

rising majestically on the mountain above the city of San Stella Diurna.

Though he had caught up on sleep in the daytime, Ray's knees were buckling slightly with excitement. The crew of the Celestine was waiting for him to come back with the shining, yellow, magical Prelloubridge.

It seemed that the Planetarium, with its huge, rounded roof, was not just soaring above the entire town, but that its cupola was touching the nocturnal starry sky itself. Ascending the seemingly countless steps in the semi-darkness, guided only by Mr. Choice's lamp, the children, finally, reached its main entrance way. The guards, all dressed in clothes dark as the night itself, opened the tall gates, letting the future starcounters into the tightly guarded heart of the city.

Pierce, who, despite his unsuccessful leap into the water, managed to hurt his leg, having cut himself on something sharp, was dragging along behind the rest. The schoolchildren, covered by capes with their stars shimmering in the darkness, slipped past the steely gazes of the guard.

The doors had only just been slammed shut, when Pierce, limping slightly, shouted: "Wait for me too!" and scurried inside through the remaining crack. For some reason, standing inside the planetarium, under the huge, dark, rounded cupola painted with golden stars, Ray felt himself to be even smaller than under the black, open starry sky.

Mr. Choice, raising his right arm with the lamp, pressed the index finger of his left hand to his tightly clenched lips, calling for silence, and the children, already frozen still in respectful anticipation, looking around themselves, huddled from the frigid cold of the inner, darkened hallways. The second hall greeted the future starcounters with its patterns of constellations, scattered on the stony firmament.

"Once upon a time, a very long time ago, so long ago that neither you, nor your parents, nor your grandmothers were yet alive, a little girl was born on this earth," Mr. Choice slowly began.

Sue listened in especially carefully.

"Time passed, she grew up and turned into a wonderful young woman whose beauty shone so brightly that even one of the Gods, who lived in the sky, was blinded by it," Mr. Choice continued.

"It is not surprising that the heart of a youth who lived near her was also aflame with love for the beautiful girl and, from his very first glance, he understood that, until the end of his life, it belonged to her. It was not her beauty that seemed a miracle to him, but that her feelings were mutual, forever granted to him," Mr. Choice scanned the children now grown quiet.

"Phew!" Brandon screwed up his face, looking over at Austin. "I can't stand love stories!"

"But the God, peering down from the sky, could not contain his own feelings for the mortal girl and he decided that, no matter what happens, he would impede the lovers, and send the poor youth on a long and dangerous journey across the sea."

Sue sighed heavily without tearing her eyes away from Mr. Choice.

"The first year passed, and after it a second, and then a third. After she had been waiting for seven years, the sky God confessed to the beautiful girl that, from his celestial height, he could see her intended. And he lives there, knowing no heartache, on the other side of the earth, where he had been charmed by a heartless witch, who made him believe that it was in her that he found his true, great love."

Sue frowned and clenched her fists, hidden under her starry cape.

"But if the enamored young woman should drink the bewitching potion, then she will be able to, having turned into a swan, fly to the other side of the earth and undo the spell on her beloved," Mr. Choice continued, scratching his bulbous nose.

"Without thinking twice, not even for a moment, she drank the magical potion. But the celestial God did not turn her into a swan, depriving her of her earthly feminine beauty, and instead only made her fall into a deep sleep, so that he could continue marveling at her beautiful features."

Sue was now petrified in impotent rage.

"A very short time passed and, contrary to the spell, her beloved returned to his native land, where only the dead body of his beloved awaited him. Tormented with unbearable suffering, he saw no other way out for himself than to drink the same magical potion in a single draft. In a moment, he turned into a swan, flew into the sky and froze still forever, spreading his starry wings on the black, nocturnal sky," Mr. Choice pronounced slowly, looking the children over.

A knot formed in Sue's throat.

"Legend tells us that, awakening from the bewitched, deep sleep, the unfortunate young woman, for the rest of her long and unhappy life, never again slept at night. And as soon as the first evening stars lit up the sky, until the very break of dawn, without shutting or tearing away her eyes, she looked upon her long-awaited swan, forever spreading in flight his starry wings in the distant and inaccessible, black firmament," Mr. Choice solemnly concluded.

"And so? What constellation is it that I have been telling you about?" Mr. Choice added unexpectedly.

"Of the constellation of the swan, Cygnus!" the future starcounters replied in a chorus.

Ray regretted not having paper and a pencil near at hand, with the strokes of which, the starry swan would have flown into the night sky. Pierce's ailing leg stopped hurting, because it had drained in the pose he had sat in too long, being fearful in his excitement to shift. Tears of betrayal were flowing down Sue's cheeks, which she, struggling with her embarrassment, secretly wiped away from her starry cape.

"And which bright stars is it comprised of?" Mr. Choice now quizzed them.

"Deneb!" Pierce raised his hand.

"Sadr!" Brandon jumped up from his seat.

"Aljanah!" Austin chimed in.

"Albireo," Sue added quietly.

The guard, dressed all in black, held the door ajar and nodded to Mr. Choice.

"We have been permitted to enter the main hall! Precisely where the telescope is located!" Mr. Choice announced solemnly.

The children raised a joyful clamor and fuss.

"Quieter please! Articus requires silence!" warned Mr. Choice, raising his index finger to his mouth.

The children, once again arranging themselves in pairs, proceeded down the dark, rounded corridor which kept turning endlessly to their left, skirting the entire Planetarium. Ray could barely contain his excitement and, more tightly than usual, he clenched Sue's palm, as though trying to charge her with ungirl-like courage. Stumbling slightly over a couple of steps leading up into the main hall containing the telescope, Ray, together with the future starcounters, entered into the holy of holies. The hall turned out to be not at all large, but the rounded cupola seemed to reach higher here for some reason. The table was cluttered with papers, and the blackboard standing a little way off was covered with calculations and drawings.

"And here he is! Our eagle eye, observing the starry sky!" Mr. Choice proudly introduced the head starcounter.

At a round little table with an ornate leg made of dark wood stood Articus's telescope, perched on a stone casket of incredible beauty, hidden within which was the shining, yellow, magical Prelloubridge.

Ray was tormented by two questions: how might he, in the presence of so many, get his hands on the stone? And how the hell did the entire crew of the Celestine, who had sent him here exactly for that purpose, think it were possible?

"It is precisely here in the not too distant future, and perhaps even very shortly, that a miracle will occur," Mr. Choice pronounced almost in a whisper.

"Our famous and respected starcounter Articus will discover a new star, the very same one he has been searching for for a very long time, each and every night, for our common benefit. Just as soon as it ceases to hide and reveals itself to Articus's watchful eye, it will remove the curse from us and we will once again be able to see the light of day, without fearing at all that we will go blind form it!" Mr. Choice promised and scanned all the stilled children with his gaze.

"Could I look into the telescope too?" Skinny Pierce with his ailing leg suddenly broke the silence.

"No!" a voice rang out. It belonged to Articus, who had only just entered the hall.

The children turned around, frightened.

"Who let the children in here?" Articus grunted irritably, crossing the hall with quick strides, wearing a long, flaring cape embroidered with stars down both sides.

"We're just here for one quick minute," Mr. Choice tried to soothe him. "The guard let us through...."

"Fire all the nitwits at the entrance to the Planetarium!" Articus shouted to no one in particular, as though issuing an urgent order.

"We were about to leave!" Mr. Choice assured him, conducting the air with his hands in the direction of the confused children, which meant: line up immediately in pairs and out of the hall on the double!

"If you can, wait for me outside by the entrance; I'll try to remain behind now!" Ray whispered into Sue's ear in a commanding tone.

Sue glanced at Ray, with an expression that was simultaneously fearful and rapturous, and nodded her head. Which meant: I have no idea what's on your mind, but I have yet to meet such a courageous boy!

Skinny Pierce, with his ailing leg, stumbled over something in his rushed excitement right at the entrance.

"What's going on now?" Articus barked out irritably, raising his head in dissatisfaction, wishing to be left alone as soon as possible.

Everyone looked over reproachfully at the bumbling Pierce, who was frightened as is already. Ray found the right moment, squatted down, crawled away on all fours, and slipped under the dark curtain, the folds of its heavy, lower edge dropping down to the floor.

The children lined up and, as there was no time now for them to pair off, obediently trudged single file out of the hall.

Hidden behind the curtain and standing on his tip toes, Ray was able to reach, at his eye level, a stripe in the curtain's thick, dark fabric that was punctuated by a fine, pitted pattern.

Articus sat down at his table with the charts and wearily stretched out his legs, as though an insurmountable task awaited him and there was no sense in hurrying to fulfill it, there being no way to complete it quickly.

"Articus! The Ruler is here!" the guard made the introduction and swung the door wide open.

Articus jumped up and flung himself toward the exit. A gaunt, wrinkled old man with long gray hair, supported by Articus's obliging arm, lowered himself into what was apparently the most honored armchair in this scantily lit hall, and wearily reclined on its soft back, decorated with an illustration formed of large and small stars.

"What does the sky tell us today?" he declared softly.

"Sirius in Canis Major is burning so bright it's no joke, and the moon has decided to linger, as though to continue gazing upon Vega in the constellation of Lyra!" Articus reported joyfully.

"You will soon find HER, is that right, Articus? You will soon find our star?" the Ruler asked him, his voice full of hope, as though imploring for help.

"I am certain of it!" Articus promised him.

"What do you think, what color will she shine with?" the Ruler asked once again.

"It will burn a bright yellow-red, reflect purple, flicker green, and glow with a blue light!" Articus replied ecstatically.

"And you suppose that its magical powers will be so strong that even I will be able to see it?" the old man pronounced timidly.

"Most certainly, Your Majesty! Its light will be so bright that even you will be able to see it, along with everything, everything, everything that surrounds you!" Articus assured him, bowing his head and respectfully holding the blind man by his hand.

Ray had grown tired of standing on his tiptoes and, unable to withstand the tension in his legs any longer, carefully and soundlessly let himself down on his heels.

Articus immediately turned around and listened in carefully.

Ray held his breath.

"I am so tired," the Ruler said quietly.

Ray, no longer able to see what was going on, heard the muffled sound of steps departing the hall, accompanied by the knocking of a stranger's heels.

Gathering up his remaining strength, Ray once again raised himself up on his tiptoes. The hall now stood empty. Ray immediately jumped out from behind the curtain and flung himself toward the table with the telescope.

"Chirp!" he suddenly heard a noise.

"Chirrup! Chirrup!" a bird's trill called out to him.

Ray turned around in incomprehension: a small, gray, insignificant little bird, somewhat resembling a sparrow, was perched on the tall, starry back of the armchair that had only just been occupied by the old, blind Ruler.

"How did you get here?" Ray said in shock.

The little bird, as though responding, hiked her tiny little head upward.

Ray looked upward: through the round opening in the high, rounded cupola of the hall, the stars winked at him from their black, nocturnal firmament.

The door, having been left ajar, was suddenly flung open.

"You, what are you doing here? They are searching for you everywhere!" Articus roared, bumping into Ray.

Ray, immediately slinging the starry cape he had borrowed from Sue from his shoulders, tossed it with all his might over the lost and chirping pipsqueak.

"I forgot my little bird!" he replied, running off with his chirping cape clenched tightly in his arms.

"Here I am!" Ray greeted everyone, flapping his star-spangled cape on the air to let the twittering birdie go free.

"If everyone is, finally, accounted for, then let us depart!" Mr. Choice commanded, reproachfully waving his finger in Ray's direction.

Ecstatic, Sue grabbed Ray by the hand, as though she intended never again to let it go.

The city of the morning star, San Stella Diurna, was ablaze with flames, the joyous and welcomed by the entire jubilant crowd, not the dangerous kind, requiring intercession. The crowd of people carrying lit torches, like burning lava oozing down the slope of a volcano, flowed out from all the streets onto the central square. Music was coming from every window, contributing to the joyful hum of blazing nighttime revelry. A woman with unruly hair and a tall, skinny man, who turned out to be the parents of Sue and Pierce, who so much resembled them, were joyfully swinging their torches, accompanying the loud, jubilant crowd.

Nimble Larry was playing dangerously with fire, swinging his torch from side to side and raptly observing how the firework sparks were scattering in the dark. Wilson had drunk too much and, hugging Archie, was bawling some sort of indigenous song. Duke and Pudgy Ike were ogling around themselves, having joined in the procession, and the torch in Hulking Bill's stretched out hand was sticking out of the crowd like a lighthouse beacon flickering at the tip of a peninsula.

"We celebrate the festival of the sacred Woody!" Sue screamed at the top of her lungs.

"Sacred Woody is just a scarecrow! They will burn him now on the city's main square. Let's run to see it!" she called out to Ray.

"Why is this scarecrow sacred to you?" Ray asked, shouting over the crowd.

"It protects our harvest during the daytime, while we're asleep!" Sue explained, rocking slightly from the endless shoving of the jubilant crowd.

"Then why must it be burned?" Ray sounded surprised.

"On this night, we burn last year's Woody, and tomorrow, towards morning, the new one will be placed out in the fields," she shouted to him.

A dozen sacred Woodies were tossed, one on top of each other, in the central square, forming a large mountain of old Woody-man scarecrows that had served out the purpose of their short lives. One more moment and they flared up, all at once, adorning the dark night of the boisterous revelry with red and yellow blazing tones and the smell of smoke.

"Archie!" Ray screamed in the captain's ear.

"I did not manage to obtain the stone! But I know the Ruler's secret!" he added.

Glimmering in his eyes, along with flaming bonfire of the burning Woodies, was a cunning plan, which would require an indomitable will to victory, as well as the assistance of many dozens of strong hands.

Someone was knocking at the door of Mr. and Mrs. Bristley's tavern.

"It is us!" the woman with the unruly hair and the skinny man resembling Sue and Pierce, introduced themselves and handed over, barely able to bear it in their arms, a mountain of bed sheets.

Mrs. Bristley was commanding the headquarters of the day's extraordinary activities.

"Don't bring any more! I think this will be sufficient!" she begged them.

Mr. Bristley, Mr. and Mrs. Harris, and the entire crew of the Celestine sat on the floor, tearing the mountains of bed sheets, brought to them from all the corners of the city of San Stella Diurna, into strips and then tying them into one long, huge rope.

"You must approach from the west!" Sue's and Pierce's parents warned.

"That area is covered with a dense and dark thicket of trees and the guards won't be able to immediately make out that someone is approaching in total darkness," they proposed.

"Well, Godspeed!" Mr. and Mrs. Bristley sighed, rising up from the floor and testing that the last segment was safe and secure.

"Faster! While there's still light!" Mrs. Bristley appealed to all present.

The strange procession, not of the boisterous, disorderly throng toward the incineration of the Woody on the central square, but of a regular file of people, moving stealthily in semi-darkness and carrying in their arms, like a gargantuan boa constrictor, a rope of extraordinary length, was advancing toward the mountain with the Planetarium towering majestically on its top.

"Faster! The guard is making its rounds! They were just here!" someone shouted out of the darkness.

The thin railings of the iron staircase ascending from the ground to the very center of the rounded cupola was now already behind them, and Ray, breathing rapidly and his heart beating faster, removed the tip of the long rope made of torn and tied together bed sheets from his shoulders. He tied it securely to the last step and jumped into the opening of the round cupola, swinging on the rope like a spider

on its gossamer web. Stretching out string-like and jumping down to the floor, he immediately ran over to the little table with the telescope, carefully slid it off to the side and opened the remarkably beautiful casket. The yellow, magical, shinning Prellowbridge lit up the entire room. Hearing strange footsteps beyond the door, Ray flung himself back towards the rope, hopped up with all his might, and grabbed onto its dangling end.

"Pull me up!" he shouted to Archie's and Larry's dark silhouettes hanging off the edge in the opening of the round cupola.

"Stand still!" the guard yelled, bursting into the hall and, pointing his long spear at Ray, snatching with its pointy tip the collar of his child's shirt.

"Pull!" Ray screamed as loud as he could, sensing himself immediately flying grabbed onto its dangling end.

"Pull me up!" he shouted to Archie's and Larry's dark silhouettes hanging off the edge in the opening of the round cupola.

"Stand still!" the guard yelled, bursting into the hall and, pointing his long spear at Ray, snatching with its pointy tip the collar of his child's shirt.

"Pull!" Ray screamed as loud as he could, sensing himself immediately flying upwards, as the guard's spear, slicing the fabric like a sharpened knife from the back of his head down to his waist, remained behind him far below.

"They are cheering, Articus!" the Ruler cried out in agitation.

"Yes, my Ruler, the people are cheering," Articus replied quietly.

"Do you hear it? It's the entire city! There are so many of them! It sounds as though they have all taken to the streets, Articus!"

"I hear them, Ruler... Yes, they have gone out into the streets, each and every one of them..."

"So, you have finally found HER, Articus?"

"...Yes... I have found HER, my Ruler..."

"Look how they are rejoicing, Articus! Just listen to them, how they are cheering!" the Ruler yelled at the top of his voice, and down his cheeks flowed tears of joy out of eyes that never did manage to see the bright, life-affirming sun of this morning, upon which the inhabitants of the city of San Stella Diurna were greeting the sunrise for the first time in many years.

The Celestine was racing full speed ahead across the surface of the sea, as her entire crew poured out on deck, exposing their gratified pirate mugs to the long-awaited sun. San Stella Diurna, the city of the very first morning star, had now been left somewhere very very far behind. A city where a boy was growing up who, every night, will observe the stars through a telescope in search of HER, that one and only.

And a girl with unruly hair, who will recall Ray, the moment the Constellation of the Swan spreads out its starry wings, frozen still in its final flight on the night sky's black horizon.

Chapter Nine

He Saves Himself Who Destroys Himself

"ell, well, so you're unsinkable!" Archie read from Cook's book. "I swear by my devil-roasted backside that your next skirmish will be your certain death! Enough chatter: you will meet an enemy who isn't any smarter than you, whose crew is not any more numerous, whose store of bullets is no less than yours. "What is the difference then?" you ask me.

IT IS THIS: ONLY ONE OF YOU WILL SURVIVE.

WHICH OF THE TWO WILL YOU CHOOSE?

A CUNNING MARK IS THE GIFT OF LIFE.

Well, yes...

HE WILL SAVE HIMSELF WHO DESTROYS HIMSELF!

Ho-ho-ho!"

Archie waited to hear the rest, but the book was silent now, and not a single other line rose up on the surface of its yellowed pages. Infuriated, Archie grabbed the book and hurled it against the wall of his cabin. The Secret Book in its dark, leather binding, plunked down on the floor. Archie picked it up, tossed it under his feet, and started stomping on it ferociously, cursing and blaspheming. Afterwards, he impotently plopped down on his knees and covered his face with his hands.

Cook Duke and Pudgy Ike were snoring peacefully, lulled by the rocking of the sea waves. Skinny Wilson, his foot jerking, kept tossing off his thin blanket. Nimble Larry dozed off at the helm.

Ray slept like an infant. Hulking Bill was snoring quietly, like a train engine after a long run, lowering its speed before breaking to a stop at a station.

Archie didn't even shut an eye. He sat on the floor by his bed and for some reason clearly understood now that he has no idea what would happen next, but tomorrow morning, his entire crew will bid farewell to this life, or he might succeed in saving them. He kept going over the last revealed lines of Cook's book in his head; he knew them by heart already but didn't at all understand what it was about them that he could grasp onto.

"Only one of you will survive..." "This was certain: either he kills me, or I kill him," Archie thought to himself. "Which of the two will you chose...." This too was absolutely clear, Archie grunted to himself under his nose. "A cunning mark is the gift of life..." "What mark?!" Archie shouted out in despair. "He will save himself who destroys himself..." "What nonsense?!" Archie whispered helplessly and banged his head against the wooden wall of the cabin. When he was overcome by sleep, half asleep, he remembered for some reason his leather raincoat and, awakening, found nothing at all remarkable about this, inasmuch as he saw that it was what he had covered himself with.

Suddenly, like a traveler who had come out of the fog onto a road, at the end of which a light flickered, he jumped out of his bed, by touch found a knife beside him, and started to fiercely cut the hem of his leather raincoat into long strips of even length.

"Everyone up! Reveille, you slackers, weaklings, nincompoops!" Archie bawled, ringing the bell.

Hulking Bill, Nimble Larry, Skinny Wilson, Pudgy Ike, Cook Duke, Ray, and Captain Archie, all of them assuming a militant pose demonstrating their readiness for battle with an unknown foe, lined up on deck at sunrise. The forehead of each of them was tied round with a strip made of the dark leather from Archie's raincoat that he had sliced into pieces that night.

"Captain! A schooner! A schooner, port-side!" Ray screamed and everyone breathed a sigh of relieve that the enemy, with whom they were already prepared to do battle, was neither a storm, nor strange beasts, nor a sea devil. All of them, all at once, rushed to the boat's stern.

"What the hell, Captain?" Ike sounded frightened.

"May I be torn to pieces by a thousand squinty-eyed sharks!" Wilson barked.

"What have I done to be cursed so?" Bill growled.

The enemy schooner was approaching at lightning speed, as though it weren't sailing but flying across the sea, and one no longer even needed to look into Cook's spyglass to be able to see that it was The Celestine, on the deck of which, glued to its stern and staring at them were Nimble Larry, Skinny Wilson, Cook Duke, Pudgy Ike, Ray, Hulking Bill and Captain Archie. Everything looked as though it were a mirror reflection: the schooner, the crew, and the captain. Only the leather strip on the foreheads of the entire crew of the genuine Celestine, the genuine mark as it were, distinguished each of them. Not even a couple of seconds had passed when both of the schooners combatively made first contact against each other's sides, like fighting cocks challenging their opponent to a tussle.

"Prepare to board the enemy vessel!" Archie screamed.

"Fight not for your life, but to the death! Do not spare yourself!" he screamed and fired a shot skyward.

The crew of the Celestine charged across the lowered gangway onto "The False Celestine," the crew of which was already also charging into the fray.

Nimble Larry with the mark on his forehead, raced across the deck after the similarly Nimble Larry, but without the mark. Skinny Wilson with the leather strip bashed Skinny Wilson without the mark on his head with a heavy board. Pudgy Ike without the mark dropped his knife when Pudgy Ike with the mark on his head twisted his arm and bopped him as hard as he could in the kidneys. Cook Duke with the mark knew where he had always kept an iron pan hidden on deck: he squatted and, crawling quickly away to avoid the pirates' brawling, found by feel the iron pan under the thick ropes and, as hard as he could, smacked it down on the head of the Duke without the strip on his forehead. Hulking Bill hoisted a barrel on his back, preparing to throw it with all his might at Hulking Bill without the mark. Hulking Bill without the mark turned out to be the quicker of the two and the barrel flew at the head of marked Bill. Ray rolled up his sleeves

and, gathering up his strength and winding up, drilled the Ray without the mark in the jaw. "Ba-am!" and Skinny Wilson with the leather strip on his forehead smacked with his heavy board one of the Nimble Larrys.

"You, id-i-ot! Can't you tell it's me-e-e-e!" Larry with the mark on his forehead howled in pain.

"You're not going to miss... You're not going to miss... You won't miss!" Archie whispered, as though praying, jumping from one side of the boat's stern to the other and aiming at the captain without the mark.

Bo-oom! And the captain without the mark tore a hole in Archie's tricornered hat.

Bo-oom! Yet another shot and hot blood spurted out of Archie's earlobe and down his neck.

Bo-oom! Bo-oom! Bo-oom! Archie fired again and the lifeless body of the unmarked, false captain swayed and toppled overboard from the stern.

"A-a-a-a-a!" Archie screamed victoriously.

"A-a-a!" howled marked Ike, being beaten with a board by marked Wilson.

"A-a-a-a!" everyone screamed in a chorus and started running, sensing "The False Celestine" having had suddenly listed and began its gentle descent to the bottom of the sea.

"Hey, you dinky little captain!" Archie, his ear bloodied, was reading again from Cook's book.

"I see that you are in no hurry to join me in hell! I wager the four yet to be found magical stones against the other three that your path will be cut short halfway through. You won't live to see the fourth stone, just as you'll never learn to shoot accurately on your first try! You're again asking for riddles, you lousy shot, you? Then, here you go:

LOOK AT THE LARGE WITH THE
EYES OF THE SMALL.

AND WITH THE EYES OF THE LARGE AT THE SMALL.

SEEK THE ESSENCE IN THE DEPTHS OF IT ALL.

And then you will find the green, magical Bowgrindle!

Farewell, captain! Till we meet again in the next world! The devils today are feeling playful; they've been tickling my heels with their pitchforks all day! Ho-ho-ho!"

"Damned Cook!" Archie barked and forcefully slammed the Secret Book shut.

"Cap-tain! La-a-and ahoy-oy-oy!" Ray screamed from the mast.

"La-a-and ahoy-oy-oy, Right on our course, la-a-a-and!" Nimble

Larry seconded him.

"La-a-and ahoy-oy-oy!" Skinny Wilson croaked in a hoarse voice, having been beaten mercilessly on his own deck for having pummeled with his board the entire marked crew during their incursion on "The False Celestine".

And all of them once again proceeded to cling impatiently to the stern.

BOUGRINDLE

Chapter Ten

San Liberi, or the Upside-Down World

"enjamin!" a little girl was speaking loudly, blocking the way to a boy who looked worried.

"That's not going to work!" she complained.

"You must forbid Sherry from planting her forget-me-nots! My nasturtiums are all dying because they can't tolerate being next to Sherry's forget-me-nots!"

"But your flower beds are separated by a fence, Hailey! How could Sherry's forget-me-nots do any harm to your nasturtiums?" Benjamin kept objecting.

"She's just imagining it all!" Sherry, barely able to keep up with both of them, jumped in.

"She's just jealous that my forget-me-nots are flowering for the second year in a row! And her nasturtiums won't even sprout," she added.

"I demand that you review this matter in court, Benjamin!" Hailey pleaded.

"Nonsense!" Sherry replied in his stead.

"It's been a year already that Mitchell is suing Spencer! And if we're going to fill a judge's working day with such mumbo jumbo, then real crime will go unpunished!" Sherry shouted in her own defense.

"If the doctor is complaining about the constant smell of soot in his house after his chimney is cleaned by the chimney sweep, that is a sufficient crime to be brought up for review by the court! Because this is gross negligence in the line of duty, and Kelvin must be punished!" Hailey countered.

The crew of the Celestine, who had only just come ashore and came upon this childish quarrel after a couple of minutes of walking, exchanged perplexed glances.

"And who are you? What are you doing here?" the deadly serious Benjamin suddenly asked them point blank. "It's nine o'clock already, why aren't the grown-ups in school yet?"

"Do all of these adults belong to you?" Hailey and Sherry asked Ray almost in unison.

"Yes, they do," Ray nodded his head, winking at Archie. "But we only just came ashore!"

"Then you must immediately register them at the city hall with the Mayor!" Benjamin commanded, hurrying on his way.

"And then take them to school, school! If you intend to stay here a while. This is no business for grown-ups to be wondering around the city willy-nilly in the midst of day," Benjamin added, looking back at them.

And he jotted down in his folder: "Nine o'clock, thirty minutes. Six adults, accompanied by just one boy, were observed in the neighborhood of Embankment Street. Sent for registration to city hall, the Mayor's office."

Mayor Fred, a pudgy boy with rosy cheeks, opened his notebook with a gesture of self-importance.

"How many are you?" Fred scanned the crew of the Celestine with his eyes.

"Six," he wrote down without waiting for a reply.

"Your ages?" Fred stared at the pirates.

"Not established," he wrote down after a moment's deliberation.

"State your profession."

Skinny Wilson scratched the back of his head.

"Uncertain," Fred scribbled with his dulled and messy quill.

"Will they all be living with you?" he asked Ray.

"Yes, we will be staying together," Ray nodded in agreement.

"Go straight along this street, then make the first left. Knock on the door under a sign that says, "Wally's and Oprah's Bed and Breakfast". And tomorrow early morning, immediately take them to school! Adults are not permitted to be loitering in the daytime!" the rosy-cheeked Mayor added severely.

The crew of the Celestine, with Ray at their head, who in this world ruled by children everyone took for their leader, obediently set off in search of the Bed and Breakfast. Children and only children were walking the streets of this sunny city, constructed out of white stone and decorated with an abundance of colorful flowers. Not one of them was moving about empty-handed. Each of them was either carrying or dragging something, or they were engaged in repairing, reinforcing, hauling, hammering, screwing in, selling, or buying. It was assumed that the grown-ups during this time, according to the words of Judge George and Mayor Fred, had to be in school.

Wally, a short, freckled boy, and similarly freckled Oprah were setting the table, having shown the crew of the Celestine to their rooms.

"Well, how do you like that!?" Duke burst out laughing, sitting down at the table and distrustfully sniffing the plate with her cooking that

Oprah had brought out to him.

"Your parents have all been gobbled up by sharks?" Wilson joked, taking his boots off under the table.

"Where are all the grown-ups?" Archie expressed his bewilderment.

"They are at school," Wally, the proprietor of the inn responded, as if this was perfectly natural.

"We know how to do everything already! You will not lack for anything!" wearing an apron, Oprah hastily assured him, carefully placing a plate with the main course on the table.

The door, that had been shoved from the outside by a foot, swung open and an out of breath boy wearing a white hat on the side of his head announced:

"Fresh buns! Fresh hot buns!"

"I'll take them, Brad!" Oprah ran over to the door and accepted the basket from the baker's hands.

"Add it to my bill, I will most definitely settle it at the end of the week!" Oprah assured him hastily.

The door hadn't had a moment's rest when another knock came on it.

A businesslike, muscular boy holding a chisel in his right hand and a set of tools in his left stepped over the threshold.

"Stanley!" Oprah exclaimed, clearly happy to see him.

"Something is wrong with our lock! Take a look over here," she invited him in, settling down beside the door.

"A couple of days ago, the key stopped turning, and then it wouldn't fit in the keyhole at all, as though it was the wrong one!" Oprah complained.

"There's nothing wrong with the key!" freckled Wally chimed in.

"I am tired of repeating it: don't bother the locksmith before you have to, just turn it slowly!" he added.

"You shouldn't have been messing around with the lock with your pliers!" Oprah shot back at him. "Nothing would have happened to the lock if you hadn't tried to fix it."

"Nothing of the sort, I didn't go anywhere near the lock! I was just tightening the door hinges, and I was using a screwdriver!" Wally defended himself.

"It's quite alright!" the businesslike, muscular boy with the tool set, who had been twisting and turning something in the door lock this entire time, reassured them.

"What a crazy week it's been!" Stanley sighed.

"Everyone is having something break or getting stuck on them! I am running off to Cobbler Paul's. And I still have to pay the doctor a visit today!" he added and slammed the door shut.

"Fred!" a boy, very serious in appearance, was addressing the Mayor.

"We have been receiving complaints from the city residents. The market on the central plaza is open on Sunday until eight o'clock. That's too late, Fred," the First Minister averred.

"But, Maxwell, Sunday is an excellent business day! The entire city visits the market on Sunday. If I close it too early, I'm afraid that the gardeners, bakers, and butchers will lose a good part of their profits!" the rosy-cheeked Mayor replied.

"The market must shut down earlier," the Second Minister shot back.

"There are many grown-ups who live in the city center. The children are complaining that the market noise, late in the evening, keeps them from getting their parents to bed on time. As a consequence, they wake up with difficulty on Monday, that is, for school the next morning. What sort of performance can we expect from them if they are sleepy and inattentive, especially on Monday!" the Second Minister added.

"We should ask Donald to shift his tests and important subjects to Tuesday!" the resourceful Mayor proposed.

"The teacher himself knows best when he needs to administer tests and what day his important subjects ought to be shifted to," the First Minister replied.

"That is true. We will not interfere in his business. If everyone were to tell others what and when they should do, then all activity would cease. Everyone will just sit around listening to other's opinions of themselves!" the Second Minister, Stanford, agreed.

"That is precisely what I was telling you! Close the market before eight o'clock on Sunday, and my merchants will be headed home with terrible proceeds. How will they then feed and clothe their grownups?" the rosy-cheeked Mayor flared up.

Maxwell, the First Minister, rolled his eyes upward.

"For each two children there are, at a minimum, a couple of grownup do-nothings! And Hillary is pulling for two alone! Or she has to explain to her chickens that they don't need to lay so many eggs, as she won't be able to sell them all at the market this coming Sunday anyway?" and the Mayor fixed his gaze at his Ministers.

"Let everyone mind their own business, otherwise everything will go to hell in a basket!" the agitated Mayor concluded and left the hall, slamming the door shut behind himself.

"That' how it always is! It's impossible to hold a single session of the Cabinet of Ministers according to plan!" Maxwell yelled out irately.

"Fred is uncooperative and short-tempered. To the proposal of the Cabinet of Ministers to cease the activities at the market on Sunday before eight o'clock he replied with a refusal. Hailey and Sherry will likely continue to inundate the Cabinet of Ministers with complaints about the noise from the city market on Sunday evenings. The problem remains unresolved. " The Second Minister wrote this down in his notebook and scratched the back of his head.

"For our next session, it would be logical to invite not only the Mayor, but also representatives of the populace, and namely Hailey and Sherry. The planned meeting can be held no sooner than in another two weeks, inasmuch as the

children are otherwise occupied with preparations for the scholastic competitions between their adults under the rubric of "Strong, Swift, and Smart". The thirty sixth session of the Cabinet of Ministers is hereby considered closed," Patrick

concluded.

"Have you recorded it?" Maxwell asked, staring thoughtfully the entire time out of the window.

"Let me sign it!" he added.

And he wrote down in his neat handwriting: "Maxwell. First Minister".

The door swung open. In the passageway stood a girl about ten years of age with a one-year-old infant in her arms.

"Have you concluded?" the Queen asked.

"We did, Meg! I wish my father had been a carpenter! Then I wouldn't have had to take his place in the Cabinet of Ministers!" Maxwell yelled out passionately.

"Oh, Maxwell, it's no easier for me... And today, Aidan won't even let me put him down!" the Queen complained about her younger brother and attentively wiped his nose with a handkerchief.

"May I enter?" Hailey peeked in through the doorway, having first knocked.

"Come in!" the doctor invited her in.

"Mitchell, I don't know what's wrong with her. Her sneezing and coughing won't go away! We've been drinking syrups, brewing herbal teas, but it's all for nothing. Thank God her temperature, I think, is normal. If she had a fever, she'd have to miss school!" Hailey exclaimed worriedly.

"Open your mouth!" Doctor Mitchell said.

The middle-aged woman who had arrived in Hailey's company obediently opened

her mouth.

"Oh, boy! Her throat is all red... She must have drunk cold water which you most likely had forbidden her to," the doctor concluded.

"Here is my prescription. Go to the pharmacist across the street. He'll prepare the new syrup for you. Give it to her three times a day. And don't forget: no cold water of any sort!" Mitchell adamantly warned her.

"Hailey," the woman whispered quietly, as though too embarrassed to speak.

"Oh yes, here's a piece of hard candy for you! You behaved so nicely to let the doctor examine your throat," Mitchell remembered just in time and handed her the promised reward.

The middle-aged woman immediately grabbed the hard candy and jumped down from her chair.

"What are you supposed to say?" Hailey inserted reproachfully.

"Thank you!" the woman remembered and obediently took Hailey by the hand.

"Hey, Paul!" Baker Brad swung open the door to the cobbler's shop.

"What am I to do with him? His sole is falling off again!" Brad helplessly flung his hands open.

A grown-up man who had come in with Baker Brad wiggled his toes sticking out of the holes in his boot.

"I have told him a thousand times already: these boots are just for school! Don't run around in them in the street, do not climb trees, don't step into puddles! It's all for nothing! First one of them wears thin, then the other!" Brad bewailed.

The grown-up man lowered his eyes guiltily.

"Let me have your boot over here!" Paul stretched out his hand.

Knock!Knock!Knock!Knock!Knock!Knock! and six finishing nails sunk into the huge sole.

"It's all done!" Cobbler Paul tossed the boot up, and Baker Brad immediately caught it mid-air.

"Well, put it on!" he ordered the grown-up man. "And don't climb trees in them anymore, or I won't buy you new ones!" Brad warned him.

"Bra-a-ad," the man drawled out plaintively.

"And, oh, yes; here is your piece of hard candy! And, please be more careful!" Paul asked him.

"Bra-a-ad," the man once again drawled.

"Well, what is it now?" Brad didn't understand him.

"A-a-ah!" Brad guessed.

"Hey, Paul, this hard candy is rose-colored... You wouldn't happen to have another?"

"Here you go, a red one!" Paul exchanged the piece of hard candy.

The grown-up raised the flat, red piece of hard candy on a stick to his eye and with rapt attention gazed through it into the light.

"Hey, Ray!" Ike burst out laughing, pointing out to Ray a small boy wearing a white dressing gown, its hem dragging on the ground, who was assiduously cleaning his business sign. "Pharmacist".

"Ray, let's check it out!" Skinny Wilson proposed.

"I've got a stomachache from eating Oprah's soup," he complained, and the entire crew of the Celestine slipped inside the pharmacy door, wide open in a most welcoming way.

"So... You have a stomachache, you say," the pharmacist Philip stopped to consider this for a moment.

"And what else did he have to eat this morning?" he quizzed them.

"Just the soup and some buns. Baker Brad's buns!" Wilson recalled.

"Buns, you say," the pharmacist thought again, flipping through a huge, thick book.

"There's nothing here about buns... and nothing about soup, either," he lowered his eyes in disappointment.

"Ah, here it is! A red rash! Does he already have a red rush?" the pharmacist Philip celebrated his discovery.

The crew of the Celestine all stared at Wilson.

"No-o-o-o!" they replied in a chorus.

"Well, there's not a clue to go on," the pharmacist complained, and once again started leafing through his book.

"Let's try this: would you show me your stomach!" the pharmacist offered.

Skinny Wilson obediently pulled up his shirt and displayed his stomach.

"And now, hop up and down on one foot!"

Wilson hopped up a couple of times and almost took a spill, having grazed against the pharmacy shelves with all their syrups.

"And now open your mouth and stick out your tongue!" the pharmacist ordered.

The crew of the Celestine could not hold it in any longer and roared with a loud, pirate laughter when Skinny Wilson obediently gaped his mouth and stuck out his tongue, jumping on one foot with his belly exposed.

The guffawing shaking the windows of the pharmacy frightened the children passing by with a self-important appearance, and it seemed to them that the pharmacy had been invaded by a herd of horses that had trampled on ten squealing pigs.

"I knew it!" the pharmacist declared triumphantly.

"Prombambrol, three spoons a day!" And the hand that he stretched out to Ray contained a green vial.

"To be delivered directly into Wally's and Oprah's hands," Oprah read the note on the envelope and sunk into her chair.

"Dear Wally and Oprah Johnson,

I am obliged to inform you that Mr. and Mrs. Johnson's performance in school leaves much to be desired. Mr. Johnson still makes mistakes in his counting. Difficult assignments do not come easy to him. He is still able to complete easy ones though. But the class is progressing ahead, together with the school-wide program, and he is among those lagging. It would make sense to transfer him into another, younger class, but then we would have to separate him from Mrs. Johnson. What are your thoughts on this? Now, about Mrs. Johnson. If I have no complaints about her concerning counting, then, when it comes to writing, things are considerably worse. Apparently, the problem is that she doesn't pay sufficient attention while listening to the question she is asked, and when she begins to answer it in writing, she makes not only grammatical mistakes, but it also becomes unclear whether she had at all heard what the subject is. I admit that Ms. Miller, from the neighboring desk, does not cease to distract Mrs. Johnson. Paying no attention to the fact that dictation is in progress, they are constantly whispering. Rumors have reached me that the subject of their conversations is Mr. Moore from the first row. There's no point to worry about him, inasmuch as he is making progress in all subjects. And if Mrs. Johnson and Ms. Miller, who distracts her, do not stop whispering, then I will have no choice but to separate the men and the women into different classes. But for some reason, neither the one nor the other want to even here about it. I ask you to speak with Mr. and Mrs. Johnson this weekend soberly.

Alternatively, if a conversation with you does not lead to some improvement, I propose that you threaten them with expulsion from the school-wide "Strong, Swift, and Smart" competition. In any case, at school, such a threat has always done the job.

Respectfully yours,

Teacher Donald."

Mr. and Mrs. Johnson sat before Wally and Oprah guiltily lowering their eyes. Mr. Johnson was tracing figure eights on the floor with the tip of his boot. Mrs. Johnson fiddled with the edge of her dress.

"Well, what are we going to do with them, Wally!" Oprah spread her arms wide. "Should we place them under house arrest?"

"Don't you understand that if you're going to be inattentive at school, you will not receive a good mark on your tests. And this means that your name will not be displayed on the honor roll of the best students in the class at the of the year!" Oprah explained in a fluster.

"And you?" Wally stared at Mr. Johnson. "How much longer am I going to have to sit with you over your counting? Isn't it time you got serious about it yourself?"

"Why do you bother going to school at all?" Oprah interjected.

Mr. and Mrs. Johnson guiltily bowed their heads even lower.

"It is not so you can be entertained and so you can chatter away with your neighbors! You go to school to acquire knowledge! And if you don't acquire it there, and your attitude toward this is irresponsible, then you will never get anywhere in life!" she concluded.

"Do you both really think that Oprah and I will be working for the two of you for the rest of our lives?" Wally sounded appalled.

"Now, go! Off to your room! And each of you in your own corner!" Wally and Oprah commanded.

"We... we...," Mr. Johnson began guiltily.

"We won't do it any mo-o-o-ore!" Mrs. Johnson started bawling and flung herself on Oprah's shoulder.

"Please welcome our new students!" Teacher Donald introduced the crew of the Celestine the next morning.

"So, where can we make room for them?" the teacher paused to think it over.

"Mr. Thompson, leave your seat for now; Larry will occupy it temporarily! And you, go sit at the third desk of the second row."

"Hey!" Ms. Martin winked at Nimble Larry, sitting down next to her.

"Mr. Clark, you're moving to the first row, and Wilson will now sit down."

"He-ey!" Ms. Robinson, with her ponytails all done up in ribbons, greeted Wilson coquettishly.

"Duke and Ike will sit at the next to last desk in the third row!" Donald commanded.

"Bill, take the last seat, next to Mrs. Hall."

Mrs. Hall shrunk back in fright.

"And Archie will sit at the third desk in the first row, next to Ms. Rodriguez. We're done with the seating reassignments now. Open your notebooks!" the teacher raised his voice.

Dark-eyed Ms. Rodriguez flung her thick black ponytail behind her back and, almost imperceptibly gathering in her dress, yielded her place to Archie.

Archie had wanted to land gracefully, but for some reason he plopped down awkwardly, glancing against Ms. Rodriguez's forearm. Ms. Rodriguez turned to face him with an expression of fright and, meeting Archie's gaze, suddenly turned beet red and, without saying a word, lowered her eyes.

"A-a-archie! Look at the blackboard and listen to what the teacher is saying!" Archie heard faintly from some far away world, unnecessary to him, now that he, incapable of looking anywhere else, was leering incessantly at Ms. Rodriguez.

"So, who are you?" Mr. Adams rapped on Nimble Larry's back.

"I'm a pirate," Larry answered truthfully.

"Oh! Me too! Mr. Adams confessed with excitement, his eyes aflame.

"Hey, Duke! Yu-uck! A bird has taken a dump on your back!" Mr. Carter squeamishly screwed up his face.

"Whe-ere?" Duke turned around, trying to get a look at his own back.

"Wha-am!" he immediately got bopped with a textbook on his head by the neighbor behind him.

Ike turned around sharply.

"Hey, fatso! Look at the blackboard, or you just might miss something!" Mr. Lewis warned him and burst out laughing, nudging his neighbor with his shoulder.

"Mr. Lewis! How much is 748 minus 526 divided by 4?" Teacher Donald shouted.

"Mr. Lewis, please rise when the teacher addresses you!" he added.

Mr. Lewis reluctantly rose from his desk and gazed up at the ceiling.

"It's useless! Hunter and Alex will receive today a letter from me, in which I will have to describe in detail your irresponsible behavior this entire past week. I don't suppose that being punished with exclusion from the forthcoming "Strong, Swift, and Smart" competition would be much to your liking," Donald conjectured.

"Then sit down and finally get to work! Your poor children are already exhausted by having to listen to complaints about you, which the school is obliged to hector them with," the teacher summed it up for them.

"Everyone, line up in pairs and, without shoving, at a normal pace, go to the cafeteria for lunch!" Donald commanded and rung a little bell.

Mr. Carter bent down, hiding behind Duke's back and, finding exactly the right moment whacked him with all his might on the head with his textbook.

Duke straightened himself out and, immediately, smashed Mr. Carter in the jaw.

Mr. Lewis grabbed his long ruler from the table and lashed Pudgy Ike's shoulder with it. Ike howled in pain, turned around, and let Mr. Lewis have it in the kidneys. Wilson, jumping up from his seat, tripped over Mr. Thompson's foot that the latter had deceitfully stuck out in the passageway, and fell flat on his face in the aisle. Having been grazed by Wilson's elbow, Ms. Lee began squealing, as though it were she who had been tripped up and had flopped on the floor. Ms. Hall shrieked just in case, to warn the rest of the impending danger. Ms. Johnson shrieked because she was a shrieker and always shrieked, even if it was just someone's book falling on the floor.

"Everyone, storm the ship!" screamed Mr. Adams, now that he thought himself a pirate. And he raised a thick stick that he always secretly carried in his backpack above his head, as though it were a sword.

Everything was turned upside down, swayed, collided, smacked, and twisted into the tangle of the deadly serious fisticuffs.

"Cease the ambush immediately! Everyone, get up! Calm on deck!" Archie shouted over the din.

And the crew of the Celestine, immediately obeying his order, slowly got up from the floor, from their knees, or from out of other people's laps.

"So, who are you?" spellbound Ms. Rodriguez exclaimed, batting at Archie her eyes full of wonder.

"I'm a captain," Archie replied in all honesty.

Mr. Lewis, Mr. Carter, Mr. Adams, and the entire crew of the Celestine sat in the office of the Headmistress, the tiny and half-blind Brooke.

"The usual suspects, Donald," she remarked wearily, addressing herself to the teacher.

"We're not to blame... They started it first," whined Mr. Lewis.

The crew of the Celestine bared their teeth and flared their eyes in the direction of the enemy.

"What am I going to do with you?" the headmistress spread her arms wide open.

"One more stunt like that and your chance of seeing the "Strong, Swift, Smart" competition is about the same as seeing your own ears!"

"We... We... We're not going to do it any mo-o-ore," howled Mr. Lewis, Mr. Carter, and Mr. Adams.

"And you, Mr. Adams! Just you try to secretly bring your club to class one more time and...!" the teacher issued his final warning.

Little Cook Mike in his white jacket and hat that had slid over his eyes was striking with his palm on the jingling bell, ensconced on a little windowsill under the window where lunch was served.

"Ne-e-e-xt! Don't fall asleep, gra-a-ab y'r pla-a-ates!" he was notifying the entire school cafeteria in a sing-song way.

"I am searching for a magical stone," someone whispered in Archie's ear as he stood in line for his lunch plate.

"Me too!" Archie immediately turned around.

"I already have three!" a grown-up man with uncombed hair baffled Archie.

And with a gesture of confidentiality he held open his large pocket for Archie to see, lying on the bottom of which were three dirty pet rocks.

"How do you like the new boys?" curly-haired Ms. Martin, who sat next to Larry, intoned.

"I'm afraid of that Hulking boy," replied Ms. Hall, next to whom the teacher had sat Bill.

"You're a fool!" Ms. Walker retorted, sitting down with her plate at the "girls'" table.

"He is so handsome! I wish they would sit him next to me!" she enviously exclaimed.

"Wilson is simply charming!" Ms. Robinson rolled back her eyes, coquettishly winding the inside of the ribbon above her ear with her finger.

"And what about you?" and, all together, they stared at the silent Ms. Rodriguez.

"When I grow up, I will most definitely marry him," Ms. Rodriguez announced mysteriously, and everyone froze still with envy.

"Everyone aboard! Line up on deck!" Mr. Adams, still thinking himself a pirate, shouted during recess.

Mr. Lewis, Mr. Carter, and Mr. Clark obediently lined up single file.

The crew of the Celestine, with Archie at their head, sprawled out flat on their backs on the hillock warmed by the hospitable sun.

"What can you see overboard, Mr. Carter?" Mr. Adams shouted.

Mr. Carter climbed a tree, folded both his palms into a trumpet, and screamed: "The surface is still! Smooth as a baby's bottom! I see absolutely nothing!"

"Fool!" screamed Mr. Lewis, climbing even higher than Mr. Carter.

"I can see sea monsters! Huge, yellow-toothed sea monsters!" he screamed from high above.

Mr. Clark, without a moment's thought, hurdled over the bodies of the crew of the Celestine sprawled out in the sun, quickly climbed up another tree, and screamed: "You, nitwits! I see an enemy vessel! An enemy vessel directly ahead!"

"No way! It's all wrong!" Mr. Adams yelled out irritably, still thinking he was the real pirate.

"Land on the horizon! A new, uncharted land, you idiots!" he added.

"You're an idiot yourself!" Mr. Clark sniped back.

"And why, anyway, is it you who is captain again?" Mr. Lewis interjected discontentedly.

"Sure! Everyone wants to be a captain! You've already been captain three times, now it's my turn!" Mr. Clark retorted.

"But why Clark? I wanna be a captain too!" Mr. Johnson, who had just walked over and joined them, blurted out.

"We're not playing with you, period!" Mr. Lewis, Mr. Carter, Mr. Clark, and Mr. Adams screamed at him in unison.

"Why?" Mr. Johnson was taken aback.

"And who reported me to the teacher about my sword?" Mr. Adams glared at him.

"I don't know," Mr. Johnson took a few steps back, just in case.

"It was you! Admit it!" Mr. Carter, jumping down from his tree, shoved him in the shoulder.

"It was him! He's the first to report everything, even if no one is asking him to!" Mr. Lewis affirmed, climbing down.

"You're too a snitch, you're a blabbermouth and a brown-noser!" Mr. Adams screamed and punched Mr. Johnson.

"Brownnoser! Snitch! Blabbermouth!" Mr. Clark, Mr. Lewis, and Mr. Carter chanted, screaming over each other, and they came out swinging.

Ms. Hall and Mrs. Johnson began shrieking at the other end of the meadow.

"They are fighting again! Run and get the teacher!" screamed Ms. Martin.

"Sic them!" screamed Mr. Thompson and Mr. Moore, who had been playing knights in shining armor nearby, as they charged into the fray.

"Where the hell is that magical green Bowgrindle?" Archie thought to himself, still basking in the sun, without opening his eyes.

"And how much longer must we linger here?" thought the entire crew of the Celestine, lounging drowsily on the lawn.

"All rise, the court is in session!" an orange-haired boy came down with a wooden hammer on the table.

Judge Benjamin, wearing a long cape that dragged along the floor, walked over to his high table. The jurors trooped after him in a pitter-patter of mincing steps: the Seamstress Heather, Market Merchant Chelsea, Cook Mike, and Blacksmith Bob.

"Defendant chimney sweep!" the Judge declared loudly.

The chimney sweep turned his face to the wall as though disinterested.

"Spencer, please, turn to face the court," Judge Benjamin asked him in a whisper.

Spencer reluctantly turned around and propped his cheek up on his palm.

"A question for the accused!" Judge Benjamin continued in a loud tone of voice.

"Who cleaned Doctor Mitchell's fireplace chimney last spring? Do you know who this man, Spencer, is?" the Judge asked the question point blank.

"So, it was me," the chimney sweep admitted reluctantly.

"What happened with the fireplace after it had been cleaned by the chimney sweep, Mitchell?" the Judge now stared at Doctor Mitchell.

"I told you a hundred times already!" Mitchell resisted.

"Don't contradict the judge, Mitchell, answer the question," the Judge asked him.

"The room is full of fumes! It became impossible to light the fireplace! Finally, this thing fell out of the chimney!" the doctor pointed at the table with the physical evidence.

A scorched, black boot belonging to someone with a large foot lay on the table.

"How is it possible, Spencer, that after your cleaning, this boot wound up in Mitchell's fireplace chimney and smoldered there, until it fell through and down?" the Judge asked the question and looked reproachfully at the chimney sweep.

"I don't know!" Spencer replied.

"I didn't throw it in there!" he screamed out.

"Cobbler Paul is called forth as a witness!" the orange-haired boy declared.

Paul squeezed his way between the rows of benches and emerged to the fore.

"Cobbler Paul! Please speak the truth, the whole truth, and nothing but the truth: is this boot familiar to you?"

Paul approached the table with the physical evidence, twirled the scorched boot in his hand, placed it back on the table, and returned to his place.

"It is familiar," Paul replied.

The audience in the gallery oohed and aahed.

"To whom, in your opinion, does this boot belong to?" the Judge asked the question directly.

"To Mr. Smith," the cobbler averred.

The audience oohed and aahed a second time.

Chimney sweep Spencer stared in confusion at Cobbler Paul.

"How could you possibly know it with such certainty?" the chimney sweep yelled out, as though in his own defense.

The audience started to whisper and fidget.

"Silence in the hall! Defendant, do not interrupt; nobody asked you anything!" the orange-haired boy shouted and started banging again with his wooden mallet on the table.

"I know this for a fact because, in this entire city, only Mr. Smith wears size forty-seven boots! And I have already had the pleasure, on a couple of occasions, to repair them!" the cobbler answered.

"Chimney sweep Spencer, where was your father, Mr. Smith, while you were cleaning the stone chimney in Dr. Mitchell's house?"

"With me, on the roof," the chimney sweep confessed reluctantly.

The audience gasped a third time.

"Defendant, are you not aware that it is strictly forbidden to bring grown-ups with you to work? Especially, to such dangerous work, on a high roof? What if your father had fallen off the roof, Mr. Smith?" Judge Benjamin shouted.

"I didn't want to take him with me! But he promised that he wouldn't touch anything on the roof!" the chimney sweep replied guiltily.

"Mr. Smith!" the judge addressed the grown-up man who was sitting on the witness bench.

"What happened in the spring of last year on Dr. Mitchell's roof?" the judge rose from his seat.

"I threw my boot into the chimney... I won't do it aga-a-a-ain!" Mr. Smith howled.

The chimney sweep Spencer shot an angry glance in the direction of his father.

The jurors whispered between themselves and handed their opinion to Judge Benjamin.

"The court has come to a decision," Benjamin announced.

"The Chimney sweep Spencer is hereby declared innocent of the charges against him! As punishment for his what he has done, Mr. Smith is to be excluded from this weekend's "Strong, Swift, and Smart" competition."

The chimney sweep sighed in relief. Mr. Smith began bawling, while loudly stomping on the floor with his feet.

"No! You will eat it!" the Queen ordered her brother, feeding him with a spoon.

"Boo!" little Aidan replied and banged the Queen on her head with his rattle.

"Please continue!" the Queen requested, addressing herself to the Ministers.

Maxwell, the First Minister, moved away from the window, from which one could see how, in the garden, the Queen's and Aidan's parents, as well as those of the First and Second Ministers, were playing hide and seek.

"The Cabinet of Ministers continues to receive complaints about Pharmacist Philip," the First Minister coughed to clear his throat.

"Baa!" Aidan affirmed, and thumped the First Minister's head with his rattle.

"They write that they come to him with a toothache, and after the visit, they suffer with an upset stomach from the medication that he had prescribed to them," Stanford, the Second Minister, added.

"Bo!" Aidan replied and bopped the Second Minister's head with the rattle.

"Aidan! If you don't stop it right now, I won't take you with me to the "Strong, Swift, and Smart" school competition!" the Queen reproached him.

"Beh!" Aidan replied and launched his rattle as hard as he could into the bowl in front of him.

Four excited teams – the Fish, the Medusas, the Tortoises, and the Octopuses – lined up single file in preparation for participating in the "Strong, Swift, Smart" competition.

"The Fish team to the starting line on the left side of the field!" Teacher Donald proclaimed on the sun-drenched meadow.

Mr. Clark forgot that this wasn't the time for bullying and stepped as hard as he could on Nimble Larry's foot. Larry turned around and stomped on Mr. Clark's foot, which caused the latter to howl and start hoping up and down on one leg.

"Competing against them is the Medusas team!" Donald declared.

Mr. Carter, out of boredom, smacked Pudgy Ike, who was standing in front of him, on the shoulder. Ike turned around and, without much thinking, walloped Mr. Carter.

"The Tortoises team is called to the starting line on the right side of the field!" the Headmistress announced to all those present.

Mr. Adams got it into his head to pinch Hulking Bill. But when he got a better look at Bill, and noted Bill glaring back at him, he had second thoughts about chancing it.

"Competing against them is the Octopuses team!" Teacher Donald added.

Archie stretched out his hands and cracked his knuckles. Mr. Lewis, standing behind Archie, immediately stretched out his own hands and also cracked all his knuckles.

"Your first task!" Teacher Donald yelled out. "Each of the team members must hop in a sack, holding it up at the waist with both hands, and, after rounding the mark, return to their team!"

"And all this must be done while there is time left in this sand hourglass!" the teacher screamed, trying to outshout the excited fans.

"Time is ticking!" Donald started the clock by turning the hourglass upside down.

"Clark! Clark! Clark!" the bleachers cheered.

"Ike! Ike! Ike!" cheered Mrs. Johnson and Ms. Lee.

"A-dams! A-dams! A-dams!" the spectators cheered.

"Ar-chie! Ar-chie! Ar-chie!" cheered Ms. Rodriguez, Ms. Walker, Ms. Robinson, and Ms. Martin.

Mr. Clark, turning red and dripping with sweat, had only hopped almost half the way to the mark. Ike was just a few feet short of the mark, a tall stick stuck in the ground and tied round with colorful fluttering streamers. Mr. Adams had just rounded the mark. Archie reached the halfway point in his sack, rounded it and was already approaching his team, completing the return trip.

"Your second task!" Teacher Donald declared, "To hop on one foot the length of this winding course!"

"And don't forget about the hourglass!" Donald added.

"Lou-is! Lou-is! Lou-is!" the bleachers cheered.

"Duke! Duke! Duke!" cheered Mrs. Johnson and Ms. Lee.

"Where is Wilson?" Mr. Clark started whirling around and looking for him. "It's his turn now!"

After the prombarol, prescribed to him by Pharmacist Philip, Wilson's stomach stopped churning entirely. Everything that had heretofore been churning or sticking in his stomach now wanted out and couldn't wait for the competition to end. Wilson, barely managing to race to the bushes in time, hurriedly pulled off his pants and screamed in relief: "A-a-a-a-a!"

Nimble Larry, rounding the cones placed in a zigzag pattern along the path, nimbly hopped on one foot, rounded the mark, and started hopping back. Mr. Adams decided to cheat and, counting on the general hustle and bustle distracting the observers, from time to time hopped over several of the cones on both his legs, ignoring the zigs and zags. All drenched in sweat, Hulking Bill, hopping on both feet, because one of them alone could not support his substantial weight, knocked down all of the cones that had been placed in a zigzag.

"Your third task!" screamed Teacher Donald. "With your eyes blindfolded, run to the little tree on the left side of the field, find by feel the piece of hard candy, and untie it from the tree!"

"Without delay, run back to the little tree on the right side of the meadow, and tie the hard candy to it!" added the Dean, the half-blind Britney.

"The more hard candies you collect on your little tree, the closer your team is to victory!" Teacher Donald promised them.

Mr. Clark, his eyes closed, ran off in the wrong direction. Duke, his eyes blindfolded, reached his little tree, but it did not have a single piece of hard candy tied to it. Mr. Adams decided to cheat and, slightly undoing his blindfold, peeked with his left eye. Archie, his eyes tied, reached his little tree, but didn't manage to find a single piece of hard candy. Ms. Rodriguez, Ms. Walker, Ms. Robinson, and Ms. Martin regretted mightily that the hard candies were not tied to themselves.

Wilson disappeared once again.

"And now, the riddle!" Teacher Donald declared.

"At home in water, at home on dry land. Walks on land and floats on the sea. And as soon as it senses danger, it hides within itself!"

"A fish!" screamed Mr. Clark.

"You fool!" yelled Mr. Lewis.

"An octopus!" Mr. Carter shouted.

"You dunce!" screamed Mr. Adams.

Ray, observing the crew of the Celestine from the spectator bleachers and seated immediately behind the row occupied by the First and Second Ministers and Queen Meg, noticed that little Aidan was smiling at him, the entire time mercilessly whacking the Queen's and the Ministers' heads with his rattle.

"Gu-bu-du!" said Aidan.

"Bu-du-gu!" Ray replied.

"Da-du-da!" Aidan said.

"Du-da-da!" Ray replied.

"Di-li-di!" said Aidan, which meant: "Can't you see? I dropped my favorite rattle!"

Ray bent down, stretched to reach the rattle that had rolled to his feet and raised it up above himself to the light. Out of its numerous winding incised patterns, streaming like rivers circling the round earth, shone a bright, green light. Ray stuck his fingers into one of the tiny holes, felt something inside it, and fished out the green, magical Bowgrindle.

"A-a-a-archie! I found it!" Ray screamed at the top of his voice.

"The Tortoises have won!" screamed Mr. Moore.

"That's ri-i-ight!" shouted Teacher Donald.

"The Tortoises team is victorious!" yelled Dean Britney.

"A-a-a-a!" the Tortoises team started screaming and hopping triumphantly.

"A-a-a-a-a-a-a-a!" came Wilson's howl of relief from out of the bushes.

The Celestine set sail, eagerly flinging herself into the water, as though it had been dying of thirst. She yearned for freedom, flirting with the favorable wind and smiling at the sun. And behind her back was the city of San Liberi, in which the children, awakening this morning, will once again set off, finally, for school. The world will, after all, turn once again, but this time, it will turn in the right direction.

Chapter Eleven

The Black Wings of the Heavenly Host

Archie carefully lowered the green magical Bougrindle into the fourth little pocket. He rolled the hem of Celestine's skirt delicately into a scroll and for some reason started looking around himself. His eyes came across his jacket and he stuffed the scroll with the stones deep into its sleeve and, having crushed the jacket, stuck it into the furthest corner of his cabin, placing a pair of his old boots in front of the improvised package. Having come into possession of the fourth stone, the smell of victory went to his head and, along with it, the strange fear of being deprived of his hard-won accomplishments.

Full of impatience, he once again opened Cook's Secret Book, but it remained silent. Archie scrolled through a couple of pages: all of them, including the story of his triumph, or defeat, to come were unwritten.

For a week already, the crew of the Celestine had been following in the direction indicated by Cook's compass.

"What the hell! Who dragged all these tree limbs up on deck!" Duke, who was swabbing the deck, cursed.

"It was Ike!" shouted Nimble Larry, bending over the helm.

"It was Wilson!" Ike shot back from the other end of the deck.

"It was Bill!" barked Skinny Wilson.

"You, idiots! I'm not giving you any chow until you clear the deck of these branches!" threatened Cook Duke.

Sitting before the Secret Book, Archie stopped to think a moment, attending to the noise on deck: "What nonsense? We've been at sea a week already; what would tree limbs be doing on our deck?"

"A-a-a-a-a!" the crew of the Celestine began to scream.

Archie ran up to the deck and couldn't believe his own eyes: the deck really was covered with dry, black, broken-off branches. At that moment, a huge tree, barely missing the mainmast, landed on the deck, its thick, centuries-old roots sticking out in all directions as though they were parallel beams. The Celestine listed on its side under its weight.

"A-a-a-a-a!" everyone screamed in a chorus.

"Toss the tree overboard!" Archie shouted a command.

Everyone immediately flung themselves at the centuries-old tree, grabbing a hold of its roots, branches, and trunk.

"Beat it!" Hulking Bill barked, shoving aside Ray, who was useless for such work, and grabbing the tree with both hands.

"We won't be able to even budge it!" screamed Ike.

"Ropes! Let's drag it with ropes!" shouted Nimble Larry and, running over to port-side, quickly tossed a couple of heavy ropes over it.

"You, idiot!" yelled Hulking Bill, straining himself. "How are we going to drag it to the ropes?"

Everyone pulled as hard as they could, while Ray clung onto the branches.

The sky suddenly darkened as though, in a single moment, midday had been replaced by night.

"A-a-a-a-a!" all seven of them screamed, seeing their own feet dangling in the air.

A black bird, its never-ending wing alone the length of the entire deck of the Celestine, clutching the centuries-old tree as though it were a tiny bough in its huge, humped beak, began to carry it away, together with the entire crew of the Celestine helplessly dangling from it in the air.

This wayward flying mass soared high above the water, and the Celestine, like the stilled surface of the sea beneath their feet, was growing more distant and distant. The sounds of the seven exhausted throats calling out for help seemed, observed from some distance, like the quiet squealing of tiny beetles, dangling on a stick of straw clenched in the bird's huge beak.

"A-a-a-a-a!" everyone screamed again in a chorus, seeing beneath themselves nothing but a bottomless black abyss instead of the sea's calm surface, and sensing that the tree, released by the flying behemoth from its beak, had begun plummeting down.

"Bo-oom!" and the tree came crashing down. The crew of the Celestine clenched their eyes shut.

Archie, realizing that they were no longer flying anywhere, was the first to open his eyes. Looking around, he found himself immersed in an impenetrable, dark forest and, seeing somewhere far beneath the branches of other, broken trees, he

got up the guts to jump down.

"Everyone, jump down!" he screamed as soon as he felt himself land on something solid.

Hulking Bill opened his eyes and jumped first, skinning his arm against a black branch. Nimble Larry jumped down, and badly twisted his ankle. Skinny Wilson jumped off having opened only one of his eyes. Pudgy Ike flopped face down and immediately screamed in pain, having fallen on a shriveled old branch. Duke at first crawled along the bough onto which he was clinging and only then dove down. Ray decided to once again scrunch up his eyes and only then jump. "Snap!" and the black branches under him groaned and, like an animal's threatening paw, scraped bloody scratches along his legs.

Archie looked up. Visible somewhere far above him, hidden by a multitude of cracked trees and branches, was a corner of the sky.

"Everyone, back up!" he commanded.

And the entire crew, jumping from one branch to another, crawling from one log to the next, breaking away one bough and immediately impaling themselves on another, scrambled upwards, crunching the branches and cursing in the thickets of a desiccated, felled forest.

Archie, having reached the edge first, raised himself on his tired arms and, grasping onto the terminal branch, looked down and froze in shock.

A nest of gigantic proportions, inside the guts of which the crew of the Celestine were clambering, hung suspended from a titanic tree, standing next to other giants just like it to its right and its left, all of them containing in their crowns nests of similarly monstrous proportions.

Thumping and rasping sounds split the air. Duke, Ike, Wilson, Bill, Larry and Ray, having reached the upper branches behind Archie, turned around and stopped in their tracks. Four huge eggs, each of them the size of several Celestines, having come into view only from here, from the edge of the gargantuan nest, ran with a network of cracks and were now threatening to split open.

"0-0-0-0-0!" they all hollered in a chorus and scrambled as fast as they could downward, crawling out of the nest and hopping to and from between the giant's boughs and branches.

Having torn their clothing, feet, and hands and reaped a mass of scratches and scrapes, the crew of the Celestine were running away across the quicksand.

"After me!" Archie screamed, not being at all sure where precisely they ought to run.

When all their strength ran out, they ceased racing about and started dragging their feet even slower, soon feeling that they only had the strength to crawl. In that very moment, when Archie understood perfectly that he would have to admit that he, just as they, had no idea in hell what direction they ought to be trudging, he was saved by providence itself: off in the distance, he glimpsed the ghostly mirage of a schooner that had foundered in the shallows.

"The Celestine!" Archie screamed.

The exhausted seven-headed crew, their smiles twisted with pain and fatigue, began trudging towards the Celestine, when suddenly, the quicksand started sinking. The sea water slowly rose to their ankles, then to their knees, their hips, their waists, and now it was already reaching up to their shoulders and touching their chins.

"Ro-o-opes!" Archie screamed, having started to paddle. "Grab onto the ro-o-pes!"

The Celestine, rising on the incoming wave as though startled out of its sleep, was meeting them with its lines dangling overboard in the water, as though welcoming her crew with her arms wide open.

"Well, well, captain! You don't burn in fire, nor drown in water? Then, welcome on deck!" the Secret Book greeted Archie the following morning.

"So, you'd like to hear my riddle, you Superman? Then, here it is:

FLY HIGH

LOOK FAR

LOVE MADLY

SAY GOODBYE PASSIONATELY.

And then you will find the blue, magical Stoublulaze!

And oh, yes! The devils asked me to give you their regards, they've already started the boiling water in a cauldron for you!

Ho-ho-ho!"

STOUBLULAZE

Chapter Twelve

The Winged City of Sant Avis

Kiara stretched her bowstring taut and aimed. The arrow, severing the air like lightening, plunged into the center of the target and the scarecrow of the black bird, stricken in the bull's eye between its beak and eyes, came crashing to the ground. She triumphantly picked up her chin and, with an anguished yearning, gazed out in the direction of the sea.

"He is already on his way. He'll be here soon. I sense it... The sufferings of your lonely heart are at an end," the Seer declared, taking delight in her triumph.

"When will it happen?" Kiara implored impatiently, as though wishing to hear him swear an oath on it.

"Be patient, Milady, the time is drawing nigh," the Seer promised and smiled.

"Land ah-o-oy!" waving his arm, Ray screamed from the mast.

"Land ah-o-oy!" Nimble Larry seconded him.

"Land ah-o-oy!" Ike, Duke, and Bill picked up the shout.

"L-a-and!" confirmed Skinny Wilson, who had been tormented by hiccups for a half a day already.

"Land ahoy!" Archie thought to himself, jumping out on deck, and his heart began racing and thumping for some reason, like a wild bird helplessly darting

about in a tiny cage.

A dozen arrows released from a bow whistled past the heads of the crew of the Celestine, who had only just cast their anchor on the unfamiliar shore.

"A-a-a-a!" screamed Duke, Ike, Bill, Larry, and Skinny Wilson, having barely had time to duck their heads for cover.

"Move away from the target!" the children shouted over one another.

Archie turned around and saw a warlike group of boys, engaged in a competition of marksmanship.

"Hey! You're not allowed to stand there!" one of them shouted to Ray, picking up a dropped arrowhead.

"Where can we stand?" Ray asked.

"Are you outlanders?" the boy with the straw-colored hair inquired, glancing distrustfully at Ray.

"Yes," answered Ray.

"Head into the city!" the boy shouted to them, interrupted by the laughter of the others.

"Lousy shot! You're a lousy shot!" they jeered and teased him, pocking their fingers in his chest.

The stone-built city of Sant Avis greeted the newcomers with its attractive, but faded facades. Visible along the stone fences and walls of all the houses were the signs of catastrophic flooding. A multitude of lines, trailing down and then rising back up, were evidence of the sea's dominion over this beautiful, strange shore. It seemed that the city had been flooded more than once, but if people were still living here then, it may be presumed, they had, each time, come out victorious in their struggle with the sea. Its inhabitants were dressed simply but in a somewhat martial fashion, as though every minute their world was threatened by violence and, so, they were obliged to be prepared to flee at any moment, or to remain and fight.

"May the devil take me! Ray!" Nimble Larry called out to him, staring at the other side of the street in amazement.

Strolling around the city among the passersby, just like "normal people," were huge gray birds. Spreading their long avian claws over the cobblestones, they were dragging their long gray tails along the ground behind themselves and turning their heads self-importantly from side to side, first left, then right, as though acknowledging the inhabitants whom they were familiar with.

"These are the Dredonts. They are our friends!" explained Mr. Luard, the veterinarian who, according to the sign on his door, had a few rooms to let. "We wouldn't be here without them!"

Just at that moment, a bird's head pocked in through the window, as though confirming what he had just said.

"This is Craig!" Mr. Luard introduced the huge gray bird. "Craig is Kelvin's friend, but he's staying with me because he hasn't been feeling well for a while. Craig lowered his huge avian eyes, as though nodding in agreement, that he is indeed unwell and not simply hanging around the veterinarian's office.

"This will probably seem surprising to you, but they are exactly like people to us. If it wasn't for them, we would all have drowned a long time ago," added

Mr. Luard, petting Craig's ailing head.

The huge gray bird circled above the courtyard of the Empress's estate and, spurred by its rider, swooped in for a smooth landing. The tall, strong man, dressed in clothes made of tanned leather, jumped down adroitly from its back and with quick strides headed towards the gates, acknowledging the welcoming nods of the guards as he passed them by.

Dylan swung the door open sharply. The Empress rose and hurriedly tossed a cape that resembled bird plumage on her shoulders over a vest made of tanned leather.

"Forgive me, Milady," the tall, strong man bowed before her on one knee.

"You've had time to think it over. What have you decided?" Dylan continued persistently, as though resuming an interrupted conversation, staring testily into the Empress's eyes.

"Don't rush me, Dylan. I am not yet ready to give you a reply," Kiara turned away in impatience, as though not wishing to return to an unpleasant subject.

"Our world is cursed. We have never yet been ruled by a woman! How long do you intend to keep tempting fate? Are you going to wait until the sea swallows us up forever?" Dylan gave her a piercing look.

"There is no more worthy companion for you than me in this world, who might take his rightful place beside you. Make peace with the idea that that man is me," Dylan insisted without rising from his knee.

"It's not your place to order me about. You are a Warrior, and not a Sovereign!" Kiara turned around abruptly to face him.

"And who, in your opinion, deserves to become Sovereign?" tall Dylan declared

rising from his knees, a note of irritation audible in his voice.

"I still don't know the answer to that ... But that is not for you decide!" Kiara shouted out indignantly.

"Then you will have to explain it to all our people the next time the sea inundates, and misfortune cover us forever under its wave!" Dylan shouted in reply.

"I am still your Empress, Dylan! And not your wife!" Kiara replied abruptly, wrapping herself more tightly inside her cape.

"Forgive me, Milady," Dylan bowed before her, as though remembering himself.

He then slowly straightened out his back, as though demonstrating all the beauty of the strong body of a Young Warrior and departed her chamber.

The crew of the Celestine wondered about Sant Avis's narrow alleyways. Its simply and somewhat martially dressed inhabitants were rushing about their business affairs. The Dredonts strolled about its streets slowly, peeking into windows and doorways, drinking from the pails and pecking at the feeding bowls placed out especially for them. It seemed that the inhabitants of Sant Avis could spoil and coddle their bird day and night, with the help of the wares offered for sale at all the shops. Small and large brushes for feathers, little leather caps for their bird heads, saddles for the companions of these birds of various sizes, from small ones for children, to medium and large ones, plain and simple ones, and ones embroidered with amazing patterns. The shopkeepers of Sant Avis offered all of these while amicably peering out of their shops, visible on the stone walls of which, on their peeling and faded paint, were the traces of this world's struggle with the merciless, salty water of the sea.

"Hey, handsome!" the plump street vendor called out to Pudgy Ike. Ike turned around smiling ecstatically.

"You're outlanders?" she immediately understood, having examined the crew of the Celestine.

"You've never fed a Dredont before?!" she was taken aback.

"Buy my little pouch! It contains his favorite seeds; I roasted them on a skillet only this morning. You will see for yourself how he gobbles them up!" she assured him, invitingly shaking the little pouch in the air.

Archie tossed her a coin. She turned it this way and that attentively, raised it up to the light, then tested it with her teeth, and only then shoved it into the deep pocket of her dark-colored apron, accepting it as payment.

"Have a go at it, handsome!" the woman smiled at Ike.

"Tweet! Tweet! Tweet!" she called over one of the huge birds striding by in a dignified manner.

The Dredont swerved from its path and approached them obediently, curiously stretching out its head. Ike was struck dumb: the huge gray bird was a couple of heads taller than he.

"Take it!" the woman handed the open pouch to Ike.

Ike carefully accepted it into his hands. The Dredont's gray head immediately bent down above his palms. Ike was afraid to breathe loudly, and the entire crew of the Celestine surrounded the Dredont, staring at this domesticated giant. Ray

gathered up his courage and stroked the gray feathers of the huge wing, now at

rest. The Dredont turned around for a moment, and Ray immediately pulled his hand away.

The large gray bird suddenly gave a start, waddled off to the side and, tucking its clawed avian paws under itself, soared into the sky, flapping its huge wings. Ray looked over at the woman with an expression of fright.

"Don't be afraid, we didn't hurt its feelings!" she smiled.

"It is midday. At midday, all the Dredonts circle in the sky above our city. They are guarding us!"

"From whom?" Archie was surprised to hear this.

"From the Arkantaurs! From the black leviathans that are three times the size of our Dredonts!" the street vendor explained, staring guardedly at the sky.

"If they pick out their pray, to feed their fledgling young, neither a child nor even a grown-up will manage to save themselves... Unless they hide in time!" she added and began to quickly gather up her merchandise.

The crew of the Celestine stared in fright into the sky, immediately feeling all their still fresh cuts and bruises, evidence of their escape from the gargantuan nest, smart.

"Djun!" Kiara cried out to him. "Do you also think that the people are suffering because of me?"

"What are you talking about, Milady?" the Seer replied.

"But it is true that a woman has never yet ruled our world. Since my father died, I have had to take his place. And what if we are indeed cursed and the sea will one day swallow us up, and even the Dredonts won't be able to save us?" in her agitation, she clutched the Seer by his shoulder.

"You did not take a vow of chastity. Your people must wait until you make your will known to them," replied Djun.

"And what if I am waiting for a ghost, Djun? And my heart has become lost, having been led astray? Do I have the right to my own personal happiness when the fate of my people rests on my shoulders?" Kiara pleaded with him.

"You cannot sacrifice your life to please your people. With an unhappy Empress, her people can never be happy," the Seer replied and gently stroked Kiara's head resting on his shoulder.

"There is something not quite right with him," the veterinarian Mr. Luard expressed his concern the following morning, looking into Craig's large eyes.

"Don't be afraid! Go ahead and pet him!" Kelvin gave his permission, and Ray cautiously ran his hand along the Dredont's long, gray feathers.

"Are there really no Dredonts where you live?" Kelvin expressed his surprise.

"No," Ray wagged his head.

"And no Arkantaurs either?" Kelvin persisted.

"None, as well," replied Ray.

"Every child here can befriend his own Dredont!" flaxen-haired Kelvin explained.

"Every day, he puts out fresh water for him and fills his bowl with seeds, and then brushes his feathers. But a Dredont isn't really a domesticated bird, so you can never be sure that it will return specifically to you again. Its love must be earned. My Craig has been with me a long time! I was six when I started taking care of him. And he has always returned to me!" Kelvin smiled proudly.

"And he never again forgot you?" Ray sounded surprised.

"Yes, I was fortunate!" Kelvin nodded. "When our Empress Kiara was still a girl, her father adopted a young Dredont for her. The bird immediately recognized her as his mistress. They became inseparable! No one knows why, but he died when Kiara had just turned nine years old..."

"And what happened then?" Ray froze still.

"The Emperor never did manage to persuade Kiara to bury him and so he ordered that he be stuffed and preserved. Her Dredont has remained with her forever, even though he has been immobile a long time now," Kelvin fell into deep thought, slowly stroking his bird's gray head.

"Kelvin, I'm afraid you must already be running off to school!" Mr.

Luard cut in.

Craig gave a start and pressed his gray head into Kelvin's lap in front of him.

"Are you offering me a ride?" Kelvin was surprised.

The huge gray bird bowed its entire body down to the ground, allowing the rider to climb up on his back.

"Ray! Do you want to come along?" Kelvin shouted with a smile.

"Am I allowed to?" Ray was dumbstruck.

"Climb on! And hold on to me tighter!" Kelvin laughed.

Ray grabbed a hold of Kelvin's leg (he had already climbed aboard), pulled himself up, and pressed himself flush against Kelvin's back. The gray mass rose

up, clicked with its clawed paws, and soared into the air, straightening out its huge wings.

"W-o-o-o-w!" Ray shouted, unable to conceal his joy, and looked down.

The entire crew of the Celestine spilled out into the veterinarian's yard and stared into the sky at Ray, who was soaring away from them into the distance.

"Craig knows the way to school by heart! If it weren't for him, Kelvin would have long ago been expelled for his latenesses!" Mr. Luard smiled.

Ray was soaring above the city. Down below, people were walking around, shopkeepers were opening their windows, the street vendors were arranging and displaying their goods, cooks were sending up clouds of steam from their pots, shoemakers were cobbling shoes, seamstresses were sewing, doctors treating their

patients, and the crew of the Celestine was ogling up at the sky. And Ray was soaring above the city. From this vantage point, the houses seemed tiny, the roofs narrow, and the people microscopic. And only the narrow confines of the sea, with its horizon receding into nowhere, could be compared with the infinity of the heavenly expanse. The cold morning air was lashing Ray's face, his hair and shirt were fluttering like the sails of some heavenly flotilla, and he had an uncontrollable urge to burst out laughing and scream to the entire world: "He-ey!

Look at me-e-e? I am fly-i-ing!"

"Thank you, my pal!" Kelvin patted Craig on the back of his neck.

Ray crawled down and stood on his wobbly sea legs, his head spinning and his throat parched. He flopped helplessly down on the ground and lay flat on his back, splaying his arms and legs outward.

"Hey, Ray! Congratulations on your first flight!" Kelvin burst out laughing.

"What must you do if you notice an Arkantaur circling in the sky above our city?" Mr. Scott surveyed the class and passed his hand over his bald spot.

"You must immediately run and hide!" tall as a beanstalk Sally raised her hand and immediately blurted out.

"Have you hidden well if you're sitting under a tree?" Mr. Scott continued.

"No! You mustn't sit under a tree! An Arkantaur might descend out of the sky and strike you with his powerful beak!" the children shouted over each other.

"You should fly away on a Dredont!" Lionel raised his hand.

"That's not quite right," the teacher replied. "Should you expose your Dredont to danger?"

"No! You must not do that!" the children shouted out once again.

"How many times larger are Arkantaurs than Dredonts?"

"Three times larger!" replied Michael.

"Can a single Dredont battle against an Arkantaur?" Mr. Scott peered out at the class.

"No!" replied Kelvin. "A single Dredont can't do it. Only three or, better yet, four Dredonts can stop an Arkantaur."

"And that's only for a time. Once an Arkantaur has picked out his prey, he will definitely return once again," the teacher added.

"Dylan, have you spoken with her?" the old Warrior stood up, welcoming his son.

"She still can't make up her mind!" Dylan replied in a tone of irritation and tossed the reins of his Dredont aside.

"Don't worry, my son. Women are silly at her age. Your mother also didn't understand right away that I was her best choice. I had to go toe-to-toe with a couple of puny weaklings before she gave me her consent," the father smiled ironically.

"Yes, but I have no equals here!" Dylan barked out in reply.

"You will prove it to her! Our city will soon be celebrating the festival of Saint Glen and, as you know, the Empress must fulfill the wishes of the champion. As the victor, you will ask for her hand before the entire people! A woman's rule in this city must come to an end. Otherwise, the sea will cover us all forever under its wave! And even the Dredonts won't be able to save us," the old Warrior replied and turned around.

"The heart of a free bird isn't subject to the will of the master of her cage," the slim, elderly woman who was leaning on the door inserted with a note of sadness.

"She'll beg me yet to be let into my cage," Dylan replied, pulling off his boots with the spurs.

"Hey, Kelvin! You've got one last chance for a rematch!" Lionel called out to him.

"If your little new friend here doesn't object, we'll compete two against three!" he proposed.

"What does the victor get?" Sam interjected.

"Kelvin's Dredont! If this weakling misses again!" Lionel replied and burst out laughing.

"You will never lay your hands on my Craig!" Kelvin exclaimed.

"We'll see about that yet, who takes whom!" Lionel snapped back.

Somebody tossed a bow with arrows into Ray's hands and all five of them marched decisively towards the target.

The meadow with the target was broad, large, and sunny, and near its edge, raised on wooden pedestals, were the dummies of birds, though not as large, yet representing the chief enemy – the Arkantaurs.

Lionel measured off thirty paces, pulled taut his bowstring, tensed up from head to toe, and let the arrow fly. The Arkantaur dummy swayed and collapsed to the ground. Lionel raised his bow victoriously above his head and let out a whoop.

Michael measured off twenty-seven steps, pulled his bowstring taut, tensed up his entire body, and released his arrow. The second Arkantaur dummy swayed and listed to the side without falling down. Michael guiltily lowered his head, and trudged off, dragging his bow behind himself.

Sam measured off twenty-five paces, pulled his bowstring taut, tensed up like a string, and released his arrow, slaying the enemy. The dummy of the Arkantaur came crashing down. Lionel victoriously raised his own bow above his head, celebrating Sam's triumph.

Kelvin counted off thirty steps.

"Forty! Count to forty! We all counted to forty!" Lionel, Michael, and Sam screamed.

Kelvin obediently counted to forty, stretched taut the bowstring, aimed and missed, not even touching the Arkantaur dummy with his arrow.

"Lousy shot! Lousy shot!" Lionel, Michael, and Sam burst out laughing.

Kelvin lowered his head, as though resigning himself to the fact that this reprehensible nickname will now stick with him forever.

Ray counted forty steps, aimed, shot and, instead of hitting the head, pierced the dummy's paw. But for some unfathomable reason, it lurched and came tumbling down.

"You hit it!" Kelvin screamed and started jumping for joy.

"No! That doesn't count!" screamed Lionel.

"You must hit the head, not the paw. Your shot doesn't count!" he decided.

The sky suddenly grew dark and everyone looked up and froze in fear. A black Arkantaur of enormous proportions, appearing as though out of nowhere, circled above the meadow, effortlessly flapping its huge wings.

"A-a-a-a-a!" the children screamed and started running.

Lionel ran in front of the rest, hoping over everything that got in his way: branches, ditches, stones, bumps, and ruts.

Michael and Sam, screaming as loud as they could, were hurtling headlong,

shoving each other, and catching on everything in their way, not feeling their cuts and bruises. Ray was barely able to keep up with Kelvin, who was running like his life depended on it, without trying to avoid any of the obstacles.

When Ray understood that he could not go on any longer and will any moment collapse from exhaustion, the huge black Arkantaur dove down and in a split second snatched Kelvin by the nape of his neck, soaring together with him into the sky.

Everyone froze still, staring at the sky in horror. A gray avian wing suddenly sliced the air just above Ray's ear. Craig gained height and nosedived like a stone, ramming into the Arkantaur's black head with his beak. The Arkantaur squawked and, opening his beak, immediately let go of Kelvin, who hurtled helplessly through the air towards the ground. A long, gray wing, faster than the wind, intersected his path, so that he landed with a thud on its familiar, broad avian back.

The enraged Arkantaur dove once again and had already opened its beak to snatch its new pray, but Lionel, Michael, and Sam barely escaped him by hiding themselves in a narrow mountain tunnel.

Ray could already see this flying, black mass swooping down in order to seize him, when he heard the shrieking of a dozen gray Dredonts, who had flown to Craig's call from all directions, and saw them fiercely swarming the Arkantaur.

The black Arkantaur, his heart set on easy pray and not wishing to tussle with this gray swarm today, dove out of the tangle of Dredonts who had surrounded him and shot upwards.

Like a stony bird's nest suspended high up on a mountain top, the monastery of the Keepers of the Shrines towered high above the city of Sant Avis.

Dressed in long, dark capes, their hoods thrown over their heads, the Keepers served the city's Shrines day and night. Only they, soaring above the city like birds, did not fear the floods, only they had been entrusted with a high mission,

for the purpose of which they had to survive, even if the sea were to swallow up Sant Avis forever.

Aaron walked across the cold stones of the dim hall, lit an oil lamp, and looked out of the window. In the inner courtyard, surrounded by Keepers, a grown-up man was rocking back and forth on a set of wooden swings.

"My friend, if we were only to succeed in learning where she hides the magical stone," Easton had quietly approached him from behind his back.

"And what if we were to have another conversation with her, before the Saint Glen celebration?" Aaron turned around to face him. "Why would she not give it to us for safekeeping, just in case the sea once again swallows up Sant Avis?"

"As soon as we succeed in depriving her of her stone, everything would change to our advantage," Easton ventured.

"Her brother is already old enough to serve his people as the new Emperor," Aaron seconded him.

"Yes, but how will we conceal from the people that he is feeble-minded?" Easton looked down and out of the window.

"My friend, we will serve him in the confines of the Emperor's estate, day and

night!" Aaron burst out laughing and, continuing to smile, waved to

Caleb rocking in the swings below them.

The people of Sant Avis were preparing for the big celebration. The city's central square, like a bride being prepared for her wedding, was obediently letting itself be decorated. The carpenters were loudly hammering their hammers, assembling the large wooden merry-go-round that was erected only once each year. Some agile fellow with brushes and paint was touching up the washed-out mural that had been painted on an ancient tree. Not a single one of these local scenes did not contain a Dredont: they soared, spreading their large wings, promenaded self-importantly among the passersby, sat in a dignified manner beside the town's houses. By all appearances, they had been here always, and it was impossible to even imagine the winged city of Sant Avis without this friendship between these people and their huge birds.

Ike and Duke were checking out this scene while munching on the local apples and complaining about how sour they were. Nimble Larry managed to take a spin on the merry-go-round that was still being assembled, stroll atop of the stands being erected for the spectators, steal a whiff of the aromatic yellow branches being sold by a plump woman who had for a moment turned away and a round-bellied fruit vendor's sweet apples.

Hulking Bill and Skinny Wilson were spitting out the husks of some sort of seeds from a little bag that someone had apparently placed out for a Dredont. And Archie was exchanging glances with a dark-haired beauty. Not awaiting help, like a huntress in tight-fitting clothing made of tanned leather, she was dragging a thick, heavy log in the direction of an open shooting gallery that was still being built.

Archie grabbed the log and raised it up; the beauty did not let go of it. They stared at each other over the top of the log that was covering the bottom half of their faces and spoke to each other in a language that only the two of them understood without ever opening their mouth even for a second.

"I have been waiting for you a long time," she said.

"I have been on my way a long time," he replied.

"I knew that one day you would come."

"I didn't know that I would find myself here one day..."

"Will you stay with me forever?" she asked silently.

"No. I cannot," he replied with his eyes only. "But I will take you with me. Because life has lost its meaning without you."

"No. I cannot come with you," she replied wordlessly.

Their hearts began to beat so forcefully that they became breathless.

"He-ey! ▯-▯-archie!" the crew of the Celestine began screaming out to him.

Someone else's pair of hands grabbed the log and it, just like the beauty with the dark eyes, quickly disappeared among the bustling throng.

"Once upon a time, a very long time ago," the teacher, Mr. Yang, began, "Long before you and I were even alive, large gray Dredonts and huge black Arkantaurs soared in circles above our city. The people of our city feared both the one and the other, and they ran to hide as soon as the birds appeared in the sky. And only one boy, in defiance of the grown-ups, began to secretly place food and water out for one of the large gray Dredonts. This was the beginning of their secret friendship. As soon as the grown-ups caught sight of the Dredont, they would immediately throw stones at it, stones so large that only they had the strength to lift them. And only the boy alone didn't do so and, each day, again and again, he waited for his Dredont. And so, once upon a time, as everyone was looking on, a huge, black Arkantaur descended from above the clouds and snatched the young boy. Not even the largest stones flung by the grown-ups could stop him. And only a single, gray Dredont, three times smaller than the black monsters, plucking up his courage, rammed the Arkantaur. Falling out of his beak, the boy survived, tumbling right into his mother's arms. But a swarm of black Arkantaurs set upon the Dredont who, fighting for his life, lost all his gray feathers until, exhausted, he collapsed and died a painful death in the arms of his friend. Since then, we cherish and coddle our Dredonts, our sole defenders. And, each year, we celebrate the festival of Saint Glen, the savior of a little boy."

"Have you already heard the legend?" the teacher asked and surveyed the children who had all grown still.

"Yes! From my parents!" Lionel jumped up from his seat.

"From my grandmother!" replied Michael.

"From my older sister!" Sam rose up to speak.

"From my mother!" "From my father!" the children all yelled out, raising their hands.

"Kiara, Milady!" Aaron bowed, crossing the threshold, "Rumors are making the rounds of the city that you have promised your heart to a certain someone. And that Sant Avis will once again soon have an Emperor?"

"It doesn't become you, Aaron, the Keeper of our Shrines, to believe marketplace gossip. Moreover, I see no reason to transfer my authority," Kiara raised her brow in surprise.

"You are as beautiful as ever!" Aaron parried.

"Forgive me, Aaron, I have much to do today," Kiara turned away from him.

"I won't keep you any further, Milady," Aaron bowed in farewell.

He crossed the reception hall, his head bowed, as though he had failed to lighten his heavy burden.

"Oh, yes... If you happen to possess something that you fear losing, don't forget that you have us, the Keepers of the Shrines, for that purpose," Aaron added and tensed up in anticipation.

"Don't worry, Aaron. Everything that is most valuable, I always carry with me, just like my heart. And no Keeper of the Shrines could protect that better than myself," Kiara replied and left the hall first.

"Hold on tight!" Kelvin shouted to Ray, who was clutching onto his back as they rode on Craig's back.

"Look over there, can you see? On our right!" he pointed with his hand.

"I see!" Ray screamed in reply.

"These are our fields of wheat! And there, to the left. That is our corn, or rather, that which remains of it after the Arkantaurs have raided it!"

"And what's that, ahead?" Ray shouted.

"It's the old lighthouse!" Kelvin yelled in reply.

"Would you like to fly up close?" he asked him.

"Yes!" Ray screamed.

A few of flaps of the large gray wings and Ray, seated on Craig behind Kelvin's back, was circling above the lighthouse, as though it were not the lighthouse that with its beam directs the way, but Ray, who is able to fly even higher than the lighthouse, who could, taking up a lamp in his hand, relay signals to the schooners and the brigantines.

"He-ey! We're over he-e-e-re! Come and see u-u-us! Come to Sant A-a-avis!"

"And over there? What's that off in the distance?" Ray screamed.

"It's the old fortification!" Kelvin replied.

"Let us fly, then!" Ray proposed.

"Yes, let us fly-y-y!" Kelvin agreed.

Another couple of minutes of flight, of cool wind in their faces, the salty sea air, the foamy waves somewhere far, far below them and they were now descending, lower and lower, towards the old, dilapidated dark stones.

"Don't be afraid! Jump down!" Kelvin commanded, and Ray climbed down from the Dredont's gray back.

Still unaccustomed to flying, he had to first stretch out his feet and lean with his back against the cold stones.

"Over here, can you see?" Kelvin called out to him, nimbly jumping from one stone to another. "Cannons used to stand here! And over here, do you see? It's the trace of an enemy cannonball in the wall."

"And now, if you don't chicken out, I will show you something that you have never seen!" Kelvin proposed, his eyes aflame.

"I won't chicken out!" Ray promised.

Kelvin hopped from stone to stone and Ray, carefully following his every step, slipped, skinned his leg, but got up immediately and hopped again. The large flat, medium-sized beveled and smaller stones, their bulging edges chiseled by time, all of them witnesses to age-old confrontations, were staring goggle-eyed at the disturbers of their peace, following them with their disgruntled gazes. The damp, narrow stone staircase descended below, deep under the earth. Ray was barely able to keep up. The light ceased to penetrate through the cracks and the realm of darkness now extinguished all sounds.

"Be careful! A couple more meters and we're there!" Kelvin, who was making his way by feel, promised.

Ray was also making his way by feel, slowly moving one foot in front of the other while sliding his palms along the cold, stone walls, when Kelvin called out: "Ray! We're here!"

Ray took another couple of cautious steps forward and froze in fear. He was standing in the passageway leading into the lowest, open underground hall. The dull light of day, penetrating from somewhere up above with its meager, thin rays, fell on a huge, dark crypt containing dozens of stone tombs, carved on the slabs of which were relieves of the fallen Dredonts.

"These are our warriors who died in battle together with the Dredonts who were helping them defend our city!" Kelvin proudly proclaimed.

Imagining to himself the mortal remains of the fallen warriors in the same grave with the avian bones of the huge Dredonts, Ray became colder still, and he wished more than anything to clamber out of here as soon as possible.

"Let's run! There's another exit here!" Kelvin commanded.

Ray flung himself after him with all the speed he could muster.

The silent walls of the stony bastion of the Keepers of the Shrines were listening intently to the sound of steps. Cole, dressed like all the Keepers in a long dark cape with a hood covering his head, was walking down the dark corridors heading toward the hall where Aaron held court. He swung open the door to the chamber of the Head Keeper and, with his permission, accompanied by a nod of the head, sat down at the long table.

"Cole!" Aaron addressed himself to him.

"You are a faithful Keeper of the Shrines of our city; you are obedient and devoted," Aaron made a pause.

"If you were to be chosen by our Order of Keepers for a higher mission than the simple, daily monastic work common to every monastery... Cole, would you be able to handle it? Would you accept it, Cole?" Aaron interrupted his speech.

"And why not?" Cole replied indecisively.

"It is a very important, but also dangerous mission, Cole," Aaron, behind whose back Easton stood with his eyes lowered, warned.

"I would try my hand at it," Cole replied and looked down himself.

"As you know, Cole, we will soon be celebrating the festival of Saint Glen and the entire city will hold competitions of agility and marksmanship?" Aaron.

"I am ready!" Cole said quickly and with relief.

"You didn't quite understand me, Cole," Aaron hesitated and paused.

"Your target is Kiara," he whispered and looked at Easton's lowered eyes behind his back.

The people of Sant Avis were making a racket, laughing, blowing into pipes, and dancing. The noises of celebration were resounding on the central square like an echo, rolling from one side to the other. The gaming attractions of the national festival, lovingly decorated with bright ribbons, flowers, and feathers shed by the Dredonts, awaited their champions.

Nimble Larry ran over to the giant sledgehammer, tensed up, but did not manage to even budge it from its place. Ike, standing in line after him, grabbed it with both hands, tensed up, quickly raised it up, and immediately dropped it, the high striker having barely reached the mark with the smiling fat lady.

Hulking Bill shoved the rubberneckers aside, confidently grabbed a hold of the sledgehammer, and slammed it down with all his might. The puck soared to the mark with the image of a Dredont. Interrupting the enthusiastic applause and smiling slightly, he bowed to the audience. The people parted unbidden when Dylan, wearing the tight-fitting leather clothing of a warrior and taking a sure step forward, approached the sledgehammer. In a practiced motion, he grabbed the handle, grew still for a moment, and slammed it down with all his might.

The puck came to a standstill on the top mark with the drawing of the huge black Arkantaur. The people burst out in applause and Dylan bowed slightly, without changing his stony facial expression.

Skinny Wilson, munching on a sour apple, was flinging darts

adorned with the gray feathers of Dredonts at a target. He kept missing, cursing out loud, and spitting out the sour apple. Duke, having stollen some sweets somewhere, was stuffing himself to the gills with them, while accurately hitting almost the center of the target.

Kiara bent over the bed of the ailing Djun, tightly clenching his fatigued hand.

"Is that you, Milady?" he greeted her quietly.

"Kiara, I ordered that you be sent for because I must tell you something," Djun whispered hoarsely. "Your life is in danger... and two great losses await you."

"I understand everything, Djun," Kiara said quietly.

"And don't forget, Milady," Djun breathed heavily. "A just ruler does not require the help of magic. Nor will the intercession of magic save a criminal who rules," he concluded his message to her and wearily closed his eyes.

"Djun! Djun!" Kiara called out to him, but the Seer replied her with only a heavy sigh.

Ray and Kelvin were rocking on the huge swings shaped like boats and painted with gray Dredont feathers.

"Kel-vin! This is too hi-i-igh! Don't swing so ha-a-ard!" Kelvin's parents were screaming to them from below.

But the general din and the laughter of the boys in the wooden boat made it impossible for their words to reach the ears of the willful and disobedient children.

Sam pulled taut the bowstring, aimed and released the arrow, missing the small Arkantaur dummy.

"A miss, kid, and you're out of the contest!" the fat man standing by the children's target smiled.

"Next up! Who's our next hot shot?" the bearded carnival barker beckoned, swinging the small children's bow to and fro.

Michael stepped forward, lifted his head with his eyes closed to the sky, as though praying for help from above, and grabbed the bow. He pulled the bowstring taut and knocked down the first of the three small dummies. The audience began to applaud the daredevil.

"Excellent, young man! Go ahead and take aim a second time!" the bearded man burst out laughing.

Pulling the bowstring taut, Michael, being afraid to miss, involuntarily closed his eyes. The arrow, without giving it a second thought, missed the second Arkantaur dummy.

"Our second contestant is out!" the fat man smiled. "Come back in a year, kid!"

Lionel, dressed like a Young Warrior in tight-fitting clothing made of tanned leather, strolled through the crowd, gathering his concentration spun the bow in his hand, as though testing its strength, pulled the bowstring taut and fired, striking one of the three Arkantaur dummies. The crowd applauded the future Warrior. The dummy stricken by his second arrow plopped down on the ground. To the applause of the audience, he pulled the bowstring taut a third time. But fortune had abandoned him, and the dummy didn't budge from its place. Infuriated, Lionel loudly slammed the arrow down, breaking it across his knee.

"The most accurate daredevil will receive a genuine Young Warrior bow and arrow set as a gift!" the bearded carnival barker beckoned, swinging the gift bow carved with the head of a Dredont.

Ray and Kelvin exchanged glances and rushed down from the swings, leapfrogging each other and slicing their way through the crowd.

Kelvin missed, not having taken his time to concentrate, and Lionel, Michael, and Sam started screaming maliciously: "Lousy shot! Lousy Shot! Lousy shot!"

Ray stepped forward indecisively, his fingers trembling, pulled taut the bowstring, the bow suddenly grown heavy as though it were made of steel, prayed to the local gods of which he knew nothing about, and let the arrow fly. Certus, the invisible God of marksmanship, observing the competition from the stands, smiled, greeting the little otherlander. And his arrow, for a reason unknown to Ray, pierced the Arkantaur dummy. The audience joyfully cheered in expectation of the second shot. Ray stared at the muscular old man winking at him from

the bleachers. The second arrow, immediately after the first, struck the second Arkantaur. Pulling the bowstring taut a third time, Ray looked at the elder, who was still smiling at him, with incomprehension. The third arrow obediently pierced into the third dummy. The crowd rejoiced, hailing the victor, Kelvin jumped for joy, and Lionel, Michael, and Sam vanished. And the elder who had been winking at Ray from the stands also disappeared without a trace.

The genuine Young Warrior bow, decorated with a little carved Dredont head, was conveyed into the hands of the champion, accompanied by dozens of pairs of children's eyes aflame with envy.

"Kelvin, I want you to have it!" Ray immediately handed it to him to the din and applause of the rapturous crowd.

Archie's dart had missed, nearly hitting the fat lady who was passing by, when his gaze fell upon the stand set up for the judges.

Wearing a royal tiara, enthroned on an armchair carved with avian wings, sat a dark-haired beauty whose arm covered in bracelets rested on a small Dredont dummy on a pedestal beside her.

The principal tournament of marksmanship languished in the absence of sufficiently mettlesome daredevils. Nimble Larry raced over to be first in line. He spun the bow around in his arms, pulled the bowstring taught, and missed five shots, one after another, not having hit an Arkantaur dummy even once. Having let a half dozen contestants go ahead of him, Hulking Bill hit one of the five in the paw.

Duke hit two of the dummies in their sides without knocking down either

of them. Wilson's arrows flew past the heads of three Arkantaurs and, infuriated, he tossed the bow aside.

Mighty Dylan, having made his way through the parting throng, pulled the string of his bow taut, aimed and, attended by the gazes of the entire hushed crowd, knocked down four of the dummies one after another.

"Arkantaurs!" the crowd shouted as Dylan released the fifth and decisive arrow.

Day turned to night, and Dylan's arrow, sailing through the dark that had descended upon the city, missed the fifth dummy. Archie froze in his tracks.

The entire city gazed into the black sky and the sun obscured by a swarm of huge black Arkantaurs in horror, and only Archie alone saw the light in the darkness that had descended upon the square: the magical blue Stoublulaze was shining from the right eye of the dummy resting beside Kiara.

The infinite flocks of the Dredonts, guarding the celebration, soared into the sky, and the black flock of Arkantaurs, preferring easy prey, slowly shifted aside, soaring away on their huge, dark wings.

The people clamored joyfully if uncertainly, celebrating the passing threat.

"Don't miss, don't miss, don't miss," Archie was praying to himself.

He squeezed his way through the crowd, pulled the bowstring taut, and exchanged glances with HER.

"Go for it, you can do it!" she said to him silently.

"And what if I miss?" he replied to her with his eyes alone.

"Today is your day. The champion's wish is the law," she added wordlessly.

"My request will disappoint you," he replied without unpursing his lips.

"I have gotten used to it," she replied.

Archie pulled back the bowstring and released the arrow, then a second, and a third, a fourth, and a fifth. And now the fifth dummy of an Arkantaur, stricken in its most vulnerable point – the spot between its eyes and beak – landed with a thud on the ground.

"Victory!" the crew of the Celestine screamed.

"Hail to the victor!" the city crowd rejoiced.

"Hurray! Hurray! Hurray!" screamed Ray and Kelvin.

Aaron bowed, standing above the Empress's armchair.

"What does the victor desire?" he relayed Kiara's question.

"The dummy of your Dredont!" Archie shouted in reply.

Kiara hesitated... and then nodded as a sign of her consent.

"Today, the champion's wish is the law!" proclaimed Aaron.

And the two guards, dressed like warriors, carried the dummy through the parting crowd towards Archie, who was stunned in his silent joy.

"Ki-a-a-a-ra-a-a!" Archie screamed, noticing the figure wearing a black cape and aiming in the direction of the royal stands.

Kiara sat beside Djun's bed.

"Is that you, Milady?" he opened his eyes.

"Don't worry, Djun, I had foreseen everything... The arrow didn't pierce my corset," she said, gazing into his eyes with gratitude.

"And the victor?" Djun asked quietly.

"You know how it is: the champion's wish is the law of the land on this day," she replied.

"Are you crying?" asked Djun.

"No," she replied, wiping away her tears.

"Kiara!" the guard called out to her.

"He brought the dummy back!" the guard announced, and the dummy of the small, one-eyed Dredont landed obediently at her feet.

"Let him enter!" she commanded.

Archie came in, got down before her on one knee and, hesitatingly, began to speak silently, in a language intelligible only to the two of them.

"Tomorrow, I will no longer be here."

"I know," she replied.

"Will you ever be able to return to us?" she asked.

"No," he answered.

"Will you ever be able to forget me?" he asked.

"Never," she said.

"Who was that, Kiara?" Djun's hoarse voice broke the silence.

"It was HE, Djun," Kiara replied.

In the morning, the Celestine was already furrowing the sea. Duke, having begun to miss his galley, applied himself to his pots, having decided to spoil all of them with something special. Ike was swabbing the deck, Hulking Bill was shuffling around the barrels of provisions in the cargo hold, Nimble Larry, manning the helm, supervised the work of the entire crew. Skinny Wilson stretched out on deck, cursing and munching on the sour apples, a couple of baskets of which he had, for some unknown reason, brought back along with him. Ray hung on the mast, imagining that he was flying on Kelvin's Dredont Craig's back, whom he would never fly upon again in his life.

And Archie locked himself up in his cabin and lay there almost the entire day, turning away to face the wall and thinking of the woman whom he will never again see for the rest of his life.

And even the shining magical Stoublulaze, hidden now in the fifth little pocket, gave no pleasure to his shattered-to-pieces heart.

Chapter Thirteen

The Ship Graveyard

The Celestine was adrift at sea, like a feral cat basking in the sun, its weary eyes shut.

Ike and Wilson were doing battle at cards. Duke was chasing after ship rats. Hulking Bill was in search of his favorite barrel of rum. Archie was gazing greedily into Cook's spyglass, expecting any second to spot an alien shore. Nimble Larry and Ray were off fishing in a dinghy.

"Hey, you! Down there!" yelled Duke.

"If you're going to be gone fishing all day, I'm not putting out any chow till nighttime!" he warned them.

"Shut up, you son of a kitchen rat!" Nimble Larry barked out in reply and got busy with his oars.

Having walked over to Celestine's portside, Ray suddenly felt a strange sensation, as though the sea water was no longer supporting them, but was agitated and rippling, shuddering in its depths.

"Pull us up! I can see your starving mug now!" Larry shouted as the dinghy began to slowly ascend upwards.

The thunder of the water shuddering in its inaccessible black depths had finally reached the upper, lit portion of its surface.

"A-a-a-a-!" screamed Ike, Duke and Wilson.

"A-a-a-a!" howled Hulking Bill.

"The devil take me!" screamed Nimble Larry, grabbing a hold of the life-saving rail together with Ray.

The underwater rumble didn't subside, but instead intensified. The Celestine was suddenly and sharply tossed upwards and she hung suspended above the sea, as though she had taken flight and got stuck in the air. Everyone to a man leaned over the rail and looked down. Instead of the sea's surface, the Celestine was resting on the back of an enormous sea monster, similar in appearance to a gargantuan whale.

"A-a-a-a-a!" all of them screamed together.

"Cough, cough!" the gargantuan throat coughed, and the Celestine flopped back in the water, rolling off the monster's mountain-sized back.

"A-a-a-a-a-a-a!" the gargantuan maw sighed, as though it were about to expel a giant sneeze.

"A-a-a-a-a!" screamed the crew of the Celestine.

And the schooner, like a tiny, insignificant minnow chased by the storm was propelled at full speed into the predator's throat. The monster suddenly decided not to sneeze after all and instead swallowed the Celestine like a small fry that had become stuck in its gaping maw.

"A-a-a-a!" everyone screamed in a chorus as they were propelled through the gigantic throat and plopped down into the muck of the pitch dark.

"Light the lamps!" Archie commanded as soon as the schooner came to rest in one place.

Ike, Duke, Wilson, and Bill started crawling on their knees in search of something to light.

Nimble Larry was the first to light a torch, and he passed it to his captain.

Archie slowly swung his arm through the air, lighting the sea monster's insides.

The Celestine was sloshing around in the massive belly, surrounded by the remnants of another three dozen or so long-ago devoured schooners and brigantines.

"A cauldron!" Archie screamed.

"Go get your largest cauldron, Duke!" he commanded.

Everyone flung themselves toward the galley kitchen and dragged over all the cauldrons and skillets they could get their hands on in the dark.

"Fire!" Archie ordered, "Start a fire!"

Ray leapt up to help out and ran off to get kindling. A hot haze hung suspended above the deck. The fire was spreading under all the cauldrons, pots, and iron skillets, shedding light on the fleet inside the monstrous belly. Duke, Ike, Wilson and Bill, having stripped to their waists from the heat, started flapping their shirts in the air, to fan the smoke away from themselves.

The monster's innards suddenly convulsed, twitched, spasmed, and once again heaved the Celestine out.

"Cou-ou-ough!" the throat coughed again with as much force as it could muster.

"A-a-a-a!" everyone screamed in a chorus as they shot bullet-like out into the fresh air like an obstinate crumb that had gone down the wrong throat and become

lodged there.

"A-a-a-a-a-a-a!" the sea monster sighed, as though it were again about to sneeze.

"Full speed ahead!" Archie screamed as loudly as he could.

And the Celestine raced away, splitting the waves like a single, stubborn fish who refused, at least for today, to spend an eternity, along with the rest of its school, in the belly of the beast.

In the morning, Archie was again flipping through the pages of the book.

"Hey, you piddly little captain!" Cook's Secret Book came to life.

"You don't burn in the fire, don't drown in water, and escape from the belly of the whale?"

"Well, here's your next riddle then!

>> SWEETER THAN THE SWEETEST
>> ARE ONLY OTHER SWEETS.
>>
>> THE SILLIEST NONSENSE IS OFTEN
>> UTTERED WITH THE WISEST GRIN.

"If you unravel this one, then just perhaps you will find the magical indigo blue Frindigoffle after all!"

"Oh, and this: your fame has reached the mouth of hell now, captain! The devils are already taking bets, which of them will impale you on their fork first!

"Ho-ho-ho!"

FRINDIGOFFLE

Chapter Fourteen

San Dulcedo,
Or
The Bittersweet Life of
a Sweet Town

"Not a one!" the King pronounced in disappointment, looking off into the distance.

"Who? Who thought up this thing, anyway, to royally welcome an uninvited guest today?" and he scanned the entire retinue of courtiers frozen still beside him.

"It was her!" the First Lady-in-Waiting pointed at the second.

"Nonsense! It was her!" the Second Lady-in-Waiting pointed at the third.

"It was him!" the Third Lady-in-Waiting pointed her finger at...

The Royal Scribbler, for one second, tore himself away from his jottings.

"I'll look it up now," he mumbled, and shuffled through several pages of his notetaking.

"Oh, yes... Here it is!" he rejoiced and set to reading the notes aloud.

"What day is it?" the King asked. "Today is Thursday," replied the Second Lady-in-Waiting. "And what is it that we do on Thursdays?" The King asked. "We catch butterflies!" replied the First Lady-in-Waiting. "Boring!" said the King. "We must think up of something more novel..." "Let us all go to the shore!" the First Lady-in-Waiting proposed. "And what are we going to do there?" asked the King. "The first ship that comes in to harbor today will be our uninvited guest!" the Second Lady-in-Waiting proposed. "Sheer genius!" said the

King. "Henceforth, we shall call Thursday "The Day of the Uninvited Guest"! The King rejoiced and all present set off for the port," the Royal Scribbler concluded.

"I told you, it was her!" the First Lady-in-Waiting yelped, pointing her finger at the second.

"He's coming! He's coming!" the Second Lady-in-Waiting started jumping up and down.

"Who's coming?" everyone asked in a chorus.

"The uninvited guest!" the Second Lady-in-Waiting averred and narrowed her eyes into slits, gazing far out in the distance.

"I don't see anything!" the King remarked, stomping his foot in disappointment.

"A spyglass! A spyglass for the King!" the retinue erupted in a coruscation.

The spyglass appeared in someone's hands and was quickly raised up to the King's royal nose.

"I see it! I see a ship!" the King nodded in agreement.

"But it is not one of ours, outlanders by all appearance," he added.

"Order all the musicians posthaste to the port!" the King commanded.

"Notify the city: the Uninvited Guest is about to arrive!" the King rejoiced, rubbing his hands together in his impatience.

"La-a-and a-ho-oy!" Ray screamed.

"La-a-and!" Skinny Wilson, Nimble Larry, Cook Duke, and

Pudgy Ike hollered.

"La-a-and a-ho-oy!" barked Hulking Bill.

"Land ahoy!" Archie thought, and glued himself again to Cook's spyglass.

Loud music, fanfares, and a jubilant crowd waving their arms in welcome greeted the Celestine in the alien port. The crew, jumping out on shore, stared in amazement all around themselves.

"Stop!" the royal retinue demanded.

"Who are you?" the Royal Scribbler asked, staring at Archie.

"I am the captain!" replied Archie.

"Did anyone invite you?" the Royal Scribbler demanded to know and looked at Archie distrustfully.

"N-n-no," Archie conceded.

"May Thursday be proclaimed "The Day of the Uninvited Guest!"" the King announced.

"All hail the Uninvited Guest!" the crowd shouted.

"Oh, he's so cute!" the King smiled in his powdered wig, staring at Ray.

"May Friday be proclaimed the day of the cute little boy from far away!" the King proclaimed and smiled once again triumphantly.

"Our Fridays are already taken, Your Majesty," the Royal Scribbler whispered in his ear.

"With what?" the King seemed truly surprised.

"Last Friday, the milk lady brought us some fresh milk," the Royal Scribbler began.

"Well, and so?" the King stared without comprehending him.

"You asked for it to be served warm," the Royal Scribbler continued.

"So what?" the King stomped his foot in impatience.

"You burned yourself on the milk, Your Majesty, and proclaimed Friday "The Day of the Prohibition Against Milk,"" the Royal Scribbler explained.

"Not a single one of the city's inhabitants is permitted to drink milk on Fridays. "I proclaim Friday "The Day of the Prohibition Against Milk,"" the Royal Scribbler read from his notes.

"So sad," the King agreed.

"Yes, Friday is, indeed taken," he now reconsidered.

"Why are the uninvited guests still standing around? Accompany the uninvited guests to their place of residence! And entertain them as the heroes of these festivities. Today is their holiday!" the King remembered himself.

And the jubilant crowd immediately surrounded the crew of the Celestine, hanging their necks with garland bouquets of freshly cut flowers and crowning their heads with laurels.

"Well, well!" Hulking Bill burst out laughing.

"Oh, they are all so cute!" the First Lady-in-Waiting smiled.

"Yes, they are all so attractive!" the Second Lady-in-Waiting nodded in approval.

"And they are probably very smart!" the Third Lady-in-Waiting supposed.

"And I think that they are very, ve-ery strong!" remarked the Fourth Lady-in-Waiting who had been silent all this time.

"Your majesty! It's them we should be asking to dislodge the log that has been blocking the road for a week already!" the First Lady-in-Waiting proposed.

"Pure genius!" replied the King and everyone flung themselves after him.

The throng carried the crew of the Celestine aloft down the street.

"Over here!" the King commanded.

Hulking Bill squeezed himself to the front and center. The log was indeed lying in the middle of the way, but in no way was it obstructing passage to its right and its left.

He shrugged his shoulders, shoved the log with his foot and it rolled away to one side.

"Strongman! Strongman!" the King praised him and smiled approvingly.

"The road's all clear now, friends!" he announced and strolled down the center in a way that attracted everyone's attention.

"Stop!" he suddenly stopped and the cheering crowd obediently grew stilled.

"And what am I to do now with my moods?" he asked, staring

again at the Royal Scribbler.

"With what moods?" the Royal Scribbler asked him in incomprehension and flipped through a couple of pages of his notes.

"You blockhead!" the King screamed at him.

"When I am in a bad mood, I pass this log on its right side. And when it's good, on the left side!" the King reminded all of them.

"That is absolutely true," the Royal Scribbler confirmed it, checking over his notebooks.

"And here I am, like a fool, trying to figure which way I am going to pass the log, when the log is no longer there?" the King sounded irate.

"Yes... The log's no longer there," the Royal Scribbler confirmed his suspicion.

"Put the log back in its place!" the King commanded.

"Pure genius!" the First Lady-in-Waiting yelped in rapture.

"Put the log back in its place!" the entire royal retinue shouted, and everyone fixed their eyes in expectation on Hulking Bill.

Bill scratched the back of his head, shrugged his shoulders, and bending over the log, effortlessly tossed it back to its original place.

"Strongman! Strongman!" the King praised him, passing around the log to its left side.

The royal entourage, without having to think too long, followed after him, gingerly passing the log on the left.

Mr. and Ms. Griffin lived in a house with the outdoor sign: "No one

here rents rooms". And it was precisely here that the inhabitants of the city of San Dulcedo had sent the crew of the Celestine.

"Deborah! Someone is ringing the doorbell; would you please go open it!" asked Mr. Griffin.

"Open it yourself, Foster!" replied Ms. Griffin.

"I can't," replied Mr. Griffin.

"Why not?" asked Ms. Griffin.

"I'm busy," replied Mr. Griffin.

"With what?" Ms. Griffin quizzed him.

"I'm thinking," added Mr. Griffin.

"About what?" Ms. Griffin expressed her surprise.

"About how it's been a nice long time since we've had any visitors, Deborah," Mr. Griffin explained.

The doorbell rang once again.

"Foster! The bell's still ringing, please go open the door!" Ms. Griffin asked him politely.

"But I already told you, I can't. I'm busy!" Mr. Griffin sounded irritated.

Ms. Griffin go up with difficulty and went to open the door.

"Didn't you read this?" she pointed to the sign on the house.

"Read what?" the crew of the Celestine were taken aback.

"This plaque!" Ms. Griffin clarified it for them.

"We haven't" the crew of the Celestine admitted.

"Then come in," Ms. Griffin invited them in and worriedly glanced from side to side.

The wooden beds, tables, and chairs in Mr. and Ms. Griffin house were all nailed down to the floor. All the goods and fixtures in their household were either carved, burned, inscribed, or embroidered with the label "Mr. and Ms. Griffin". Because more than anything else in this world, Mr. and Ms. Griffin feared that their temporary lodgers would carry all their possessions out of the house, down to the last teaspoon. Each lodging room had its own key, the use of which was absolutely impossible, inasmuch as, to avoid the prospect of these ever being lost, the foresighted Mr. and Ms. Griffin affixed them high above each of the doors, having providentially secured the rope each was hanging on with several nails.

Hanging on hooks on the left side of Mr. and Ms. Griffin foyer were their household goods. Above each hook was a helpful wooden plaque. Hanging above the first was "Fine Weather". This is where a light jacket, light boots, and Mr. Griffin's light hat belonged. Above the second hook was the sign: "Bad Weather". Prepared for use here were a long coat, worn down boots, and a broad hat with a sloping brim. Above the third hook hung the sign "Inclement Weather" but no clothing of any kind hung on this. It was possible to conjecture that Mr. Griffin never ventured outside of the house in inclement weather, and if he ever did do

so, then, most likely, it was without any outer garments. Perhaps the most remarkable thing was that the footwear here was organized on the upper shelf and the hats lay on the floor, where the knee-length boots and the work boots would normally be.

When the crew of the Celestine came down for breakfast, it turned out that the windows of the dining room were firmly nailed down, inasmuch as, according to Ms. Griffin's explanation, last year, a powerful downpour and wind had mercilessly hammered the wooden, latticed storm shutters against the exterior of the house, threatening to tear them off forever.

Duke, Ike, and Bill, sheerly out of politeness, were chewing on Ms. Griffin's baking, left over, it would seem, from the previous week. Wilson wanted to spit

out the slop burning his tongue that, on Nimble Larry's suggestion, he had only just taken a swig of from the jug. Archie was mixing some sort of hot swill in a glass with a spoon that had been tied round with a tag with the inscription "Mr. and Ms. Griffin" on it. Ray was squinting through the grate of the closed shutters

that let the sun's rays into the room, when suddenly the door was swung open and two identical, obese boys stumbled into the dining room. They were tightly clenching their cups and round bowls filled with a hot porridge. All their dishes were embossed with the initials "B.G."

After they had emptied the bowls of porridge, before them appeared plates, each with two-three blintzes with jam. Two similar plates filled with the fresh baked goods vanished after these, chased down with some sweet jelly-thickened juice. Incapable of stuffing themselves any more, and namely, with the flagels powdered with sugar that were served to them next, the brothers Bryan and Brandon rolled out from behind the table, sucking on their hard candies on a stick.

On the large-as-a-wardrobe shelf clock in the dining room, the numbers were distributed in reverse order, so that on its right side, twelve was followed by eleven, and on the left side, correspondingly, was one o'clock. The hands advanced slowly, changing their position on the clock face in the direction opposite to the hour hand that Ray's eyes had grown accustomed to seeing.

In a world were, in the opinion of Mr. and Ms. Griffin's new lodgers, the Devil himself had broken a leg, and a sea demon had bitten all, right after they were born, the sun shone quite brightly, and so the crew of the Celestine set out to

explore the city with Archie in the lead.

Walking down the embankment were two who considered themselves to be great fishermen. They were carrying their boat upside down on their shoulders, over

their heads; the legs of each of them were facing, and moving, in two opposite directions. The first couple of steps were won by the right pair of work boots, and the upside-down boat would shift a few steps in the right direction. The next couple of steps, the waders sticking out on the left side proved victorious, and the boat was tugged a couple of meters of the way to the left side. Ike, Duke, and Bill passed the walking upside-down boat on the left, and Larry had collided head on with it, while the boots that were sticking out from under the boat to the right side had temporarily led the scoring.

On a porch, under an awning that read "Mr. Jenkins's Repair and Impair Shop" sat a jocular mustachioed man who was forcefully hammering a seventh leg onto the same and only one footstool. Soon, he was whopping away with a hammer on one of the legs of an upturned second footstool, apparently wishing to demolish this no longer needed object by mightily seeking to smash it to smithereens.

On the steps of the little shop with the "Mr. Sanders's Pince-Nez and Walking Sticks" awning, warming himself in the sun, was a well-groomed gentleman, his arm leaning on an elegant, wooden cane, his eyes closed beneath a pince-nez planted on the bridge of his nose without any glasses in them.

Nimble Larry immediately planted on his nose, from among the many displayed in the street case, a pince-nez without prescription lenses in them, and twirled a walking stick in the air, barely missing swiping the other customers. Ray and Hulking Bill were dying of laughter nearby, trying to convince Skinny Wilson to try on one of the powdered wigs that all the walls of the neighboring street vendor's shop were hung with from ceiling to floor.

"And what would you do, gentlemen, if you were to lose your right boot, while still being in possession of the left one?" the

proprietor posed his question point blank, taking no note of the confusion of the crew of the Celestine, who had stopped in front of his shop, in which offered for sale was footwear exclusively for the right foot.

"The right boot may become misplaced, or worn out, or it may even be, God forbid it, stolen!" the salesman reasoned, raising his bushy eyebrows in a conspiratorially conversational matter.

"Where else could you go? Of course, you come to me, Mr. Right's shop! Here, you will most definitely find a replacement for your favorite right boot, whether it be a child's little booty, or a lady's high-heeled calf-length boot, or a man's loafer! There is no right foot in existence that would leave the confines of my shop barefooted!" and Mr. Right burst into maniacal laughter.

On the opposite side of the street, Ike, Duke Bill, and Wilson stumbled into the shop of Mr. Left, doing a brisk business selling footwear exclusively for the left foot, and who confided to the outlanders a secret, and namely, that having quarreled with Mr. Right, they hadn't exchanged a single word already these past two years.

No one succeeded in escaping the attentions of the "Shop of Useful Suggestions" awning, and so the crew of the Celestine proceeded to slip inside.

There was not a soul in the dimly lit establishment. Nimble Larry jerked the string of the bell, which promptly came off in his hands.

Having made his appearance, the owner, Mr. Cunning, showed Larry how it may be tied back on to the bell and asked him to pay a pretty penny for this service. Hulking Bill pulled the door handle, and it remained in his palm; for a coin, the master enlightened Bill about how he may insert it back in the door without the use of any tools. A pail of flour was dumped on Duke, sparing only his eyes, which he had clenched shut just in time. For a gold piece, Mr. Cunning immediately sold Duke a brush. Skinny Wilson tramped with both of his feet into a puddle of glue, and for another coin, Archie had no choice but to purchase a concoction that served as a solvent, so that Wilson could again move his feet. Ray asked to use the restroom, and, for just one gold piece, the proprietor suggested, through a crack in the door, how he might be able to open the secret lock that had suddenly closed behind him. Having taken their leave of the "The Shop of Useful Suggestions," the crew of the Celestine discovered that they had blown through an entire palmful of gold pieces, having not acquired a darned thing from the entrepreneurial Mr. Cunning.

"Rook to D4!" the King announced.

A Lady-in-Waiting in a tall wig looked around herself in confusion.

"Rook to D4!" the King repeated irately and stomped his foot.

The ladies-in-waiting, who were serving as pawns on the huge chess field in front of the royal estate, sprung into a flurry of commotion, directing the rook to her new place.

The rook, wearing a tall wig, raced across to her new position.

"Knight to F3!" the King decided and ran over to the other half of the field.

The Royal Scribbler, who served as the knight, giddied up to his new place.

"The white King to B6!" the King declared and ran off to reposition the white King.

"Black King to G3!" he shouted again and ran over to his new place, repositioning the black one.

"Your Majesty! The harpsichord teacher is awaiting you for your lesson!" the butler announced.

"Tell him to go to hell!" the King replied and fell into contemplation over his next move.

"He refuses to go away!" the butler soon relayed the message.

"Off with his head!" replied the King and sank back into his deliberations.

"The teacher has disappeared!" the butler relayed the new development.

"What do you mean disappeared?" the King let out a squeal.

"And what about my harpsichord lesson? Chop off the lout's head, as soon as you find him!" the King raged.

"Anyway, what else is on our schedule?" the King exclaimed.

The Royal Scribbler, afraid to move an inch, or even to shift in his position, only spread open his arms, directing his glance at the stack of his jottings he had left out on the chair before the chess game had begun.

"The knight may temporarily leave the field!" the King issued his permission.

And the Royal Scribbler, exhaling in relief, raced over to his stack.

"On Mondays is the King's birthday, Your Majesty. On Tuesdays, the flogging of the contrite."

"And what if no one had trespassed?" the King wondered aloud.

"There will be flogging anyway," the Royal Scribbler shrugged his shoulders.

"On Wednesdays… I can't quite make this out," and he flushed red, not daring to pronounce it aloud.

The Lady-in-Waiting who served as the rook left her place, with the King's nod of approval, and whispered in the King's ear: "Women's Fashions Fitting".

"Oh, yes. Oh!" the King chuckled.

"We will continue the game on Wednesday!" he immediately declared and ran off in the direction of the royal chambers, accompanied by the squeals of the ladies-in-waiting racing after him.

"Bob! Bob, please take your starting position," the commentator announced.

"Hugh follows him in the second position. Who will be third? Yes, Phil is third! The tension is rising! And who will be racing in the fourth position? Ah, Floyd! Fourth is Floyd! And who, who is brave enough to claim the fifth position? Sean! All the starting positions are taken! Please, make your wagers, ladies and gentlemen!" the commentator appealed, the entire time hooting, whooping, and winking to the public to attract attention.

"I wager one gold piece and a bowl of my dinner bouillabaisse on Bob!" wearing a rumpled suit, Mr. Long made his bet.

"Two gold pieces and my right shoe on Hugh!" declared bald Mr. Bennett.

"Half a golden on Phil, the other half on Floyd, and a leftover slice of Ms. Took's birthday cake!" offered Mr. Cooper, who was distinguished by his slight height.

"Sean! Sean is my favorite!" Ms. Price shrieked. Three goldens and a powdered wig on Sean!"

The wagers in the "Flea Races" at the seaside casino were all placed, and the fleas took off like banshees. Duke, Bill, and Archie exchanged glances, never having managed to distinguish a single one of the participants of the race in the box, over which, with such dogged ardor, a dozen of the local inhabitants were bent over.

A table was set in a small and narrow street, in a not very large public space courtyard. Eight men with knitted eyebrows, their arms crossed before their chests, were curiously looking around everywhere without exchanging a word with each other.

"Hey! Kiddo! Take a look around the corner, will you! You don't see Mr. Cage coming, do you?!" one of the skulking men asked, having noticed Ray.

"Someone in a striped suit with a cane happens to be walking here right now!" Ray confirmed.

The silent men were startled and exchanged malevolent glances with each other, but still didn't open their mouths.

"So, what's going on?" Mr. Cage asked them as he sat down with the silent group, adjusting on his nose a pince-nez without any lenses.

One of the fat men with their arms crossed against their chests straightened them out only in order to explain with silent gestures that he would say not a word and pointed with his index finger at the gentleman to his left.

"Matthew, help us settle this," the neighbor to the left interrupted the silence. "We gathered here to play poker. Because we already had played Boston last week."

"Nonsense! I won at Boston, and three weeks had passed already since then!" inserted Mr. Gilbert.

"Rubbish! I lost at bridge only two days ago! According to our agreement, we must now play whist!" Mr. Myers slammed his hand down on the table.

"They are both lying! They had lost their shirts at whist only three days ago! Take a look under the table, Matthew!" the fat man broke his silence.

Mr. Gilbert and Mr. Myers hurriedly withdrew their shoe-less legs under and wrapped their jackets tighter around themselves, concealing in that manner the absence of shirts on their backs, evidence of their debacle in the last contest.

"Well and, what did you decide?" Mr. Cage asked, lowering his eyes to look at the legs that the losers had withdrawn between their tails.

"Nothing!" the fat man admitted. "We have been sitting here three days already without exchanging a word with each other!"

"I propose that we draw lots," Mr. Cage suggested, tentatively scratching the back of his head.

"The short straw - we play bridge, the middle one - it's poker, the long straw - and it's whist," Mr. Cage proposed, breaking the three straws into fragments of absolutely identical length, to avoid any possible new controversies.

There was a great hubbub on the town's central square.

"Dear Ladies, there are no losers in this competition! Please, come to your senses!" Ms. Melrow, the chairwoman of the Cross-stitching Club, entreated everyone.

"Not true! My tablecloth is longer than Ms. Barnes's!" Ms. Fine insisted, ready to fight tooth and nail.

"Shame on you, Brenda! Everyone can see for themselves that I am the victor, that mine is longer than yours by an entire inch!" Ms. Barnes defended herself, prepared to do battle.

"Well, what have we got here?" the invited Mr. Cage took an interest.

"Matthew!" Ms. Melrow, the chairwoman of the Cross-stitching Club, began.

"You have probably already heard that for the past week, we have been holding a competition for the longest cross-stitched tablecloth," she explained.

"So, who won?" Mr. Cage interrupted her, glancing impatiently at his pocket watch, racing relentlessly in the opposite direction from the hour hand.

"That is precisely what we have been unable to determine, Matthew!" Ms. Melrow proclaimed in desperation.

"By some strange and unexplained coincidence, Ms. Barnes and Ms. Fine started stitching the very same tablecloth, only from different ends. Now, that they have met in the middle, we are unable to determine whose half is longer!" the chairwoman of the club admitted heatedly.

"Hmmm," Mr. Cage scratched himself behind his ear.

"The answer is simple!" he joyfully raised his index finger and pointed it up at the sky.

"Both of them must start to undo their stitching from the middle back to their ends. The one who requires more time to do it is the one who had stitched the greater half!" decided Mr. Cage and everyone exhaled in relief.

"And what day of the month is it today?" the King was contemplating something, slouched on his throne.

"It is Friday, the thirty third," replied the Royal Scribbler.

"And what do we have on Fridays?" the King inquired, having forgotten, after the fashion fitting, to take the earrings off his earlobes.

"It is the day of important deliberations," the Royal Scribbler read aloud.

"Aha," the King once again fell back into his own thoughts.

"And what haven't we done in a long time?" the King appealed for help and glanced around himself, expecting to be prompted.

"We have not gone to war!" the First Lady-in-Waiting remembered.

"Yes, yes! We haven't gone to war in a long while!" the King rubbed his hands in glee.

"Who shall we go to war with?" the King pursed his brow.

"Of course, with our neighbors!" the Second Lady-in-Waiting not so subtly hinted.

"Pure Genius!" the King agreed.

"And who are our neighbors?" he wondered aloud once again.

"To the North – the Brits, to the South – the Duncans, to the East – the Trullers," the Royal Scribbler read aloud.

"Whom shall we begin with?" the King lowered his eyes absentmindedly.

"With the Trullers!" the Third Lady-in-Waiting proposed.

"Brilliant!" the King rejoiced.

"Declare war on the Trullers immediately! No! Without declaring war, attack the Trullers! This very evening!" the King ordered, taking pleasure in the martial tones of the sound of his voice.

"Your Majesty," the Fourth Lady-in-Waiting, who had been silent too long, interrupted.

"What's the matter?" the King, who had just already imagined himself triumphant, having conquered the Trullers, discontentedly replied.

"This evening we have already planned to play hide and seek in the dangerous and dark garden behind Your Majesty's estates," she reminded the King.

"Oh, yes! Of course!" the King recalled.

"And why didn't anyone remind me of this earlier?" he expressed his irritation.

All the courtiers froze still, afraid of being punished.

"But we could play war ourselves!" the First Lady-in-Waiting promptly found a way out.

"What do we need the Trullers for? They are so far away! We would have to pack up our things all day, just to be able to observe the battle on location," she complained.

"Brilliant!" the King could not be any happier now.

"What I want to know is, why hasn't anyone proposed this earlier? Let's play war! I'll be the Commander-in-Chief!" the King proclaimed, and jumped up on his throne with his feet, triumphantly hiking his arm with an invisible sword skyward.

"Hand the King his Sword!" the Second Lady-in-Waiting shouted out just in time, and all the courtiers surged and were off to the races in search of a suitable sword.

The city's main street was blocked by a slow-moving funeral procession. People dressed in dark clothes thronged, walking behind a tall gentleman who was ceremoniously carrying in his arms a sealed vase reminiscent of an urn. The sounds of a funeral march split the air, washing upwards in a way contrary to the smiling sun and the bright daylight.

Curious, Nimble Larry joined in, in the back, Hulking Bill, Duke, and Ike, followed behind, and Skinny Wilson trudged last.

"Who are they burying?" Archie expressed his interest to a miss with the sad face who was walking last in the procession line.

"Are you an outlander?" she raised her eyebrow, looking at him.

"We are the residents of Eighteenth Street. You, most likely, don't know anything about it, but we are always being oppressed by sad thoughts. No matter what happens, we always find a reason to be upset," she explained.

"We've already tried moving! Earlier, we had all lived on Sixteenth Street. But the sad thoughts found us in our new place as well, and now they are oppressing us at Eighteenth Street," the miss with the sad face confessed.

"Mr. Cage advised us to bury them. And so, we all wrote them down on little notes and placed them in an urn, which is now being carried by Mr. Parsons," she pointed to the man carrying the vase.

"Well, and so? Did it help?" Archie asked.

"So far, no," Ms. Mercer admitted in disappointment.

"But perhaps this is only because we have yet to bury them," she supposed.

"And you know, we don't really have time to think about it at all. It's already the second week that all we've been doing is organizing the funeral," Ms. Mercer added.

"We have already burned, drowned, and thrown them off roofs. So far, it's all been useless," Ms. Mercer from Eighteenth Street sadly lowered her eyes.

"Here I am, looking at you, and I'm thinking, that poor, poor man... What a long and difficult path had brought you here... and what a long and difficult one still awaits you," Ms. Mercer sighed.

There was nothing, beside the fact that this was all precisely so, that Archie could have said to her in reply.

"Attack!" the King screamed and rushed out from behind a bush in the palace garden.

"You're dead!" he whacked the gardener's back with his wooden sword.

The gardener, who was not taking part in the proceedings, decided to collapse dead anyway, pretending to have been slain.

"Ho-ho-ho!" the King chuckled triumphantly, passing the tip of the wooden sword back and forth across the man's chest, as though to make sure that the enemy was

no longer breathing.

"He's dead!" the First Lady-in-Waiting, now dressed in men's clothing, shouted and raised her sword triumphantly upward.

"But where are the Trullers?" the King paused.

The ladies-in-waiting, acting in the role of the Trullers, cowered, scattering around the garden.

"Let us advance, my general!" the First Lady-in-Waiting proposed.

And hopping up and down in a gallop while rhythmically clicking their tongues, they all set off in search of the enemy.

"Emily!" the Royal Scribbler called out quietly.

"Emily! Please take mercy on me, I beg of you!" he moaned to her.

"Simply just one squeeze of your little snow-white hand and I am already in heaven!" the Royal Scribbler pledged, clenching his eyes shut in expectation of the anticipated pleasure.

"Please be quiet, I ask you, Edward!" the Fourth Lady-in-Waiting placed her index finger to her lips imploringly.

"We can meet, but only later! Head toward the labyrinth; I will wait for you there. But please, be careful, Edward!" she whispered.

Drunk with ecstasy, the Royal Scribbler glanced all around him and, avoiding a direct path, weaving and zigzagging, flung himself in the direction of the palace labyrinth consisting of dense, green bushes that had been neatly trimmed by the gardener.

The Second and Third Ladies-in-Waiting depicting the Trullers stretched themselves out in the meadow, closing their eyes and smiling at the sun.

A gallop accompanied by the clicking of tongues was heard in the bushes.

"They are coming!" the Third Lady-in-Waiting jumped up.

"Lie back down!" the Second one commanded.

The Third Lady-in-Waiting, obeying her command, immediately flung herself in the grass, crushing her unruly, puffy skirt.

"There's no one here!" the First Lady-in-Waiting, still dressed in men's clothing, shouted.

"Advance, my general!" she proposed and quickly hopped over a low-lying bush.

"Ride in the lead, my friend!" the King commanded.

"I will outflank the enemy from the south and you will surround him!" he added.

"Brilliant!" the First Lady-in-Waiting agreed and quickly hopped away.

"Emily! I beg of you, have mercy on me!" the King whispered.

"Just simply a single object from your wardrobe and I am already in heaven!" he moaned.

"But, Your Majesty...," the Fourth Lady-in-Waiting froze still in confusion.

"If you must insist... Please take this!" and she offered him her lacy glove, pulling it off her hand.

"Oh, you are so generous, my dear!" the disarmed King pressed the trophy to his nose.

"Just like you, it smells of violets!" he purred, clenching his eyes shut.

"Quieter please! People are coming!" the Fourth Lady-in-Waiting warned him and the King, loudly clicking his tongue, immediately rode away, raising his knees inordinately high.

"Stop!" the King shouted.

"You are dead! You poor, miserable Truller!" the King commanded and poked at him with his sword.

The Royal Scribbler, as if on command, collapsed in the grass, shutting his eyes and not stirring.

"Charge! Victory is at hand!" the King screamed and rode on, clicking with his tongue.

The Royal Scribbler cautiously raised his head, waiting to make sure that the coast was clear, and then leapt up and flung himself toward the labyrinth, the entire time glancing from side to side.

The First Lady-in-Waiting, dressed in men's clothing, lay stretched out in the meadow, her eyes closed.

The King rode by, without noticing her, the wooden sword in his raised hand. The First Lady-in-Waiting hid and, once the danger had passed, shifted to her side.

The hem of the royal frock became stuck in the labyrinth's bushes, which the King was trying to squeeze himself though, planning to take the disarmed enemy by surprise.

Not finding any help, he forcefully tugged on the edge, but the hem did not budge. He pulled harder and, cursing quietly, felt about with his hand in the dense foliage.

"The sun! You are the sun shining in the heavenly firmament! No! You are a seagull soaring above the sea! My Lord, your aroma! You are a little flower, a little heavenly flower from the Garden of Eden!" and the Royal Scribbler showered the royal wrist, garbed in the Fourth Lady's in Waiting lacy glove, with kisses.

"Nincompoop!" the King shouted, jerking away his arm and squeezing his head though the dense bushes.

"You've been killed already!" he remembered.

And the Royal Scribbler gladly dropped dead, not stirring an inch and tightly clenching his eyes shut.

Pudgy Bryan and Brandon were reading from a book the next day at school, as was the custom in the city of San Dulcedo, from its end to its beginning.

Their eyes, gliding along the lines on the page from the bottom to the top, did not register the least bit of sense, given such a reading, just as they did from their entire topsy-turvy school program. And so, both of them hopped off the windowsill, as it was permitted to sit anywhere one wished in the classroom, and with difficulty started peeling off their hard candies out of their pockets, long ago stuck there to their lining.

The teacher, Mr. Watson, was reading the local paper, his legs stretched out on

the teacher's table, marveling at the events that did not fit in with his own worldview.

"Just you look and see!" the teacher exclaimed.

"At the Flea Races, in the final race, the victor was Sean." Ms. Price had told me: Bet on Sean! But, no, the Devil got me to bet on Bob! And I lost! I got totally crushed!" Mr. Watson shouted, grabbing his head in his arms.

"Mrs. Watson won't let me back in the house today!" he collapsed with his entire body on the table and covered himself with the Trivial News newspaper.

"Mr. Watson! How long will this go on? Each time, we have to sit through your performance, so that you can coax a couple of gold pieces from us!" the disgruntled class shouted.

"But you know, I manage pretty well each time," the teacher winked cunningly with one eye, peeking out at them over his paper.

"This is the last time we are lending you any money. And stop betting on the Flea Races, especially on Bob," Morgan warned him.

"Bob and Hugh are dragging their tiny little paws already. This is their final season; they've already gotten old and are about to retire. Make way for the young, you know, Mr. Watson!" the children explained to him.

And then they reluctantly passed around a cap, tossing some gold pieces in it, for the deeply indebted teacher.

"Thank you! You really saved my life!" Mr. Watson bowed his head gratefully.

"And don't you forget," he warned them.

"We know, we know!" the students interrupted him.

"No gallivanting about, you just sit at home doing nothing, no reading, eat as many sweets as possible, no doing homework assignments and, in no instance, ever listen to a grown up!" he ended the class.

"Yes, yes, you are my golden ones! Everyone, everyone today gets an automatic D! As you already know, you don't have to learn anything, but I will give them to you anyway!" and the teacher smiled at all of them in farewell.

Pudgy Bryan and Brandon were trading their hard candies, providently stashed for them in their school bags by Ms. Griffin, for chocolates. The stick-thin brothers Louis and Lloyd, impatient to possess the desired candy, were stretching out their arms to them with their own melting pieces of chocolate.

"Are you going to be finished anytime soon?" Mr. Goodman called them to attention.

"Can't you see for yourself? We haven't finished eating yet!" the brothers Griffin growled in irritation.

"And we still haven't gotten the hard candies back from them!" complained skinny Louis and Lloyd.

"We don't want to play football today anyway!" shouted Bryan and Brandon.

"We don't want to either!" skinny Louis and Lloyd insisted.

"Nor do we-e-e-e!" the entire class started shouting over each other.

"If you only knew how much I don't want to either" replied Mr. Goodman, and he flung the old pumpkin that served as a ball way out in the bushes and plopped down on the grass relieved.

"Does anyone have something sweet for me today?" Mr. Goodman ventured meekly.

"Mr. Goodman! Stop begging!" Bryan objected.

"Yes, our mother warned us about this: don't even get it into your head to share your food with anyone, especially with the wily Mr. Goodman!" Brandon added.

"How long will this go on, Mr. Goodman?" complained Louis. "I shared my chocolate with you every day last week! And you still did not give me the D you promised!" he explained.

"No wa-a-ay? He still hasn't? He had promised me a D for my hard candy just two days ago! And it was my very last one, and just, you know, my favorite!" Morgan recalled fondly.

"Liar! I brought him a piece of cake every day for a whole month!"

"And I brought him licorice for a week!" the children yelled out, interrupting each other.

"OK, OK, already, everyone gets a D, just as I promised you!" groaned Mr. Goodman.

"Only, please, somebody, give me something sweet to eat right away?" Mr. Goodman begged them.

And Pudgy Bryan and Brandon both reluctantly stuck their hands back in and resumed scraping their old hard candies from the lining of their pockets.

On Saturday, the sweet city of San Dulcedo was deep in preparations for its sweetest holiday. Tables had been set up on both the right and the left sides of its narrow lanes and smaller squares. All of them were loaded with the exquisite delights produced by the town's pastry chefs. Multistory meringue cakes, with a thousand little sugar roses resting on them. Countless platters of all sorts of pastry: vanilla, strawberry, raspberry, chocolate, all decorated with a cream curlicue, a drizzle of transparent gelatin, or the dark splash of a cherry on top. The chewy caramel, powdered with sugar, like twisted snakes with their sweet tails retracted, trailed down in rings from the wooden trays. Every table was temptingly beckoning you to it, promising sweets, heavenly delights, and confections that melt immediately in your mouth. The central square was blocked off by a table placed perpendicularly, proudly displaying a truly great sample of culinary art. On a round and humongous plate, raised up high on a silver base, the city's inhabitants were greeted by a likeness of their king's sweet head, wearing a wig made of meringue, powdered with powdered sugar, with sour cherry eyes, and a yellow-green smile made of translucent apple sauce.

"Long Live the King!"

"Long Live our Sweetest King!" the inhabitants hailed the royal retinue, with the Ruler at its head.

The King exactingly inspected every table, modestly smiling and marveling at the novel confectionery inventions before him, and picked off, here and there, a cherry or two from the pastries that he found most appealing.

"To your health, Your Highness!" the First Lady-in-Waiting meowled, obediently opening her mouth to meet the royal cherry.

"My dear, I will save the sweetest pastry for you!" the King whispered into the ear of the Fourth Lady-in-Waiting.

Emily turned beet red and lowered her eyes. Secretly fondling her hand, the Royal Scribbler, gleefully took this to be on account of him.

The crew of the Celestine went stumbling about, their empty stomachs churning, among the many riches of the kingdom of sugar.

"Hey! Outlander!" a smiling roly-poly saleswoman called Ike over to her.

"Try my pastries, you won't regret it!" she winked at him.

"I'll bet mine are sweeter?" her neighbor interjected, temptingly raising her plate up to Skinny Wilson's nose.

"Hey! Are you the captain?" a dark-eyed beauty called out to Archie, showing off her table buckling under the weight of her cream-filled delicacies frosted with all the shades and hues of chocolate.

Archie glanced over at the meringue and cream-filled mountains and drowned in the slightly Asiatic eyes of the stunning brunette. The sweet ladies, playfully nestling in the men's laps, were laughing haughtily while teasingly stuffing the open and starving mouths of the pirates with their bittersweet concoctions.

Apparently, inasmuch as it proved impossible to stuff oneself with so much sweet stuff, even for an entire city, the Festival of Sweets always concluded in a wild, pie-in-the-face tossing, free-for-all fracas.

Those with their heads already white with whipped cream, from the cakes that had just been flung at them, in revenge, would wind up and hurl back plates of sugar-powdered pastries at their opponents.

Everything went flying and made a muffled thumping sound, splattered, or sluiced down the faces, clothing, and hair of the participants. A white sugary haze hung suspended in the alleyways between the houses, through which it was impossible to see either the victors or the defeated, all of them blindly palpating the tables in search of the as yet untouched sugary trophies.

Under the central table of the festivity, rescuing herself from the sweetness of skirmish, her face smeared with white cream, the Fourth Lady-in-Waiting kept obediently opening her mouth, allowing the King to hand feed her the twenty-fifth cherry. Having noticed the Royal Scribbler crawling towards her under the table, his face similarly smeared with cream, she managed to swerve in time, and the twenty-sixth royal cherry landed in the mouth of the Royal Scribbler, who had gaped it for a secret kiss.

In the morning, Ms. Griffin sent Ray, who had risen before the rest, off to the candy store to buy licorice, that had run out. Ray wandered down the powdered streets that had yet to be cleaned by anyone, and the sweet smell of yesterday's sweet combat sickened him.

"Good morning!" Ray greeted the inexplicably frowning Ms. Swift, the door to whose pastry shop was for some reason propped open, so that the silent doorbell did not announce the visitor.

Contrary to Ms. Griffin's order, Ray had an irresistible urge for a plain, old unsweetened white bread bun and he handed over to Ms. Swift his coin having entirely forgotten about the licorice.

"A bun? You'd like a bun?" Ms. Swift jerked up her eyebrow.

Ray nodded, and guiltily shrugged his shoulders. Leaving the pastry shop, Ray's gaze was suddenly directed downward. The door with the silent little bell above it was being propped up by the needed by no one and entirely meaningless in this world magical blue Frindigoffle, which had dulled from all the gray roadside dust mixed together with the powdered sugar. Clenching in his hand the little paper bag with the plain bun, Ray sank down to his knees and retrieved the magical stone. The door immediately slammed shut, striking the little bell, which did not fail to let out a ring.

"Guards! Catch the thief!" Ms. Swift screamed.

And, as if out of nowhere, two tall guards dressed in iron armor lifted Ray up and out into the street under his armpits and immediately dragged him away.

"The clock on the city tower struck two and a half minutes past ten. The brass hum of the bell still hung suspended in the warm air, just as the most distinguished members of the court, raising gingerly the hems of their long, dark robes, were climbing up its dust-covered stone steps, their heads drooping low, as though weighed down by worldly concerns. Their black hoods, entirely covering their foreheads, draped down almost to their eyelashes, hiding even their gazes from the prying eyes of the crowd.

The somewhat befuddled members of the jury and a sea of the curious faces of the onlookers, flowing together like columns of ants, were already filling the great hall of the courtroom. The sun's rays were trying to tickle their serious faces, but the thick, pale yellow, stone walls barely admitted them through the narrow slits of the tall oval windows.

The iron-clad sentries with their tall and pointy spears, their faces covered by masks with only a slit for the eyes, carried in the heavy cage. Huddling inside it, like a hunted animal, quivering in fear in its furthest corner, was the body of a small child.

"Your Majesty, the Laws of our Grandest of States were violated in the most horrible manner and, moreover, deliberately and cold-bloodedly, by this wayward child! I call upon you to declare the boy guilty of all of the seventeen charges of the indictment!

Charge the First. After the "Festival of Sweets," in accordance with our King's latest proclamation, all are supposed to sleep in till noon. Rising before the time designated is permitted only to pastry chefs, so that they may distribute their freshly baked goods. This rude boy was found wandering around the city alone in ignorance of the aforementioned decree.

Charge the Second. In accordance with our King's declaration, the customary morning greeting after the "Festival of Sweets" is "Good evening!"

This urchin dared to greet Ms. Swift with a "Good morning!"

Charge the Third. On the morning of the "Festival of Sweets," only licorice is bun!

The senseless charges read out by the prosecution were stringing themselves together, one on top of each other, forming an endlessly long verbal

boa constrictor that was now stretching itself towards Ray's youthful neck. Like a pyramid made of a child's play cubes, all the nonsense was piling up in the courtroom until it reached its vaulted ceiling, accompanied by the reproachful wagging of all the heads stuffed with this gibberish. This kingdom of the absurd, ruled over by the royal fool himself, determined everyone's fate, like a careless infant, waving around a dangerous, sharp dagger in his tiny little hand.

Ray already knew what would happen next, having previously opened the book in this terrible place.

"Taking into consideration the uncertain origins of the foreigner boy, who does not possess knowledge of the Laws of our Most Sacred of States, I ask the court to be lenient in its sentence. And to substitute the public quartering on the city's main square with an execution by hanging on the smaller square, behind City Hall," the defense interceded.

The morning of the execution was slightly chilly, fragrant, and piercingly silent. The child's bare feet, bound in shackles, barely surmounted the damp and cold steps of the dungeon. The early morning breeze fluttered the heap of the child's hair, and it seemed that for the breeze alone, the crude iron grating was no obstacle in this. The cart kept bouncing over and over on the pavement cobblestones, and the guards, sensing the importance of the impending hour of retribution, stretched to their full height as though on a string, as though it were an entire enemy army and not a single lonesome, little boy, that was being led to its execution."

"Hey, Ray!" Nimble Larry quietly called out to him from below, sticking like glue to the bottom of the cart.

"Hey, Ray!" a saleswoman passing by raised her headscarf to reveal Pudgy Ike's face.

"Hey Ray!" a pauper with a dirty hood called out to him, before pulling it off to reveal Archie's face smeared with soot.

"Away with you, you iron devils!" Hulking Bill barked out, falling down from somewhere up above and, like a log, knocking down the two iron guards at once with one stone.

The guards collapsed to the ground like mowed down grass, and the spooked horses neighed and reared on their hind legs. Nimble Larry found by feel the right key in the bunch of them on one of the steel hips. Cook Duke and Skinny Wilson whopped the shinning helmet with something heavy as it tried to get up.

"[]-[]-archie!" Ray shouted, having jumped out of the cage.

"I have i-i-i-it!" he burst out laughing in exultation, wiping away tears of joy and taking out of his pocket the magical indigo blue Frindigoffle that was not needed, and would not be missed, by anyone in this world.

The Celestine was flying along the smooth surface of the sea like a strong, daring, young animal issuing its challenge to the entire animal world.

Remaining far behind them was the sweet city of San Dulcedo, in which, as soon as the haze of powdered sugar dissipates after the latest pie-in-the-face, free-for-all fracas, according to the King's latest decree, in honor of his triumph over the Trullers, everyone will consume licorice at breakfast, followed by a cream puff, and drink it all down with some bittersweet lemonade. And the obstinate Mrs. Watson will, finally, pay off her spouse's, the teacher Mr. Watson's, debts to his students. Of course, only if Bob, gathering up his remaining strength, before his well-earned retirement, gives the Flea Races an encore performance, and shows Sean, Floyd, Phil, and Hugh who among them is the real boss!

Chapter Fifteen

A Hair's Breadth from Certain Death

The magical indigo blue Frindigoffle slipped softly into the sixth little pocket in the hem of Celestine's skirt. Archie could not believe his eyes, but only the seventh pocket still remained empty. The prospect of victory now seemed palpable, one only had to stretch out one's hand to welcome it. The pages of Cook's Secret Book were silent, but the pride of having overcome the long and arduous path behind them made Archie feel invigorated. The crew of the Celestine was bustling about, having come to miss working together on deck, as though it had grown closer during their journey and, for no reason in this world, would wish to be deprived of a single one of the links in its chain.

"Hey, Duke! What are you going to do with your money?" shouted Nimble Larry, smiling cunningly.

"I've had second thoughts about opening a restaurant!" Duke replied, launching a peeled potato into the kettle pot.

"I'll probably sign up as a cook on some brigantine! Things would be too painfully dreary without the sea," Duke confessed.

"Ike and I will probably buy a brigantine!" Larry chuckled.

"Will you take me on? I will miss your pirate mugs!" Hulking Bill barked out.

"And you, Wilson?" shouted Nimble Larry.

"I'll buy myself an island," Skinny Wilson's face twisted into a smile.

"And retire to my well-earned rest!" he burst out laughing in a leery manner.

"You lose again, Wilson!" Pudgy Ike yelped with excitement and, slinging cards with Wilson, plunked down an ace.

"Pull off your boots, you old sea devil!" Ike burst out laughing.

"You're the one that's lost, fatso!" Wilson scowled.

"You take off your jacket! You little shark snack!" he snapped back.

"You, ugly mug," Ike got up and, barely having had time to roll up one sleeve, punched Wilson full force in the jaw.

Skinny Wilson flew back, raised himself slightly, passed his sleeve over his bloodied mouth, and spat out a loose tooth.

"I'm gonna get you, you rattlesnake," Wilson hissed out and flung himself with all his might at Ike, prepared to punch holes with his sharp fists in his fat stomach.

They tangled in such a tight coil that it was impossible even to distinguish whose fists were now swinging away or whom they were pounding.

Boom! A cannon ball flew by them, barely missing the Celestine's stern.

Bang! And another one flew by, plopping down thunderously in the water.

Archie jumped out on deck.

"Return the enemy fire!" he screamed.

Pudgy Ike, Hulking Bill, and Nimble Larry ran over to the cannon.

"Load it!" Archie commanded.

Hulking Bill carried the incredibly heavy cannonball over.

Boom! The Celestine fired back but missed the enemy vessel. Bang! Another incoming enemy fire came crashing down beside the stern. Boom! The Celestine replied, missing once again.

Ray rushed about on deck, carrying over reloaded muskets as they were needed.

Such a curtain of smoke hung above the deck that it was impossible to take aim, and the thunder of the incoming artillery rounds drowned out all the other sounds.

The cannon balls were raining down to the right and to the left, and it seemed that the enemy was playing a mean joke on the Celestine, trying to frighten its crew without ever actually sinking the ship. Boom! Another round came smashing down, barely missing portside. Suddenly, the smoke started to clear, and Archie immediately glued himself to Cook's spyglass. Laughing maniacally on the deck of the galley that was firing at them was the Black Devil and doing a little victory dance around him was the one-eyed man who, now and then, would take a suckling swig out of a bottle he was carrying.

"Hey, you, my piddly little captain!" In the morning, the pages of Cook's Secret Book again began to speak.

"Why choose such a difficult path? Wouldn't it be easier for you and your blockheads to simply croak under fire? After all, one can only die a single death. Or do you wish to experience an entire hundred? Here is your riddle, you, stubborn mug, you, if you're still even searching for the last magical stone, that is!

TIME IS A BIRD; IT CAN'T BE KEPT IN A CAGE.
AND HE WHO DOES SO, WILL
LANGUISH FOR A CENTURY.

If you puzzle it out, then just perhaps you will find the violet magical Floviolesbel, after all!

The devils have pulled a good one! They fried up two musicians last night but left the basses for later. The grating here is so unbearable now, I tell you, that the new recruits are begging to be boiled in oil themselves! Ho-ho-ho!"

FLOVAILSBEL

Chapter Sixteen

Sanct Tempus, the City of the Most Precise Clocks

"Vincent," the Emperor barely managed to raise himself up.

"When I am no longer alive, and I have a feeling that this will happen very soon, you will have to assume the reigns of our city," the Emperor whispered in a hoarse voice.

"Father!" Vincent was stunned, jumping up from the edge of the sick man's bed.

"So be it, Vincent. Remember my instructions: never trust anyone and...," the Emperor's voice broke and he once again dropped back heavily on the pillow, while still clenching his son's hand.

The monkey Chichi, nimbly descending down the dark bed canopy that surrounded the head of the bed, jumped down on the Emperor's legs covered by a blanket and started repetitively waving her head.

"La-a-and aho-o-oy!" shouted Ray.

"La-a-and aho-o-oy!" exclaimed Ike, Duke, and Larry.

"La-a-and aho-o-oy!" confirmed Skinny Wilson.

"La-a-and aho-o-oy!" barked Hulking Bill.

"Land ahoy!" Archie thought to himself, staring greedily into Cook's spyglass.

A strange sound – tic-toc, tic-toc, tic-toc – that hung suspended in the air, greeted the crew of the Celestine as soon as they moored.

Ike and Duke stopped in their tracks and listened in, having just come ashore from their ship.

Ray ran, hopping and skipping, in front of the rest, and Hulking Bill and Wilson were looking around themselves this way and that. Archie closed his eyes, trying to guess which direction the wind that was carrying this quiet, monotonous striking of a clock was blowing from.

The crew of the Celestine was walking down the sidewalks of the city of Sanct Tempus, a city that could not be recognized by either the cries of sea gulls, nor by the shouting of women street vendors, nor by the quayside cursing of sailors, nor the noise of public carousal. The city of Sanct Tempus was ticking like a single, gigantic clock and this sound – tic-toc, tic-toc, tic-toc – hung suspended between its plazas, houses, and streets, huddled in its alleyways, and soared up under its roofs. It seemed that, any time soon, the next hour would be rung by a huge, invisible pendulum forcefully striking their cornices.

"Abigail! Abigail! Abigail!" a woman on the embankment was calling out in confusion and waving her head.

A young girl with fiery red hair suddenly jumped down from somewhere up

above, nearly knocking Ray off his feet.

"Where have you been? Were you climbing the tower again?" her mother yelled angrily.

"No-o!" Abigail lied.

"Can't you see? I was helping the outlanders find the way to Mr. Parker's!" she immediately came up with an alibi, giving Ray a nudge.

"I noticed you a long time ago from up above! I can see everything from the tower!" she whispered into Ray's ear, pointing with her eyes in the direction of the city's clock tower.

"Are you looking for Mr. Parker?" the woman with the tightly pulled back hair asked.

The crew of the Celestine exchanged glances shrugging their shoulders, Archie nodded in agreement.

"Just follow us, we are going the same way," the woman called out to them, looking reproachfully at her daughter.

Tic-toc, tic-toc, tic-toc followed after them wherever they went.

"Where is that sound coming from?" Archie asked, raising his index finger skyward.

"Don't you know?" Ms. Hudson expressed her surprise.

"We produce the most precise clocks in the world! And we also send them across the entire world!" she explained, graciously smiling at the ignorance of these foreigners.

"Isn't it the reason why you came here?" she glanced mistrustfully at Archie.

"We are visited by many foreign ships. They buy so many clocks from us that we must immediately assemble new ones, or we would have nothing left to offer our next customers!" Ms. Hudson bragged.

Ray's stare lingered on the old city clock tower.

"Oops!" he cried out having tripped over a cobblestone.

"Are you staying with us a while?" Abigail asked, staring at Ray.

"I'll come for you!" Abigail immediately promised, smiling and not waiting for a reply.

In the window of every shop one could see a clockmaker at work bent over his or her table.

"This is Mr. Bush; he fashions the thinnest clock hands in the world! And this is Ms. Dickinson - she paints the numerals onto the clock faces. This is Mr. Day - he decorates our clocks with natural crystal. And this is Mr. Charleson - he attaches to our clocks the most beautiful chains in the world!" Ms. Hudson explained, pointing to the shops on her right and her left.

"And here are Mr. and Mrs. Parker! They make the most beautiful boxes in the world for our clocks! And they also happen to rent out rooms," Ms. Hudson smiled, knocking at the door.

All of Mr. and Mrs. Parker rooms were piled with little boxes, or more precisely, in Mr. and Mrs. Parker's house, a thousand little boxes of all colors and sizes were piled accurately into multi-story towers, rising from floor to ceiling.

"Some people think that what we do isn't very important!" Mrs. Parker complained angrily, ladling out the hot soup for the crew of the Celestine.

"But what would they sell their clocks in, if it weren't for our little boxes?" she objected to the injustice.

"Brenda!" Mr. Parker grunted unhappily.

"Our visitors have only just landed on our shores and don't want to hear all your problems! Besides, they've come for our most precise clocks in the world, and not for idle gossip," and he winked at Archie.

"Damn it!" Duke burned himself on the hot soup.

"Last year, the order for the round boxes for pocket watches went to Mr. and Mrs. Bailey! Can you believe what is going on?" Mrs. Parker could not calm down.

Hulking Bill got the last, crusty butt of bread and, deciding to dunk it, accidentally drowned it in his bowl of soup.

"Damn it!" he cursed, burning his fingers trying to fish out his sodden crust out of the scalding hot soup.

"Bailey is making boxes only for the second generation! Mr. Parker and I are already the fourth!" Mrs. Parker raised her eyebrows in indignation.

"Darn it!" Wilson, burning his tongue, started sucking on his cool spoon.

"The world has been turned upside down, when they start handing out such important requisitions to incompetents and upstarts!" Mrs. Parker concluded angrily.

The cupboard in Mr. and Mrs. Parker's dining room was covered with clocks of all shapes and sizes. It was clear that they, like a tiny but proud cog in the larger mechanism of production of these most precise clocks in the world, could not but feast their eyes on the principal good of their city, seeking, day and night, to sense themselves an important component of the greater, communal whole.

"Harold," the Emperor called out.

"When I am no longer alive, Vincent must take my place," he whispered quietly in a hoarse voice.

"But, Emperor, it is too early for you to think of your demise." The servant of time bowed his head.

"My days are numbered, Harold... But the people need an Emperor. Vincent is still a child; Jordan and you must help him. Authority that is placed in weak hands is placed in danger," the Emperor said quietly and slumped back down to his pillow, having exhausted himself.

Harold stood a while with his eyes lowered at the head of the sick man's bed. He then tugged on the tassel that gathered in the canopy of the bed and, as soon as the heavy, dark fabric obscured the helpless Emperor, gingerly left the room, quietly closing the door behind himself. Chichi, having followed Harold with her gaze, quickly hopped down from the windowsill and, having raced around the foot of the bed, instantly jumped up on it, landing squarely at the Emperor's feet.

"Jordan!" Harold whispered, face to face with the Servant of Time, who was awaiting him anxiously.

"The old man senses he doesn't have long to live," he smiled cunningly.

"Luck won't be smiling on us, if we don't get him to drink the potion one more time... We must serve him from this goblet," Jordan replied quietly, his eyes jubilantly twinkling.

"Just a little while longer and the path to the throne will be ours! Oh, Dear Lord, when will he finally do us a favor and get out of the way,"

Harold implored.

The dark walls of the Emperor's chambers shamelessly listened in on this private conversation, powerless to interfere with its malicious intent.

Mr. and Mrs. Parker's doorbell rang and then, getting no reply, the door was almost immediately impatiently knocked upon.

"Thirty-three little boxes for Mr. Day!" Abigail announced as soon as Mrs. Parker appeared in the doorway.

"No, not you! What's your name again?" and she glanced behind Mrs. Parker's back.

"Ray!" Ray replied, peeking out from behind their hostess.

"Get your shoes on, quickly, and follow me, you bench-warmer, you!" fiery-haired Abigail ordered him impudently about.

And Ray was off and out the door almost immediately, pulling his jacket on on the run.

"Tic-toc, tic-toc, tic-toc," the sound followed after them wherever they ran.

The girl with the fiery red hair was racing down the streets, taking kitty-corner shortcuts to cross them, jumping headlong on the curb stones, hopping as high as she could to see if she could touch all the windowsills, walking along the tops of the roadside stones, holding her arms out to balance herself.

Ray had no idea where they were running too and, just in case, he kept on turning to look back, and asking himself: could he, if he ever had to, find his way back?

"Mr. Day! Thirty-three little boxes from Mr. and Mrs. Parker!" Abigail reported, as soon as Mr. Day flung open his door.

"Abigail, you're wonderful! If you should happen to drop in on Mr. Charleson today too, please tell him that for our next batch, instead of the usual gold chains, we will need bronze once!"

"Abigail!" a very skinny kid peeked out from behind Mr. Day's back.

"Vincent!" she said, happy to see him.

"Get your shoes on, quickly!" Abigail burst out laughing.

"Hey, Vincent! A couple of more lessons and Sanct Tempus will have a second master crystal maker!" Mr. Day smiled, praising him in farewell.

Pale and scrawny Vincent, Abigail with her fiery red hair, and Ray were racing down the city streets, taking kitty-corner shortcuts to cross them, jumping headlong on the curb stones, hopping as high as they could to see if they could touch all the windowsills, walking along the tops of the roadside stones, holding their arms out to balance themselves.

"Tic-toc, tic-toc, tic-toc," the sound followed them wherever they ran.

"Here you are, little cogwheel," Mr. Carroll whispered, handling his pincers with a barely noticeable tremor.

"And here's another... And here are the tiny screws...And here's the gear... And now the little hand, and...." A pocket watch, in Mr. Carroll's masterful hands,

seemed a soulless bauble until that moment when it suddenly came to life, when its heart began to beat.

"They're ticking, my precious!" Mr. Carroll greeted them as though they were a newborn, smiling benevolently at his own creation.

Vincent, Ray, and Abigail bent their heads over the table – the tiny little screws, cogwheels, and gears seemed, obedient in the master's fingers, tiny, barely visible dots, that scattered in all directions from the slightest breath of air from the mouths of the three curious and attentive children.

"Hey, Ray!" redheaded Abigail was pointing at a street sign, barely catching her breath, having just ran over there from around the corner.

"The Street of Silence," Ray read the tablet.

"This is where all the clock mechanisms are calibrated, it is forbidden to even speak aloud here," Abigail whispered to him quietly.

Ray nodded knowingly, while Vincent and Abigail, holding their index fingers up to their lips, got up on their tiptoes. Having gone half-way down the street communicating with each other only through gestures, they suddenly burst out laughing and jeering as hard as they could.

"You fell for it! You fell for it!" they teased him good-naturedly, doubled over in laughter, while Ray was still treading cautiously on his tiptoes, peeking into random windows with bated breath.

"I'll race you to the clock tower!" Abigail proposed, and two more sets of flashing heels immediately flung themselves after hers.

The dark, weathered stones of the old city tower gawked at the fearless visitors with interest.

"Hey, Ray!" Abigail shouted. "Be careful! The step here has

collapsed!"

"The next one, too!" Vincent added.

Ray, stepping slowly, placed his foot still higher, carefully finding by feel a dependable stone under his foot.

"Why is it that in your city, where there are so many clockmakers, the clock on your main tower isn't working?" Ray expressed his surprise.

"They stopped on the day that my mother died," Vincent replied.

"And then my father, the Emperor, decided that that is how it should remain, in her memory...," he quietly added.

"Hey! Everyone, come over here!" Abigail called to them from somewhere far above.

Ray and Vincent rushed up towards her and froze still beside the tiny window. The sea was caressing this small corner of the gently sloping shore, and the old stone tower rose up like a lighthouse over the quiet embankment, its clock hands forever stilled in memory of the early and dearly departed wife and mother.

"Hey! Watch out!" yelled two giants, dragging in their muscular arms a wooden cog twice the size of Ray himself.

"Now that's a wheel!" Ray was stunned.

"Our best clockmakers are competing to show off their skills today!" Abigail rejoiced.

"Let's run! You won't get to see this anywhere else!" she winked at Ray.

"Mr. Day says that, in a couple of years, I will be able to take my place among them," skinny and pale Vincent added proudly.

"Wa-atch ou-ut!" screamed two fat men, who were rolling two huge winding knobs along the ground.

The central square, decorated for the competition, was thronged with people. At the tables that were set up around it sat clockmakers, their heads bent low, working their magic on the mechanisms, as they competed for the title that was awarded annually.

"Hey, Ray! Just look at this!" together with the entire crew of the Celestine, Hulking Bill was staring in amazement at the gigantic cog wheel that had now been rolled into place where the clock was going to be assembled.

The two giant strongmen, obeying the master's orders, were dragging huge wooden screws for what, according to the clockmaker, Mr. Brooks, would be the world's largest clock.

"Cogs – to the right, screws – to the left!" Mr. Brooks commanded.

"And where do we put the hands?" the two giants stared at him expectantly, barely holding up the giant clock hands, longer than long ship oars, on their bowed backs.

"Be careful! Put them over here!" Mr. Brooks yelled out, anxiously circling around the two workhorses.

"Hey Ray! Look over here!" Nimble Larry called to him, pointing with his finger at the neighboring table.

The master craftsman's table was surrounded by curious onlookers so that Ray and Nimble Larry were with great difficulty barely able to squeeze through the crowd. The wooden box opened to welcome everyone, and music came sounding out of its round base, slowly rotating to the beat, as a shepherd playing a pipe rolled out of his enclosure. After the little shepherd moved on, three little rams, who were slowly nodding their heads, came into view. After the little rams, there appeared a shepherdess with a basket of flowers who was spinning around rhythmically together with the rest of the figures. The long minute hand budged and the little shepherd with the pipe, the rams with the nodding heads, and the shepherdess with the basket of flowers all hid from view until the top of the next hour. The rapt audience began to applaud, as Ray and Nimble Larry exchanged surprised glances.

As though entirely uninterested in the mechanical wonders on display and the victors awarded the title of master clockmaker, by the roadside, a dark-haired beauty was selling from a basket of green apples.

"Hey, stranger! Taste these, you won't regret it," she smiled coquettishly, batting her black eyelashes.

Archie turned around and, stunned, froze in his tracks, wanting, more than anything else in this world, to taste her green apples.

Duke, Ike, and Wilson were staring at Mr. Allen's table.

Mr. Allen sat hunched over his work, from time to time straightening his back out and then again sticking his nose practically into the table. A plump madam with two restless children, a young couple, a man with a wiry mustache, and a couple of stick-thin acquaintances were waiting for the performance to begin. Mr. Allen waved his hand, and everyone bent low over his table. Spinning around to the sound of music on the round circus arena was a juggling monkey and the figure of an elephant, rising up on its hind legs and catching rings on

its trunk, stretched out and upwards, that were being flung by a cat dressed in a hat and a woman's dress. The minute hand budged and the circus performers vanished until the next full hour, leaving the size-of-an-apple circus arena empty again. Duke, Ike, and Wilson froze still in amazement. Ray and Nimble Larry exchanged stunned glances and shook their heads at this marvel.

Jordan's trembling hands raised a tiny vial up to the light. The dark mixture filled it barely half-way. Having struggled to unseal its round lid, he carefully squirted twelve drops into a tall, shinning goblet. Standing behind his back, Harold listened cautiously to the sound of the receding steps and stretched out his hand towards the filled-to-the-rim goblet.

The dark walls of the Emperor's chambers followed him with a reproachful glance, being powerless to save a life that had now been placed in danger. Chichi, suddenly anxious, started hooting and hollering, but Harold immediately shoved her out of the way with a powerful sweep of his leg.

"Harold," the Emperor called out to him.

"I am here, my Master," the Servant of Time replied, raising the heavy curtains of the canopy bed.

"And this year's winner and holder of "the Master of knavish intent and magic fingers" title is... The title is awarded to...," the self-important Ms. Ball shouted out, but Ray could no longer hear her voice, because the bell on the city clock tower had, for some reason, began ringing in alarm, drowning out the general hubbub on the plaza.

"Where is Archie?" Nimble Larry suddenly started looking around for him.

"He went off to buy some green apples from that brown-eyed beauty!" Hulking Bill burst out laughing.

"Her name is Jenna," Abigail turned pale.

"Who?" Ray was frightened by the expression on her face.

"It's the Black Widow," confirmed the skinny, pale Vincent.

"Only once each year does she descend out of the mountains to choose her intended. But no one has ever again seen the men she has led astray this way into the mountains," Abigail replied and, growing silent, stared at Ray.

"Archie! Archie! A-a-r-chie!" Ray screamed.

But his helpless scream was muffled by the accelerating ringing of the bell and the unexpected exclamation of the throng: "The Emperor! The Emperor!"

"Father!" Vincent cried out.

Out of dread, and because nothing else had come into his head at that moment, Ray started running away. He ran down the sidewalks, cut corners, crossed streets, and passed entire neighborhoods. The road led him uphill and then back down, and he didn't know which way he ought to run in order to find Archie. When twilight had crept in upon the city, he came out on an embankment and helplessly drooped down on a large, cold stone. Tucking in his tired legs under himself, Ray didn't even have time to notice that he was overcome by sleep.

"Tic-toc, tic-toc, tic-toc," the sound reached Ray's ears and he only managed to open his sleepy eyes with great difficulty.

"Ray, can you hear that?" Nimble Larry asked him, listening intently and raising his finger in the air.

Ike and Duke, walking out in front, stopped and also listened in. Archie closed his eyes and bowed his head, trying to guess what direction the wind that was carrying this quiet, monotonous ringing was blowing in from. Ray jumped up and saw that the entire crew of the Celestine was standing around him.

"◌-Archie! ◌-◌-Archie!" he shouted joyfully.

"Shhh!" Archie whispered, still attentively listening in.

"Tic-toc, tic-toc, tic-toc," the sound reverberated in the morning air. The city of Sanct Tempus was ticking like a single, huge clock.

"Abigail! Abigail! Abigail!" a woman was crying out in distress on the embankment and shaking her head.

The girl with fiery red hair, suddenly, jumped down from somewhere above them, almost knocking Ray down off his feet.

"Where were you? Were you climbing the tower again?" the mother shouted out angrily.

"No-o!" Abigail lied.

"Can't you see? I was helping the visitors find their way to Mr. Parker's!" she immediately came up with an alibi, nudging at Ray.

"I could see all of you from the tower a long time ago! I can see everything from the tower!" she whispered into Ray's ear, pointing with her eyes in the direction of the city clock tower.

Ray could not believe his own eyes: this abominable, cursed, bedeviled day was beginning to repeat itself all over again! He pinched himself painfully to make sure that he wasn't still asleep. Nothing changed, except for the pain in his arm.

"Are you looking for Mr. Parker?" asked the woman with the tightly pulled back hair.

The crew of the Celestine exchanged glances, shrugging their shoulders, and Archie nodded in agreement.

"Follow us, we are going the same way," the woman called out to them, looking over at her daughter reproachfully.

"Tic-toc, tic-toc, tic-toc," the sound followed them wherever they went.

"Where is that sound coming from?" Archie asked, raising his index finger in the air.

"Don't you know?" Ms. Hudson said, sounding surprised.

"We make the most precise clocks in the world! And we export them all over the world!" she explained.

"Wasn't it for them that you came here?" she looked distrustfully over at Archie.

"Many foreign ships come to visit us. They buy so many clocks from us that we must immediately make new ones, or we wouldn't have anything to offer the next customers!" Ms. Hudson bragged.

Ray turned his head and looked at the old city tower with the with the forever stilled clock hands.

"Oops!" he exclaimed, stumbling over a cobblestone.

"Are you going to stay with us a while?" Abigail asked, staring at Ray.

Ray looked at Abigail attentively and silently shrugged his shoulders.

"I'll come back for you!" Abigail immediately promised and smiled.

In the window of every shop one could see a clockmaker at work bent over his or her table.

Ray was staggering about, barely dragging his feet and not raising his head, and he wanted to stuff his fingers in his ears, so that he could finally stop hearing this dull, monotonous ringing.

"Hey! What's with you?" Hulking Bill nudged him playfully.

"Some people think that what we do isn't so very important!" Mrs. Parker complained angrily, ladling out the hot soup for the crew of the Celestine.

"But what would they sell their clocks in, if it weren't for our little boxes?" she objected to the injustice.

"Brenda!" Mr. Parker grunted unhappily.

"Our visitors have only just landed on our shores and don't want to hear all your problems! Besides, they've come for our most precise clocks in the world, and not for idle gossip," and he winked at Archie.

"Damn it!" Duke burned himself on the hot soup.

"Last year, the order for the round boxes for pocket watches went to Mr. and Mrs. Gibson! Can you believe what is going on?" Mrs. Parker could not calm down.

Hulking Bill twiddled his piece of crusty bread and, deciding to dip it in the soup, accidentally drowned it in his bowl.

"Darn it!" he cursed, burning his fingers trying to fish his sodden bread crust out of the scalding hot soup.

"The Gibsons are making boxes only for the second generation! Mr. Parker and I are already in the fifth!" Mrs. Parker raised her eyebrows in indignation.

"Darn it!" Wilson, burning his tongue, started sucking on his cool spoon.

"The world has been turned upside down, when they start handing out such important requisitions to conmen and deadbeats!" Mrs. Parker concluded angrily.

Somebody rang Mr. and Mrs. Parker's door and, not getting a reply, immediately knocked on it impatiently.

"Forty-four little boxes for Mr. Day!" Abigail blurted out as soon as Mrs. Parker appeared on her threshold.

"Hey you! I've forgotten your name?" she peeked behind Mrs. Parker's back.

Ray didn't say a thing.

"Hey! I'm taking to you!" Abigail was surprised by his silence.

"Ray... I'm Ray," Ray replied quietly in an even tone of voice.

"Get your shoes on, quickly, and follow me, you bench-warmer, you!" fiery-haired Abigail ordered him impudently about.

Ray pulled his jacket on slowly and reluctantly followed after Abigail.

"Tic-toc, tic-toc, tic-toc," the sound followed them wherever they went.

The girl with the fiery red hair was racing down the streets, taking kitty-corner shortcuts to cross them, jumping headlong on the curb stones, hopping as high as she could to see if she could touch all the windowsills, walking along the tops of the roadside stones, holding her arms out to balance herself.

Ray trudged after her slowly and indifferently.

Abigail kept having to constantly stop and wait for the boring outlander to catch up.

"Mr. Day! Forty-four little boxes from Mr. and Mrs. Parker!" Abigail reported as soon as Mr. Day's door swung open.

"Abigail, you're wonderful! If you should happen to see Mr.

Charleson today, tell him that, for our next order, we'll need bronze chains instead of golden ones!"

"Abigail!" a very skinny kid peeked out from behind Mr. Day's back.

"Vincent!" she said, happy to see him.

"Quickly, get your shoes on!" Abigail burst out laughing.

"Hey, Vincent! A couple more lessons and Sanct Tempus will have a second master crystal maker!" smiling, Mr. Day praised him in farewell.

Pale and scrawny Vincent, Abigail with her fiery red hair, and Ray were racing down the city streets, taking kitty-corner shortcuts to cross them, jumping headlong on the curb stones, hopping as high as they could to see if they could reach all the windowsills, walking along the tops of the roadside stones, holding their arms out to balance themselves. Ray was barely able to drag his feet, so that Vincent and Abigail had to, now and then, stop and wait for him. They kept jumping up on the large roadside blocks to call back and wave to him: "Hey, Ray! Would you step on it, already!

"Tic-toc, tic-toc, tic-toc," the sound followed Ray wherever he went.

"Here you are, little cogwheel," Mr. Carroll whispered, handling his pincers with a barely noticeable tremor.

"And here's another one...And here are the tiny screws...And here's the gear...And now the little hand, and...." A pocket watch, in Mr. Carroll's masterful hands, seemed a soulless bauble until that moment when it suddenly came to life, when its heart began to beat.

"They're ticking, my precious!" Mr. Carroll greeted them as though they were a newborn, smiling benevolently at his own creation.

Vincent and Abigail were mesmerized, their heads hanging in amazement over the table, their breath, baited. Ray stared indifferently out of the window, his eyes glazed over.

"Not everyone is meant to be a future master clockmaker!" Mr. Carroll smiled, benevolently winking at Ray.

"Hey, Ray!" redheaded Abigail was pointing at a street sign, barely catching her breath, having just ran over there from around the corner.

"The Street of Silence," Ray thought to himself.

"This is where all the clock mechanisms are calibrated, it is forbidden to even speak aloud here," Abigail whispered to him quietly.

Vincent and Abigail held their index fingers up to their lips and got up on their tiptoes. Having gone half-way down the street communicating with each other only through gestures, they now turned around to look for Ray.

"Let's climb the tower," he proposed, and without even getting on his tiptoes or switching to a whisper, turned around and walked off.

Vincent and Abigail silently exchanged glances, shrugged their shoulders, and ran after him.

The dark, weathered stones of the old city tower gawked at the fearless visitors with interest.

"Hey, Ray!" Abigail shouted. "Be careful! The step here has collapsed!"

"I know, I know, this step has crumbled," Ray replied.

"And the next one, ..." Vincent started adding.

"Not another one," Ray wondered aloud.

"Hey! Everyone, over here!" Abigail called out to them from somewhere up above.

Vincent rushed up towards her and the two of them froze still beside the tiny window. The sea was caressing this small corner of the gently sloping shore, and the old stone tower rose up like a lighthouse over the quiet embankment.

"Vincent, do you think your father will ever allow anyone to repair the clock on this tower?" Ray said pensively and stared off into the distant sea horizon.

"Hey! Watch out!" yelled two giants, dragging in their muscular arms a wooden cog that was twice as large as Ray himself.

Without even raising his head, Ray walked off to the side indifferently.

"Our best clockmakers are competing to show off their skills today!" Abigail rejoiced.

"Let's run! You won't get to see this anywhere else!" she winked over at Ray.

"Mr. Day says that, in a couple of years, I will be able to take my place among them," skinny and pale Vincent added proudly.

"Wa-atch ou-ut!" screamed two fat men, who were rolling two huge winding knobs along the ground.

The central square, decorated for the competition, was thronged with people. At the tables that were set up around it sat clockmakers, their heads bent low, working their magic on the mechanisms, as they competed for the title that was awarded annually.

"Hey, Ray! Just look at this!" together with the entire crew of the Celestine, Hulking Bill was staring in amazement at the gigantic cog wheel that had now been rolled into place where the clock was going to be assembled.

The two giant strongmen, obeying the master's orders, were dragging huge wooden screws for what, according to the clockmaker, Mr. Stevenson, would be the world's largest clock.

"Cogs – to the right, screws – to the left!" Mr. Stevenson commanded.

"And where do I put the hand?" one of the giants stared at him expectantly, barely holding up the giant clock hand, longer than a long ship oar, on his bowed back.

"Be careful! Put it over here!" Mr. Stevenson yelled out anxiously.

"Where's the second one?!" he stared irately at the working stiffs.

"Hey Ray! Look over here!" Nimble Larry called out to him, pointing with his finger at the neighboring table.

The master craftsman's table was surrounded by curious onlookers so that Ray and Nimble Larry were, with great difficulty, barely able to squeeze through the crowd. The wooden box opened to welcome everyone, and music came sounding out of its round base, slowly rotating to the beat, as a boy playing a flute rolled out of the enclosure. After the little boy receded, three little chicks with tiny little heads, their tiny little beaks pecking slowly on millet seeds, came into view. After the chicks moved on, a girl wearing a long dress and a wreath on her head of woven field flowers slid out and spun around rhythmically together with the other figures. The long minute hand budged and the little boy with the flute, the pecking chicks, and the girl in the long dress with the wreath on her head all hid from view until the following full hour. The mesmerized audience began applauding. Duke and Nimble Larry exchanged surprised glances. Ray walked on by all of this with indifference.

As though entirely uninterested in the mechanical displays of wonders and the victors awarded the title of master clockmaker, by the roadside, a dark-haired beauty was selling from a basket of green pears.

Hulking Bill, Ike, and Wilson could not tear themselves away from Mr. Olson's table.

Mr. Olson sat bent over his work, straightening his back from time to time and then once again sticking his nose into the table. A stout man with a mustache and his two silent daughters with identical hairdos, both of them unmarried, a man with a curly beard, and two other fidgety damsels were waiting for the performance to begin. Mr. Olson waved his hand, and everyone bent low over the table. On a round circus arena, spinning round to the sound of music, a calico cat stood on its rear paws and juggled balls in the air. A figurine of a white horse spun around, rearing on its hind legs, and two little monkeys dressed in brightly colored, puffy skirts were tossing rings, then taking turns stretching their necks out to catch them. The minute hand shifted, and the circus artists vanished again until the next full hour, leaving the barely-the-size-of-an-apricot circus arena empty. Bill and Ike froze still in amazement. Nimble Larry and Wilson exchanged stunned glances and shook their heads at this marvel. Ray stared off into nothing and then trudged slowly away, making his way through the crowd with difficulty.

Harold's shaking hands raised a tiny vial up to the light. The dark mixture filled it barely half-way. Having struggled to unseal its round lid, he carefully squirted thirteen drops into a tall, shinning goblet. Standing behind his back, Jordan listened cautiously to the sound of the receding footsteps and stretched his out hand towards the full goblet.

The dark walls of the Emperor's chambers followed him with a reproachful glance, being powerless to save a life that had now been placed in danger. Chichi, suddenly anxious, started hooting but Harold immediately shoved her out of the way with a powerful sweep of his leg.

"Harold," the Emperor called out to him.

"I am here, my Master," the Servant of Time replied, raising the heavy curtains of the canopy bed.

"And this year's winner and holder of "the Master of knavish intent and magic fingers" title is... The title is awarded to...," the rail-thin Mrs. Wagner shouted out, but Ray could no longer hear her voice, because the bell on the city clock tower had begun ringing in alarm, drowning out the general hubbub on the plaza.

"Where did Archie go?" Nimble Larry suddenly started looking around for him.

"He went off to buy some green pears from that brown-eyed beauty!" Hulking Bill burst out laughing.

"Her name is Jenna," Abigail turned pale.

"Who?" Larry asked again.

"She's the Black Widow," the skinny and pale Vincent confirmed.

"Only once each year does she descend out of the mountains to choose her intended. But no one has ever again seen the men she has led astray this way into the mountains," Abigail replied and, growing quiet, stared at Larry.

"Archie! Archie! A-a-ar-chie!" Hulking Bill and Nimble Larry screamed together.

But their cry was muffled by the accelerating ringing of the bell and the exclamations of the crowd: "The Emperor! The Emperor is dead!"

"Father!" Vincent cried out.

Ray did not run, his eyes full of hopelessness and despair. Instead, he trudged slowly in the direction of the waterfront. The devious glimmerings of twilight had crept in upon the city, slowly spilling down its streets and squares like coffee spilled on a pale-colored tablecloth.

"The tic-toc, tic-toc, tic-toc," the sound reached Ray's ears and with difficulty he opened his eyes.

"Ray, can you hear that?" Nimble Larry asked him, listening intently and raising his finger in the air.

Ike and Wilson, who were walking out front, stopped and also listened in. Archie closed his eyes and bowed his head, trying to guess what direction the wind that was carrying this quiet, monotonous ringing was blowing from.

"Tic-toc, tic-toc, tic-toc," the sound reverberated in the morning air. The city of Sanct Tempus was ticking like a single, huge clock.

"Abigail! Abigail! Abigail!" a woman was crying out in distress on the embankment and shaking her head.

The girl with fiery red hair, suddenly, jumped down from somewhere above them, almost knocking Ray down off his feet.

"Where were you? Were you climbing the tower again?" the mother shouted out angrily.

"No-o!" Abigail lied.

"Can't you see? I was helping the visitors find their way to Mr. Parker's!" she immediately came up with an alibi, nudging at Ray.

"I could see all of you from the tower a long time ago! I can see everything from the tower!" she whispered into Ray's ear, pointing with her eyes in the direction of the city clock tower.

All of a sudden, Ray rushed out front, pushing the crew of the Celestine aside, and started running away.

"Hey, Ray? What's with him?" Ike and Larry exchanged confused glances.

"Are you looking for Mr. Parker?" Ray heard the disembodied voices being carried by the wind.

"Where is that sound coming from?"

"Don't you know?"

"We make the most precise clocks in the world..."

"Didn't you come for them?"

"Many foreign ships visit us...."

Ray ran and ran, racing as fast as he could to get away from all these words. He didn't know what direction to run in so that this damned, cursed day would stop repeating itself over and over again.

Getting weary, he dragged himself towards the city tower and started climbing the old familiar steps. Sitting alone, beside the open window, he looked out with longing onto the open sea, feeling like a small, defenseless animal locked up in a new cage.

The cold sea breeze blew into the window and Ray turned around to search for his jacket he had dropped somewhere in the darkness. Finding it resting on the huge cog wheel of the long-ago deactivated clock mechanism, he tried jerking it downward, but the jacket was caught. He pulled on it even harder, but the sleeve, stubbornly stuck, firmly resisted all his attempts to get it to slide off. Bending down to get a better look at it in the dim light, Ray was forced to open and close his eyes not once but twice in disbelief, to make sure that he wasn't mistaken. The vision repeated itself: between two sets of old, stilled cogs, obstructing the progress of Sanct Tempus's passage of time, resplendent, was the magical, violet Floviolesbel.

Stretching his fingers out towards it, he still couldn't quite reach it. He climbed down and, carefully, planting his feet wide to brace himself against the iron teeth, with great difficulty, pulled the magical stone out. The cog wheel, liberated from its fetters, moved and Ray's foot slipped, and he almost fell into the dark abyss, managing to grab a hold of the life-saving ledge just in time. Pulling himself up, he finally again felt the stone floor under his feet, but, too exhausted, with a smile, slid down his back, leaning against the cool wall.

"Hey! Watch out!" yelled two giants, dragging in their muscular arms a wooden cog twice the size of Ray himself.

Ray forcefully squeezed his way between the two giants and ran off.

"Wa-atch ou-ut!" screamed two fat men, who were rolling two huge winding knobs along the ground.

At the tables that were set up around it sat clockmakers, their heads bent low to work their magic on the mechanisms, as they competed for the title that was awarded annually.

"Hey, Ray! Just look at this!" together with the entire crew of the Celestine, Hulking Bill was staring in amazement at the gigantic cog that had now been rolled into place where the clock was going to be assembled.

Ray wanted to sprint through the middle of the huge winding knob, but having thought better of it in time, headed around the thing. The central square, decorated for the competition, was thronged with people. At the tables that were set up around it sat clockmakers, their heads bent low, working their magic on the mechanisms as they competed for the title that was awarded annually.

"Hey, Ray! Just look at this!" together with the entire crew of the Celestine, Pudgy Ike was staring in amazement at the gigantic cog wheel that had now been rolled into place where the clock was going to be assembled.

"Where is Archie?" Ray screamed.

And without waiting for a reply, he started waving his head in disbelief. Shoving the crowd aside, he ran after Archie, whose back was now flashing in front of him.

As though entirely uninterested in the mechanical display of wonders and the victors awarded the title of master clockmaker, a dark-haired beauty was selling from a basket of black plums by the roadside.

"Hey, stranger! Have a taste of these, you won't regret it," she smiled coquettishly, batting her black eyelashes.

"0-0-0-Archie!" Ray screamed as hard as he could and, in a dash, knocked the basket out of her arms.

"He-ey, you! Where are you in such a rush to get to?" the Black Widow knitted her eyebrows angrily at him, casting her eyes down at the plums he had scattered all over the roadway.

"Ⅱ-Ⅱ-Ⅱ-ar-chi-e-e-e!" Ray screamed again.

Archie turned around, happy to see him.

"I have it!" Ray shouted over the noise of the crowd and grinned from ear to ear, waving his arm jubilantly in the air.

The tears of joy that had welled up were now tied in a knot and sticking in his throat.

The sky suddenly turned dark and began to rumble, as though a dozen dragons, enraged at being awakened, had opened wide their gigantic throats. Bolts of lightning, flashing as though they were the dragon's steely canines, pierced knifelike into the heart of the celestial dark. Abruptly, the downpour began flogging the ground with its powerful, icy spouts, as though, having bidden its time, the celestial ocean finally came crashing down, smothering the suffocating earth with its superhuman strength. The crowd scattered in a fit of howls and cries, and Ray, having been immediately soaked to the bone, was left behind, standing alone as though his feet were planted in the ground, clutching the seventh magical Floviolesbel tightly to his chest.

Jordan's trembling hands raised the tiny vial up to the light. The dark mixture filled it barely half-way. Removing the round lid with difficulty, he carefully squirted fourteen drops into the tall, sparkling goblet. Harold, standing behind his back, listened cautiously to the sound of the receding footsteps and stretched out his hand towards the filled goblet.

The dark walls of the Emperor's chambers followed him with a reproachful glance. Chichi, suddenly become anxious, started hooting and hollering, but Harold immediately shoved her out of the way with a powerful sweep of his leg.

"I am here, my Master," the Servant of Time replied, raising the heavy curtains of the canopy bed.

"Father! Father!" Vincent, who had suddenly burst in, yelled, almost knocking Harold off his feet having overturned his full goblet.

"Vincent!" the Emperor raised himself from his bed.

"Father! They are moving once again! The clock on our city tower, it is moving again!" pale, skinny Vincent smiled.

"Just as when mother had used them to teach me how to read the time!" Vincent was shouting joyfully, as though once again feeling his dead mother's proximity.

Just as the Emperor was smiling at his son, Chichi dropped dead, having licked clean the red puddle beside the goblet Harold had spilled.

The Celestine was racing across the dark, stilled surface, offering its sails, that had so long pined for the sea, to the wind. Archie was manning the helm, as Sanct Tempus remained far behind them, ticking like one large, over-sized clock. There, where a girl with fire-red hair will continue, for a long time, to climb a tall tower, where a scrawny and pale Vincent will grow up to become a strong and handsome young man and take his father's place. Where the clockmakers, tirelessly competing against each other, will fashion and cause to beat the very largest clock and the smallest watch in the world. This city, in which time, that had come to a stop, finally, once again, began its relentless march forward.

Chapter Seventeen

Escape From Safe Haven

or an entire week now, the Celestine, like a predator preparing to strike, springing on its nightly prowl into a decisive pounce, waited out the endless storm in the mouth of a quiet, nameless, rocky bay.

"Hey, Duke!" Pudgy Ike called out, getting himself ready to go to sleep.

"While we were in port, the entire time, I kept thinking I was seeing the Black Galleon," he whispered.

"You too?!" Duke jumped up immediately from his seat.

"What do you think it means? Could the Black Devil have plotted to swindle us? And go down into the grotto to retrieve the treasures by himself?" Pudgy Ike raised his eyebrow.

"The fewer people there are, the less he will have to share... And we, idiots, will be used for shark bait!" Ike hissed out.

"Hear me out, Ike. Larry swore to me today that he saw Wilson huddling with the one-eyed man!" Duke whispered, his eyes aflame with indignation.

"Wilson? Could that skinny sea devil of a rogue, have schemed to lay his hands on our gold?" Pudgy Ike flew into a fierce rage.

"Quieter!" Duke grunted, and both of them listened in, clenching their fists in anger.

"Hey, Wilson!" Nimble Larry called out in the dark.

Wilson played deaf and dumb.

"Wasn't it you I saw hobnobbing in the port with the one-eyed man?" Nimble Larry blurted out, no longer able to keep his secret.

Wilson started snoring loudly, pretending to be asleep. Nimble Larry could not fall asleep and, just in case, sneaked quietly across the cabin, felt about in the dark and, finding Wilson's pants and jacket, placed them under himself as bedding, plopped down on them, and went to sleep.

The seven magical stones lay before Archie on the table in the captain's cabin. Mesmerized, incapable of taking his eyes off their shinning eyes, Archie managed to force himself to carefully stow each of them away in his pouch made of the hem of Celestine's skirt. And, having rolled up the fabric into a scroll, stuffed it deep into one of his boots, tossing his jacket over them.

At midnight, sleep overcame the entire exhausted crew of the Celestine. Only Ray, thinking of the mysterious island of Tuki-tuki, of the seven magical stones, of the untold treasures, and of home, never did manage to fall asleep. And, tiring of twisting and turning, he quietly sneaked out of the cabin, leaving Hulking Bill alone with his snoring.

Hanging over the port side, he gazed out with fascination at the moonlight reflected in the black sea water. Suddenly, a rustle along the starboard side forced him to grow still and prick up his ears. Holding his breath like that for a full minute, he proceeded to cautiously tip-toe across the deck and was stricken dumb: splitting the black, nocturnal, still sea surface and pulling away from the Celestine was a dinghy with the dark silhouette of Skinny Wilson wearing a tricorn hat.

"Wilson?" Ray exclaimed.

"A-A-Archie!" Ray screamed and raced over to the captain's cabin.

"Wilson has run off!" Ray blurted out, prodding and pulling at the still snoring Archie.

"Wilson! Wilson has run off!" Ray kept screaming, while slapping sleepy Archie across the cheeks.

Archie jumped up and immediately flung himself in the corner. Tossing aside the jacket, he saw that one of his boots was missing. Looking around, he discovered it in the other corner and started to shake all over, cursing and burning up with anger. Flinging the empty boot at the wall with all his might, he ran up on deck and raised the alarm.

The Celestine was racing into the night, the entire enraged crew hanging threateningly overboard, holding at the ready a huge iron hook, which could easily have snagged not just Wilson in his dinghy but a whole enemy brigantine.

"Stop! You, sea devil! Stop, you, skinny little sea devil!" they all screamed in a chorus, catching up with Wilson.

Skinny Wilson helplessly retreated and holed up in the corner of the stollen dinghy, pressing the precious pouch to his chest.

Having lost yet another couple of teeth and rolling himself into a ball, his stomach that had been pummeled by the fists of the entire crew knotted in pain, huddled in the boat's stern Wilson, suddenly screamed: "You, idiots! You rotten pieces of shark snack! You obey your beloved Archie, and he himself has already probably planed how he's going to cheat all of us! And you're never going to see, you, knuckleheads, your lousy treasures! And if you don't believe me,

then ask your beloved Archie! Yes, yes! Ask him, you, numbskulls, what deep secret your beloved Archie has kept to himself? And if you don't believe me, ask the one-eyed man!" Wilson was screaming without letting up, covered head to foot in blood.

"You expect an equal division of the spoils from someone who's intimately connected with Bloodthirsty Cook?" Wilson blurted out and stuck out his broken finger in Archie's direction.

"Shut up!" Archie snapped back abruptly and again let Wilson have it in the jaw.

For some reason, all of them froze still then and stared at Archie searchingly.

Archie lowered his eyes and grew silent.

"Spill the beans, Archie! What is this about, captain?" they all groaned out in a chorus.

"Bloodthirsty Cook... Bloodthirsty Cook – is my father..." Archie grunted under his breath, and the entire crew of the Celestine froze in their tracks.

"Yes! He's my father!" Archie kept screaming, surrounded by his pirate crew, who were belligerently clenching the handles of their pistol and the hilts of their swords.

"But he abandoned me and my mother when I was a little boy."

"What kind of a father could a Bloodthirsty pirate be, always away at sea; his name alone inspires a shudder! I was never strong enough for him, brave enough, accurate enough, that he could be proud of me!"

"I am a weakling, a klutz, a ne'er-do-well! The captain of a sunken brigantine! Ask those dead men what sort of a daredevil I am! Why did I have to be washed overboard by that cursed wave then?! I had no right to survive, when all of them went down with the ship!" Archie suddenly covered his face with his hands and his shoulders began to tremble, betraying his despair.

The crew of the Celestine slumped, lowering their heads, and Nimble Larry, with Ike's, Duke's, and Hulking Bill's nodded approval, tossed the pistol they had just taken away from him at Archie's feet.

"Take the helm, captain!" screamed Nimble Larry.

"Take it, Archie!" yelled Pudgy Ike.

"Lead us, captain! We're not fated to see any treasures without you, no more than a shark to see neither hide nor hair of my backside!" Hulking Bill winked at him and then tossed his sword into Archie's arms.

Skinny Wilson spat, squinted, and quietly pleaded:

"I'm back in, right? I have my share again?"

Pudgy Ike, Hulking Bill, Nimble Larry, and Duke turned around, looked at Wilson, and rolled up their sleeves...

Chapter Eighteen

The Paradise Isle Of Tuki-Tuki

The sunrise was aglimmer, confident in its triumph over the realm of gloom. Cook's compass kept pointing the way. The Celestine was swallowing the waves beneath her and rearing up in its progress towards the final victory.

"Island! I can see an island!" Ray, who was hanging off the mast, once again glued to Cook's spyglass, screamed.

The entire crew piled out on deck and stared off into the distance. The mysterious Tuki-tuki, the island of untold hidden treasures, shone alluringly green directly ahead of them.

"Archie!" Ray suddenly exclaimed and, rushing headlong down from the mast, handed the telescope into the captain's able hands.

A vessel was already moored beside island of treasures. The Black Galleon, having arrived first, was already there, awaiting The Celestine.

"Oh, well, it's either he gets us, or we get him..." Archie uttered quietly, lowering the telescope in his hand.

"Ow, ow, ow!" "Dwee, dwee, dwee!" "Wok, wok, wok!" The yet to be seen beast and birds of the mysterious island of Tuki-tuki were already warbling and chirping. Ike and Duke, stripping to their waists as a defense against the heat, scored their stomachs with the sharp-pointed leaves of the indigenous fauna. Skinny Wilson was fanning himself, now and then, with his tricornered hat, also drenched with sweat. Hulking Bill was dying of thirst and could barely keep up fanning away the persistent no-see-ums. Nimble Larry fashioned a turban out of his shirt to cover his head. Dripping with sweat, Ray and Archie, their shirts sticking to their backs, walked in front of the rest, using their swords like machetes to clear a path through the overgrown tropical forest. The day was coming to its end, the hot sun was releasing the mysterious island into the domain of night, and there was not even a hint yet of the grotto, or the one-eyed man, or the Black Devil, with his thugs. Having started a campfire by the shoreline, the crew of the Celestine collapsed on the sand, not even noticing how sleep had overcome them.

Archie and Ray were awakened by the hooting and drumming of the savage islanders, their singing, resembling the chanting of shamans. Duke, Ike, Bill and Nimble Larry, got up immediately after them. Exchanging silent gestures, they shoved the still sleeping Wilson in his side, and set off in the direction of the noise that disturbed the quiet of the sweltering night.

Stealing through the bushes, they cautiously pushed aside the foliage and went numb. The entire crew of the Black Galley, all of them bound hand and foot, was helplessly huddled together beside the huge, flaming campfire of the natives.

Three shamans with tattooed faces and closed eyes were giving thanks to their idols for this rich haul.

Stomping their feet in a malevolent dance, the islanders whirled around the disarmed prisoners. Covering up the opening through the foliage, Archie gave everyone the sign: turn back! And the entire crew, numb with horror and quietly shuffling their feet, flung themselves into retreat.

"Gar, gar, gar!" the night birds cried.

"Oooooo, ooooo, oooo!" the wild beasts howled.

The frightful, dangerous, uneasy night of the mysterious island of Tuki-tuki cunningly embraced the crew of the Celestine, pretending to be a warm, summery, peaceful, and verdant paradise.

Wilson, heeding the call of nature at sunrise, came running back howling wildly. Incapable of describing what he had seen, he only kept waving his arms about and pointing at the bushes. Everyone ran to follow after Archie, who led the way.

"There's nothing for you to do there!" he shouted to Ray, who was deeply hurt by this.

Duke and Pudgy Ike returned with faces white as snow. Hulking Bill vomited in the bushes. Impaled on two of the islanders' spears were heads deprived of their torsos. The Black Devil and the one-eyed man were not fated to ever leave the mysterious island of Tuki-tuki.

Hesitation in this green Eden could cost one one's life and, just in time, Archie's face lights up with a bright idea. He reaches into his bag for Cook's compass. Its arrow begins spinning around, as though curiously examining its new location, and stops in its track, pointing with absolute certainty to the southwest.

"Follow me!" Archie gives the command.

Looking around themselves from side to side, not knowing what they ought to fear more – being torn to pieces by wild beast or being served for dinner to the natives – the entire crew of the Celestine set out in the direction pointed out to them by the arrow.

Bright yellow parrots, staring at them from the high branches, were swinging their heads in rhythm with the crew's steps.

"A-a-a! A sna-a-ake!" Wilson hollered, hopping up and down in one place.

Boom! Archie's shot rang out and the exotic viper, hiding its immeasurably long body under the foliage, impotently dropped its head to the ground.

The long, strange-looking leaves, their edges lined with sharp spikes, extended on stalks towards them from all sides, like hands holding daggers and lying in wait for their victims.

"A-a-a-a-a!" Duke, Pudgy Ike, and Hulking Bill screamed, falling into a pit trap that had been covered with huge, green branches.

Ray, Archie, and Nimble Larry reeled backwards. A liana vine struck Archie in the face, and he immediately grabbed it and jerked it downward, to see if it would reach the edge of the pit.

"W-a-a! W-a-a! W-a-a!" the liana cried out.

A huge orange ape jumped off to the side, yanking its twisting tail out of Archie's arms.

"Branches!" Nimble Larry shouted, cautiously tugging at the thick, long green stalks.

Cursing and swearing, Duke, Ike, and Hulking Bill crawled up and out. Ray suddenly sensed in his palm someone's small, soft paw. Not having had time to even let out a peep, he turned around and saw a little marmoset that had grabbed his hand and was impatiently pulling him off to the side. He stared at Archie for guidance.

"Forward!" Archie gave the order, deciding to follow the monkey.

He had hidden from the crew the fact that he had no alternate plan at the moment. The marmoset guided them off to the side and a long-ago trodden path through the impassable tropical forest opened before them. A gigantic purple dragonfly, its wing the same length as Ray's entire body, whirred loudly, flying past them, barely missing Skinny Wilson's head.

"O-o-o!" the pugnacious marmoset whooped and again darted off to one side.

The entire crew of the Celestine came to a complete stop, full of anticipation and barely catching their breath. Gaping in front of them was the black entrance to the underground grotto that lay hidden, together with all its untold treasures, on the mysterious verdant island Tuki-tuki. Archie looked around himself, found a thick, desiccated branch and used it to fashion a torch.

Lining up in a single file and stepping carefully, not believing their own eyes, the crew of the Celestine set out after him into the dark.

The long, black tunnel was replaced by a cramped, circular underground hall. Dark, old waistcoats, torn dirty shirts, crushed tricornered hats, adorned the skulls and bones of the unfortunate treasure hunters who would never again get to take leave of this grotto.

The crew of the Celestine shuddered and, staring intently ahead, followed after Archie.

"Archie!" Ray, who was walking in front, shouted.

The flame in Archie's hand lit the stilled surface of an underground lake, and the seven, dark, forged chests, bound with cobwebs, resting on its shoreline.

Just as the one-eyed man had promised, visible inside their keyholes were deep sockets that have been awaiting the insertion of the magical stones that would finally open them.

Archie handed his torch Hulking Bill, pulled up his roomy shirt, and unwound the hem of Celestine's skirt from around his stomach. Carefully removing the magical stones, one after another, with their dirty fingers, Ray and Archie took turns inserting them into the mysterious chests.

"Click!" the magical, red Credisford clicked into place.

"Clack!" replied the orange, shining Plorangestone.

"Cleck!" the yellow Prelloubridge cut in.

"Clock! Clyuk! Clack!" the shining magical Bougrindle, Stoublulaze, Frindigoffle echoed them.

"Clyak!" the violet Floviolesbel put the matter to rest.

A seven-colored rainbow, just like fireworks, for a moment lit the dark hall of the grotto. Grunting, as though awakening from a long sleep, the seven dark, forged lids yielded to the prying of the crew of the Celestine and, as though yawning, creaked their hello in the underground silence. Resting on the bottom of each was a fragment of a map. Their hands shaking, Archie, Ray, Ike, Duke, Bill, Larry and Skinny Wilson each carried one of these over to the center of the earthen floor and assembled them into one complete map. The heretofore dismembered words coalesced into legible lines.

"Archie White! I always knew that it would be you!"

Archie read Bloodthirsty Cook's familiar handwriting and froze in his place. The entire crew of the Celestine stared at him intently.

"You came here in search of infinite treasures, but please forgive me, I did not accumulate them," Archie read aloud in an unsteady voice.

"I blew through everything that fell into my arms, enjoying my life of roaming and rambling. But how could you fail to understand, having reached this far, that you possess something far more important than all the world's treasures? You found faith: you came to believe in yourself! You are accurate, daring, and brave, my son! And I am proud of you! And all one needs to find genuine treasures is a fast schooner, a courageous captain, and a few incorrigible rogues!"

"He-ey, Archie," Hulking Bill stammered, not understanding what was happening.

"So, where's the money?" Ike stared uncomprehendingly at the letter.

"And the gold?" Nimble Larry added, waving his head.

Archie shrugged his shoulders in bewilderment and resumed reading.

"Should restlessness and wanderlust ever consume you, as once upon a time they did me, then inside the seventh chest you will find a scroll that contains a magical spell. It will bestow on eternal life and magical powers on you."

Everyone flung themselves toward the seventh chest beside which Skinny Wilson was sitting and immediately fished out a dark, leather case that had rolled off to the side. Struggling to open its fragile, desiccated cover, Archie dislodged a scroll that had become yellowed with time and was tied up in something strange. Not the usual piece of rope, but with several little tails, reminiscent of those of mice, tied together into a single longer one.

"I didn't bother chasing after eternal life, captain. With a nickname like "Bloodthirsty" on this earth you're not going to earn an easy fate in the afterlife!"

"Archie!" exclaimed Ray.

And everyone turned around, having heard the sound of a body plopping into the water.

Wilson's tricornered hat was floating on its disturbed smooth surface.

"The scroll!" shouted Nimble Larry, staring at the empty leather case beside Archie, who was kneeling down.

"This scroll! I had seen it somewhere before!" Ray racked his head, struggling to remember that strange, long cord, tied together out of a dozen shorter, desiccated little tails resembling those of mice.

Suddenly, he saw in his mind Mr. Fox's kitchen, with its sweet, raspberry mixture bubbling over in pails and pots ...

And that scroll! Yes, the scroll standing on the upper shelf, with its long, drooping cord!

"Our Wilson, what's his name?!" Ray suddenly exclaimed.

"Wilson!" replied Ike.

"Skinny!" Hulking Bill barked out.

"Fox! Wilson Fox!" yelled Archie.

"Mr. Fox?!" exclaimed Ray.

More than anything else in the world, Ray was afraid of diving. But he didn't think twice, not even for a second, as he threw himself into the water.

"Mist-e-e-er Fo-o-o-o-o-x!" Ray screamed, jumping in after Wilson.

The cold water immediately paralyzed his arms and legs, but he kept courageously diving down deeper and deeper.

"Fo-o-o-o-o-o-x!" Ray kept screaming under the water, blowing bubbles from his mouth.

His wet clothes were sticking to his body and, as though trying to free himself from them, he started twisting and turning in place and suddenly ... he once again felt the solid ground beneath himself. Fearfully opening his eyes that had been clenched shut, he saw the ceiling of his own room.

"Ray!" He could hear the sound of his mother's voice.

Ray jumped up and stared down at his soaked clothes, at his arms and feet, all scratched by the spiky leaves of the tropical forest.

"Ray!" His mother called out to him once again.

Grabbing a dry t-shirt from the back of a chair and sliding his head through its neck in one swift movement, he ran to the kitchen in his bare feet, leaving behind himself a track of wet footprints.

Having knocked his father's portrait off the cabinet, he turned back and righted it back in its place.

"Hey, Ray!" his father smiled, winking at him.

"Did you see that?! Did you see that, Buddy?!" Ray stared into the eyes of his beloved pet, who had rapturously flung himself at him.

The kitchen beckoned and tempted him with its long-ago forgotten appetizing odors, and his mother's voice was humming some sort of vaguely familiar melody.

Ray got down on his knees in front of the dog and, joyfully stroking the shaggy fur behind his ears, burst out laughing:

"Hey, Buddy! It's been a long time since we dropped by Mr. Fox's place!"

"Your breakfast is ready!" his mother shouted, heartily spooning out a generous dollop of the brightly colored, transparent raspberry jam out of the jar and spreading it thickly on his piece of toasted bread.

Printed in Dunstable, United Kingdom